THE DOUBLE MAN

A JACK WIDOW THRILLER

SCOTT BLADE

Black Lion Media

Published by **Black Lion Media**.

CHAPTER 1

The helicopter was a Sikorsky MH-60 Jayhawk, a twin engine rescue aircraft capable of reaching speeds of two hundred and seven miles per hour—for maximum short distance missions. The United States Coast Guard depended on it for deepwater rescues. It was the workhorse of the US water and mountain rescue operations. The bird was designed to fly three hundred miles out to sea loaded with a crew of four, and could hoist six people from the ocean and carry them all back to shore. It could hover over a rescue site for up to forty-five minutes before needing to return home to refuel.

The man was called Gary Kloss. Although no one would know that because he didn't have a wallet on him. No identification. Nothing. The only way to know who he was, was to ask him. The only way to know *anything* about him was to ask him, which was why he was out here.

Kloss was strapped into a CMC Rescue Disaster Response Litter, a highly durable stretcher fused together with powder-coated steel, metal wire, and mesh. The US Coast Guard used it to pluck up survivors from disastrous situations, like capsized boats stranded in the ocean or injured climbers on the side of a mountain. It was an essential piece of equipment for any rescue unit. No doubt about it. Without it, hoisting people out of choppy waters after their boat capsized was near impossible, especially for survivors with broken limbs. And Kloss had two broken limbs. Both of his legs were broken at the kneecaps. He felt the pain. It wasn't numb. No way could he survive treading water for long, not on his own, not without a life vest, which he wasn't wearing. Under normal circumstances—normal weather and sea conditions—the Coast Guard helicopter would be a welcome sight. But these weren't normal circumstances—far from it.

Kloss's stretcher dangled from a retractable cable rigged outside the helicopter to a winch. Nylon cloth belts strapped him into the stretcher tight. His movement was completely constricted, and he couldn't move his legs. The straps were so tight that he barely had room to breathe and wriggle, and that was about it. Since his legs were broken, he could only squirm from the waist up. Not much good that would do him. He couldn't swim, not with the broken legs. He wasn't much of a swimmer, anyway. Even if he could swim, even if his legs weren't broken, he still couldn't escape the litter. The straps were too tight. And his hands were pinned underneath them.

The only thing he could do that mattered was he could take deep breaths, which was good. He needed them.

Gales of cold wind howled and shrieked all around him. A lightning bolt flashed and electrified the sky for one long, bright second. Kloss dangled in the stretcher. The wind swayed him from side to side under the helicopter. He looked up and saw the undercarriage of the Jayhawk. He saw the rotor blades whopping fast like the wings of a dragonfly. He stared past the aircraft and the blades and saw the underbelly of enormous storm clouds above. They hung in the sky like massive creatures. In comparison, he felt like a bug.

A lightning bolt flashed, brightening the sky. Then it vanished, and the skies died back to near darkness. All except for the Jayhawk's exterior navigation lights, but not for long. More lightning crackled and coruscated above the Jayhawk. It continued like a light show in the sky. There was no pattern to it. The lightning was completely random, as lightning is. He knew that, but it seemed to spark the sky every five seconds. Thunder rumbled above. Torrents of rain engulfed the helicopter. The wind pummeled him with huge squalls. Rainwater gusted everywhere. It slapped across Kloss's immobile body, across his bruised and battered cheeks.

Kloss's legs were broken, but that wasn't all. His face was a wreck. He had two black eyes, one of them mashed shut. His nose was broken. There were bruises on his arms and chest. He was sure he had a fractured rib or two.

The Gulf of Alaska was thirty feet below the helicopter. The water below swelled and crashed. Huge waves rose and fell and churned below him. Whitecaps crashed into each other in a chaotic rhythm that only the sea understood. The water was dark and gray. It was just as terrifying as deep space, but far more alive. Below the surface lay the unknown, but he knew it would kill him. There was no escaping it, not for Kloss. He couldn't swim to shore, not even if the conditions were calm. It was too far. And again, his broken legs wouldn't allow it. The only thing that waited for Kloss below the water was death.

Kloss, the litter, and the basket dangled in the harness from the Jayhawk about fifteen feet above the crashing waves. The waves splashed and billowed up. The spray slapped across his cheeks and into his eyes. Saltwater stung his face. He tasted it on his lips and in his mouth. He swallowed some of it. He inhaled some of it. It couldn't be helped.

The Jayhawk's rotors spun. Rainwater ricocheted from the rotor wash and spat back out away from the helicopter. The night was cold and wet in every direction. The cargo cabin doors were slid all the way open. Two men leaned out. Their hands held onto grips near the door. They didn't want to fall out. One guy wore a ball cap. He operated the winch. The other stood over and peered down at Kloss like he was supervising a deep water rescue.

The man supervising wore a leather jacket in place of a blazer over a crinkled dress shirt and tie and black chinos. His tie whipped in the violent wind gusts, slapping his neck and shoulder. His gray hair was slicked back from the rain.

Behind him were three other guys, all built like human pit bulls, only taller. All of them wore casual, warm clothes, except for the pilot, who wore a flight suit. The pilot was the only guy out of the six who didn't have broad shoulders underneath his suit. He was more of a desk type than the others. Even though he didn't sit behind a desk all that much. His life was sedentary. The other five were different. They were built like former football players. They were built like former Special Forces operators, only bigger.

If someone could see them from shore, it would appear that the US Coast Guard was rescuing a man from drowning, but they weren't. That's not what the guys in the Jayhawk were doing at all. Not that it mattered, because the shore was too far away for anyone to see them. Even in daylight, they would've been a speck in the sky, a dot on the horizon. But there was no one onshore watching them. No witnesses. No onlookers. Not in this weather. They were closer to a passing cargo ship than to anyone standing on the beach. They knew that because the pilot had logged the ship from radar. He told his leader, the guy in the leather jacket, about it. But the cargo ship was far away. The ship's crew knew of the helicopter presence—probably. They could see it on their own equipment, but they didn't know who was onboard or why it was there. The pilot monitored the radio just in case the ship's crew tried to be Good Samaritans and offer help. But they didn't. They never radioed.

The Jayhawk hovered fifty miles from the south shores of Kodiak Island—Alaska's biggest island and the second biggest under the umbrella of US territory. Only Hawaii was bigger. No one could see them, not from the ship, not from shore. Maybe the helicopter's navigation lights would've been visible on a clear, dark night. Maybe they could've even been seen with a high-powered scope, like a telescope or a camera lens. Maybe it was possible to see the lights with the naked eye as a faint, distant twinkle. Maybe, from the nearest ship, sailors on deck could catch a faint hint of the beacon light that blinked from the Jayhawk's undercarriage. But this was no clear, dark night. And no one was looking at them with a high-powered scope or camera lens. No one was looking with thermals. No one was looking out at them— period. Why would they? Not during a storm like this. Not at the end of an Alaskan September.

Kloss stared up at the man with the whipping tie leaning out of the helicopter. Lightning crackled again. Even without the instant flash of light, Kloss saw him. The Jayhawk's interior cabin lights illuminated his face. There was one distinguishing feature about the man with the whipping tie. It was his expression, the look in his eyes. It was horrifying. A malicious smile cracked across the man's face. It resonated like pure evil, the kind seen once in a lifetime.

Kloss would never forget that look. He would remember it for the rest of his life.

"Who did you tell?" the man with the whipping tie yelled down to Kloss.

Another large swell crashed below him, and water sprayed up across his face again. The swells continued like relentless drumbeats, constantly pounding below.

Kloss shouted, "No one!"

"You're lying," the man with the whipping tie said, and he paused a beat. Then he called out, "Take a deep breath!" He glanced at the guy controlling the winch and said, "Do it."

The guy controlling the winch smiled under the ball cap and hit a button on a control panel. Instantly, the cable slacked, and the winch released, and Kloss and the rescue litter went crashing down into the waves below, into the black water. The guy controlling the winch pressed the button again and stopped the slack. The helicopter hovered. The man with the whipping tie stared down. Glee danced in his eyes like dancing candlelight. He watched. He was impressed because even though Kloss was old and his legs were broken and he was strapped into the litter, he thrashed and flailed about from the torso as best he could. He tried to free himself, tried to get loose.

The man with the whipping tie could see the water splash violently from Kloss's struggling. It was impressive. The man had been impressive all around so far. He'd given up some information, like his name. But the man with the whipping tie knew Kloss was holding something back. There was more information to get. And so far, he'd been unable to get it. The man with the whipping tie couldn't remember the last time a subject held out on him. It had been decades, probably.

Kloss wanted to live, so he squirmed and wriggled under the weight of the water, under the tight straps. But it did no good. His efforts changed nothing. He was fighting against immense undertow, while his legs were broken and his arms were strapped down. He didn't stand a chance.

The man with the whipping tie watched. The glee in his eyes continued. The thrashing below continued. He didn't know how long Kloss could hold his breath. Not long, he bet. But that didn't stop the man with the whipping tie from keeping Kloss down there. If the guy died, then he died.

The man with the whipping tie waited. *Thirty seconds. Forty-five seconds. One minute.* The thrashing continued.

The guy controlling the winch asked, "Now?"

The man with the whipping tie said nothing.

One minute, thirty seconds.

The guy controlling the winch repeated, "Now?"

Silence.

One minute, forty-five seconds.

The thrashing slowed like the drip from a loose faucet until it stopped.

The man with the whipping tie said, "Okay. Now."

The guy controlling the winch hit the button, and the winch cranked, and the cable retracted and reeled back up. The litter surged up out of the water. Seawater dripped off the sides. The litter came back up several feet out of the crashing waves. The man with the whipping tie peered down from the Jayhawk and waited to make sure Kloss was still alive, which he was.

Kloss coughed and wheezed and spat up seawater violently. His lungs hurt. His throat hurt. His body ached, but he couldn't tell the difference between pain that came from his broken legs and pain that came from the barbaric water-boarding.

"Stop," the man with the whipping tie said.

The guy controlling the winch hit the button again, and the winch stopped cranking, and the cable and the litter froze in place. Kloss and the litter swayed to one side from the wind.

The man with the whipping tie called out, "Who did you tell?"

Kloss coughed and gagged and breathed. *Did he already tell them? Didn't he already break?* He couldn't remember. The last twenty-four hours had been the longest of his life. All the pain and torture made a lifetime of memories run together.

He shouted, "No one! I swear! No one!"

Didn't I tell them already, he asked himself. The answer was no. He never broke. He told them nothing that they couldn't find out on their own. But he lied about who hired him. He never gave them a name. At least, he hoped.

The man with the whipping tie called out, "Who hired you?"

"I don't know," Kloss lied.

The man with the whipping tie paused. The wind continued to push the litter to one side. The man with the whipping tie looked at his wristwatch. Then he tucked it back under the leather jacket sleeve.

He spoke under his breath. "I don't have time for this." Then he called back down to Kloss. "How do I know you're not lying?"

Kloss spat seawater out of his mouth. He lied, "I'm not! I swear! It was anonymous."

The man with the whipping tie said, "Dip him again."

Kloss didn't hear the order, but he read the man with the whipping tie's lips and understood the gesture. He shouted back in protest, shouted up into the noise of the rain and wind and thunder and rotor wash, but he wasn't heard.

The button was pressed, and the winch cranked, and the locking mechanism released the cable, and the litter dropped several feet at once and went back into the water. Kloss vanished under the swells.

The man with the whipping tie stared down and smiled. The same glee danced in his eyes. But the thrashing in the water wasn't the same at all. This time, it was barely a struggle. It was more apt to a death rattle than to a man fighting for his life. It was like Kloss was defeated. It took all the joy out of it for the man to watch. It was pathetic. Kloss had given up. They always did.

The man with the whipping tie's smile faded, and the glee in his eyes died down to nothing. He was disappointed. Kloss had been an army veteran. He knew that from a simple background check. Anyone could discover that about Kloss, but the man with the whipping tie's resources were a lot more than what most people could access. Not that he needed to do a background check because Kloss had already told him enough, all but who hired him.

Every man has a breaking point, even a retired Army veteran. When breaking a man's legs gets you nothing, injecting him with narcotics often will. The man with the whipping tie hadn't injected him with any narcotics, however, because he had neither the time nor the proper equipment, not on Kodiak Island. The island itself wasn't the middle of nowhere, but it was remote enough. Having the proper equipment on standby took time to prepare. He didn't have that time.

Taking Kloss out on a dip from a helicopter seemed to be enough to get the job done. Sometimes it was the crude measures that worked best. Plus, the man with the whipping tie enjoyed the hell out of it. But that sensation had passed. And he had better things to do. If Kloss hadn't told him by now, he wouldn't tell him at all.

"Pull him up," the man with the whipping tie said.

The operator nodded and hit the button, and the winch cranked to life again and reeled the cable up. Kloss and the rescue litter came up out of the water.

The man with the whipping tie looked over at the operator controlling the winch and nodded at him again. The operator nodded back and hit the button again. The cable stopped cranking, and Kloss was left dangling again several feet over the water.

The man with the whipping tie gave it one last go and called down. "Who did you tell?"

Kloss coughed and gagged and nearly vomited, but didn't because his abdominal muscles were beyond the point of straining.

Kloss shouted up, "No one! I swear! Please! Let me go!"

The man with the whipping tie stared down and yawned. He felt tired, partially from the long flight to Alaska just to deal with this guy, and partially from the long torture of Kloss. He called out, "Okay. I believe you." Though he didn't.

The man with the whipping tie stepped back and stood straight and tall. He stretched his arms out and looked at the guy controlling the winch. He yawned again.

He said, "Bring him back up."

The operator nodded and did as he was told. Once again, he pressed the return button. The winch motored and cranked. The cable took several seconds to lift all the way.

The guy controlling the winch stopped it as soon as Kloss and the litter were within grabbing distance.

The man with the whipping tie turned to the pilot. He said, "Take us up higher."

The pilot said nothing. No affirmative response. No nod. No look. He just did as he was ordered. The Jayhawk climbed.

The man with the whipping tie got back into the cabin and dumped himself down in an empty jump seat behind the cockpit. His tie stopped whipping. He looked at his watch.

Without eye contact, he barked an order to one of his guys. "Help him."

One of the large guys, the one closest to the doors, unbuckled his safety belt and stood up. He clambered over to the open door and helped the other crew member drag the litter in and unharness it from a large hook at the end of the cable.

Kloss breathed in and breathed out. Rainwater and seawater drenched his face. There was saltwater in his stomach and lungs. No doubt about it. His skin was pale blue. The bruises on his face were wrinkled and had turned purple. But he said nothing. He felt lucky to be alive.

The helicopter climbed higher and higher.

Kloss stared at the man with the whipping tie. The two large guys dragged the litter into the cabin and set him down in the middle of the floor. They checked the straps on his hands, made sure they were fastened tight. He didn't struggle or thrash about like he did before, because he didn't want to piss them off. They were letting him go. He had told the man with the whipping tie enough.

Kloss thought he had convinced the man with the whipping tie to let him live, and that was victory enough. His broken legs would heal in time. His bruises would heal. Now they were going to let him go. They'd probably dump him at an emergency room somewhere, probably in Kodiak or Homer.

Whatever, he didn't care. He just wanted to be rid of them. He could regroup later. He could get the FBI involved after he was safe and sound.

The helicopter climbed.

The man with the whipping tie stayed quiet. The two large guys that set Kloss down stayed near him. One unhooked him from the cable. The cable whipped back out into the night. It dangled from the side of the winch. The operator stayed near the open doors but did not close them.

One of the large guys kept a massive hand laid across Kloss's chest like he was keeping him restrained with it. The hand was the size of a shovel, and heavy as a rock. Kloss looked them all over carefully like he was taking notes about them. He recorded their faces for his statement to the Feds later. Then he paused a beat and glanced back over his shoulder out the open doors. Lightning cracked the sky again. He stayed fixated on the rough sky beyond the doors until a question popped into his mind. It was a question he couldn't ignore. So he asked it.

He asked, "Why is the door still open?"

No one answered him.

A fear crept up on him. Kloss's heart raced. He asked again, "Why is the door still open?"

No answer.

"Guys, close the door," he said.

No response.

"Close the door," he begged.

No answer.

Kloss asked, "Where are we going?"

He got nothing but silence from the men and the howl of the wind and rumble of the thunder and the *whop-whop-whop* of the rotor blades. No talk. No speeches. Nothing else.

The man with the whipping tie turned in the jump seat and looked back over his shoulder at the pilot. His tie started whipping violently again. It was from a draft that blew through the open door.

The man with the whipping tie asked the pilot, "Where are we?"

The pilot called back, "Fifty miles out from the island."

"How high?"

"Over three thousand feet."

The man with the whipping tie turned back and faced his crew. He glanced down at Kloss. He said, "Okay. We're going to let you go now."

Kloss stared at the man's eyes. He saw that evil glee return.

The man with the whipping tie looked at his guys. He said, "Do it."

The two guys standing over Kloss, including the one with his shovel hand on Kloss's chest, stood up from their perches. They both grabbed hold of opposite sides of the litter and hauled him up off the floor. The litter was in the air. They shuffled him over to the open doors. A third guy unbuckled his seat and reached under it and came out with a heavy object. He shambled over to the stretcher. He lifted the object into Kloss's view. It was a fishing boat anchor. There was no chain attached to it. There was only the hole where one would go. The third guy hooked the anchor onto the stretcher's railing and dropped it on Kloss's lap.

Kloss's heart raced faster, like a fast telegram with an urgent message. He squirmed and struggled and whipped his head back and forth. He asked, "What're you doing?"

No answer. No one listened. The large guys hauled him to the edge of the helicopter and the empty sky. They wrenched him back and then started swinging him forward like they were about to throw him out. They swung him forward and back repeatedly. At the end of each swing, he feared that would be the last one until they tossed him out.

"No! Wait! I told you everything! Wait!" he cried out.

It was no use. On the fifth swing, they tossed him out the open doors. Kloss and the litter went out into the storm, into the darkness, into the night.

CHAPTER 2

Seven days later, it still rained. Although it had slowed, it never stopped. Not really. It was more like it had paused a few hours here and there.

This time, it was October rain. It fell sporadically like soft ash from a volcanic sky. The sky grayed under a bright sun, leaving the impression of an atmosphere that couldn't decide. But that's what Alaskan weather was like. It's always changing, always defiant, always sullen, always glum—or not.

The old man stood alone in the water, close to the banks of a remote part of the Karluk River. He wore waders to keep the clothes underneath dry. The river water was up to his knees, and the mud on the riverbed was up over the heels of his boots. His fishing line was cast. He waited. He had been waiting. So far, he had been there all morning, since well before sunrise. He got there on a four-wheeler from an old road around four o'clock in the morning. Of course, he'd had to do some special maneuvers to sneak away. He would reap the repercussions for sneaking out. He knew it. But it was totally worth it. Every man needs some time to himself. Plus, there was another incentive. It was his second reason for coming out there alone. He had a satchel with two large silver salmon.

He enjoyed fishing enough to risk the punishment. Fishing was one of the draws to living on Kodiak Island. Kodiak was one of the best fishing spots in North America. Hell, it was one of the best in the world. Especially for salmon.

Kodiak Island was a part of the Kodiak Archipelago. It was the largest island in the archipelago and the eightieth largest island in the world, spanning nearly three thousand, six hundred square miles. There were seven communities on the island, seven hamlets. The biggest was the main town called Kodiak. The south part of the island was filled with rugged terrain, but was fairly treeless. That's where most of the population lived. The northern and western parts were more remote parts, like thick forests and forgotten fishing villages. There was a lot of wildlife in the northern and western parts.

Fourteen thousand people inhabited the island, with millions passing through for tourism, bird-watching, hunting, and fishing over the course of a year. The island was originally inhabited by the Alutiiq people—Alaskan natives. They're more commonly referred to as Pacific Eskimos.

The old man knew some of them personally.

The old man waited quietly, watching his fishing pole, hoping for a bite, before he realized he had lost his bait to a silver salmon that was more cunning than your average fish. He thought about tossing the line out again with fresh bait, but he glanced at his watch and then up at the clouds. The rain fell slow and steady. It was a light drizzle, as it had been all morning, but he knew it would get worse. The afternoon often brought heavy weather. He realized he better make the long hike back to his four-wheeler. Not that it mattered in terms of his being caught sneaking out. He was busted no matter what time he got back. Heading back now or heading back later made no difference. His caretakers would know he had gone. Hell, they already did. They may have sent out a search party for him. But they wouldn't find him. Not before he returned. There weren't many people living on the island, and there was plenty of space to hide.

The old fisherman scooped up his hook and line and hooked it to the end of the rod. He took big steps to wade back through the river water and onto the muddy shore. He passed through the mud and stepped up onto long blades of grass. He stomped his feet and raked the soles across the grass to remove most of the mud. He shook both of his legs, one at a time, to shake river water off his waders.

The old man scooped off his ball cap and brushed his hair back. His gray hair was getting long. He'd have to convince Peter to take him into town soon to get it cut. It swooped over his scalp to one side, like it had nowhere else to go. He took more big steps back toward the direction of the parked four-wheeler, which was about a hundred yards back through waist-high grass and behind a cluster of trees. He didn't want to chance getting stuck in the mud, so he had parked his four-wheeler back on the old road and walked to the river, carrying his fishing gear.

About twenty yards in, he realized everything was quiet. He paused and stopped and wondered: *Why is it so quiet?* It was weird. When he first arrived and walked through the grass down to the river, he heard nature sounds. But now, he heard nothing. No birds. No insects. Nothing but the slow breeze in the cold air.

He looked left and followed the grass, the tree line, and the horizon with his eyes. He traced it all the way back to the river and saw nothing. He took a breath.

He took a step forward, and abruptly, there was a noise. A skein of Northern Shovelers took off from out of the grass.

They launched fast and furious like they sensed a hunter, like someone fired a gunshot to scatter them. And that's the first thought that fired through the old man's head. He wondered if he wasn't alone. He wondered if there was a hunter nearby. But he heard no gunshots. He looked around curiously at first. Then he realized he wasn't wearing a bright-orange vest or any other bright color to show hunters he was out there. It was an amateur thing to forget to wear it out in the Alaskan wilderness. Then again, why would he wear a safety color? Hunting wasn't allowed, not on this part of the river. Anyone caught hunting during off-season or in protected areas would face steep consequences. The Alaskan Department of Fish and Game wasn't to be trifled with. Not in his state.

Nervously, because he didn't want to get shot, the old man checked left and checked right. He circled his head and looked in every direction. He saw nothing. He saw no one. No hunters. No signs of human life. Not anywhere.

Unexpectedly, the Shovelers weren't the only birds in the sky. A raft of nearby ducks did the same thing. They flew off in a frenzy—squawking and flapping their wings frantically like their lives depended on it.

Suddenly, the old man froze in terror—dead in his tracks. He heard the reason behind the fearful ducks and the fleeing Shovelers before he saw it. The reason wasn't a hunter. It wasn't a human.

A roar that would rock a lion to its core erupted nearby, like a cannon blast. Before he turned all the way to look in its direction, a ten-foot-tall, fifteen-hundred-pound Kodiak bear came pushing past the tall grass out of the gloom.

The old man stayed frozen. The first thing he did was drop his ball cap. Then he instinctively reached for his belt, right side, where he kept a can of bear spray clipped to it. He snatched at it to immediately jerk it off his belt. Only his hand came up empty. He reached down again to swipe the bear spray up; again his hand was empty. He patted the place on his belt where it was supposed to be. But there was nothing there. He patted again, desperately. It still wasn't there. He stopped patting and remembered it was still on the four-wheeler. He'd forgotten it.

The bear closed in and stopped fifty feet away. It stopped and stared at him. It stared into his eyes. The bear's eyes were brown and deep, nearly black. They weren't lifeless, not like a shark's eyes. These were full of life and thoughts. The old man knew instantly the single thought that ran through the bear's mind. It was food. He could only imagine that he looked like a walking chicken drumstick to the animal, even though, in reality, the old fisherman was pretty bony. The bear could do better. But when you're starving, you will eat anything.

The old man tried to remember what to do. Should he run? Should he play dead? The only answer his brain would give him was to spray the bear with bear spray.

Before he could make a decision, the bear made it for him. It reared up on its hind legs and stretched up to its full height. A looming ten feet of muscle and fur and claws and teeth. The old man froze more than he had. He felt his heart stop for a long second, and then he dropped his fishing pole and swung around and ran as hard and as fast as he could. The heavy waders didn't do him any favors. They slowed him down. But he had to press on. No choice.

The old man ran, and the bear chased after him. The bear stomped on the man's dropped fishing pole, and he heard it snap under the heavy weight of the giant beast. He didn't look back. There was no time to be upset. Fishing poles were replaceable. His life was not.

The old man ran back toward the river. He knew the water would slow the bear down. His heart was no longer still. It beat hard and furious in his chest, pumping blood hard through his veins, igniting him with adrenaline. His brain slipped into survival mode like it was just the flip of a switch. The old man's boots pounded on the riverbank and then into the water. He felt the mud squishing under him. The water splashed up and across his face and neck. He waded through the river as fast as he could. He heard the bear behind him. It followed. It splashed and panted. It wasn't slowing down. He knew it. He felt it.

The old man crossed the river to the other side. He took a quick glance over his shoulder. The bear was right there. Twenty feet. Fifteen.

The old man kept going, kept running. He headed toward nearby heavy rocks and trees. He stomped through more tall grass and didn't stop. He kept running. His satchel beat across his hip. The caught salmon inside shuffled around. He kept running. His waders slowed him down. His age slowed him down. He felt himself getting winded. He wasn't making much distance. His feet hurt. His legs ached. He was getting tired. But he continued.

He ran past the tall grass and into a cluster of big rocks. He continued on until he was stomping through more mud. He didn't turn back. He heard the bear's feet stomping on the ground behind him. He heard the bear breathing and panting. The bear roared again. It sounded like it was furious. Now the old man had made it mad. The old man needed a break. He needed to catch his breath. He wasn't a young man anymore. Those years were decades behind him.

He ran.

The bear's heavy weight echoed with each step it took. And then it got worse. The old man heard the bear's steps get louder and louder and faster, like it was galloping.

The short time he bought himself gave him the chance to remember something about bears. Bears could run fast. He recalled a show on the Discovery Channel about grizzlies. They could clock in at thirty-five miles an hour on foot. He couldn't beat that. No man could. He had to escape. Outrunning it wouldn't work.

The old man took a sharp left at a huge rock and headed for some tall trees. He kept going, but he heard the bear gallop harder and harder, faster and faster. He twisted in the mud, and the bear did the same with no problem. The bear turned like it was the easiest thing it had ever done. He wasn't going to outrun it, and he wasn't going to outmaneuver it.

The old man's heart raced. His chest heaved. His legs burned. His knees ached. His one bad knee felt like it was on fire. The trees were right there. He had one chance. Maybe he could lose it in the trees? Maybe he could climb a tree? Not that it would save him. He also remembered from that same Discovery Channel special that bears could climb. And if they didn't feel like climbing, they could shake a tree with so much force and power just by pounding on it they could uproot a tall tree out of the ground. They could knock an entire tree over. It happened all the time.

The old man heard the bear's breathing getting heavier and heavier. Now it sounded like it was on his heels, like it was right behind him.

The old man turned his head and glanced back. He couldn't help it.

He saw the bear. His eyesight was hazed over by the gloom and the running. The detail was fuzzy, but he saw fifteen hundred pounds of evolution's most fearsome land predator.

With his eyes staring back at the bear, he wasn't watching where he was running. And he made a huge mistake, one that could be the end for him. He slammed right into a thick, hard tree and fell back on his butt. The wind knocked out of him. His eyes stayed on the bear even as he struggled to catch his breath.

The old man thought the bear was going to pounce on him right then. He thought it was all over. He had lost. He was bear food. It was the end.

But the bear didn't pounce on him. Not yet. It stopped right in front of him. It dropped its mouth open wide and roared in his direction.

This is it. Feeding time, he thought.

CHAPTER 3

The Kodiak bear could've eaten him right there. The old man slammed his eyes shut, expecting it to. He breathed in and breathed out. His heart raced. He waited to feel the teeth and the claws. He expected to hear the heavy breathing over his dying corpse. It was going to happen. There was no equation where he walked away from this. No sense in resisting. No chance to run. He hoped it killed him before it started eating him, and fast.

But the bear didn't kill him. It didn't eat him. There were no claws, no teeth, no heavy breathing over his dying body.

He opened his eyes.

The bear wasn't eating him at all. Instead, it reared up on its hind legs again. This time it stretched all the way out as far as it could. It raised its paws and roared. Its head was the size of two bowling balls. The mouth opened wide. The mouth opened so wide it appeared it could swallow most of the motor on his four-wheeler easily.

He tried to remember that Discovery Channel documentary again. He remembered seeing something about bears doing this to intimidate other bears or other large predators. But why? He wasn't a predator. He wasn't a threat to the bear. He was nothing, barely a whisper to the bear.

Just then, the old man felt something else, like a third presence looming behind him. The third presence was the tree that he slammed into when he was running at full speed with his head turned back to see the bear. He had thought he slammed right into a tree, and it had knocked him on his butt, knocked the breath out of him. But it wasn't a tree. It couldn't have been because it walked. The tree moved into view. It walked out in front of him, stopped, and stood there at his feet, facing the enormous bear.

His first instinct told him it was another Kodiak bear. He looked forward at it, his vision still blurry from the running and panting. The thing in front of him that knocked him over wasn't a bear, either. He knew that because it didn't move like a bear. It was a living, breathing thing that walked upright and was bipedal. The thing in front of him raised up its paws and stretched them up to the sky like the bear was doing. It was another beast—that was for sure—but not a bear.

The beast stretched its body out to full height, same as the bear. It mimicked the same aggression and rage, and it was like two bears encountering each other out in the wild. It was a turf war. They could've been fighting over who would eat the old man.

The thing at his feet roared back at the Kodiak bear, only the roar didn't sound like a bear at all. It sounded like a man—a savage jungle man, but a flesh-and-bone man. It was a beast man.

"Arrrrrggggggghhhh!" the beast man roared.

The Kodiak bear responded with another earth-shattering roar. The roar echoed over the trees and rocks. It was heard beyond the grass and the river. More terrified birds launched from out of the trees and scattered into the air.

The beast man at his feet wasn't like any creature he had ever seen before. It was too humanlike. His first thought was it might be the legendary Bigfoot come up out of the woods. The thing was massive. From the ground, it looked somewhere between six foot five and seven feet tall—hard to tell with it fully stretched all the way out like it was.

The beast man was all muscle and bulk. He had broad shoulders, like he was wearing NFL armor. His arms were solid, like tree branches. His fists were thick, like the business end of a Louisville Slugger. He had a long reach, like the wingspan of a California condor. The reach from shoulder to fingertip made it appear nearly the same height as the bear from the old man's perspective.

Abruptly, the Bigfoot did something unlike any Bigfoot legend he ever heard of. It spoke.

"Go away!" the Bigfoot shouted to the bear.

The Kodiak bear didn't roar back this time. It stayed standing, but looked back at the beast man. Confusion streamed across its face. It pawed at the air with one mitt like a dog might. It was utterly perplexed.

The Bigfoot glanced over one shoulder, keeping one eye on the bear, and spoke to the old man. "Toss your satchel," the Bigfoot said.

The old man stared up at the Bigfoot. His vision came more into focus, and he realized it wasn't a Bigfoot either. It wasn't some legendary creature from out of the woods. It was a man —a large man, but a human man.

The old man could see how he was confused at first. Not only from his blurred vision and his seated perspective, but also, the guy was so big. That part hadn't been an illusion. The guy's frame was large and muscular, like he was born with a suit of armor instead of muscle and bone. His face was covered in a thick beard, not as long or thick as a mountain man who'd never stepped out of the woods before, but like a beard that had grown over weeks. His dark hair was disheveled, and his eyes were ice blue. They pierced through the old man like heat-seeking missiles. For a moment, only a moment, he feared the guy more than the bear. After all, man was more dangerous than any apex predator on the planet, and this guy seemed at the top end of the food chain.

The old man had seen scary men before. He knew scary men all too well. He knew more scary men than he cared to remember. This guy seemed different. This guy was something out of a horror comic, like the ones his granddad had read to him as a child. He mostly paid attention to the pictures. Out of all the terrifying men the old man had known in his life, this guy took the cake as far as physical appearance went.

The large man snapped his fingers, fast, snapping the old man out of his train of thought.

He said, "Hey! Pay attention! Throw the bear the satchel!"

The old man looked at the Bigfoot man and then down at his satchel. It hung around his torso. He paused a beat and stared at it like it held great sentimental value. Then he nodded without looking up and reached down and fumbled with it. One of the fins from a silver salmon poked out of the opening. He pulled the satchel off him and got up on his feet, slow, and stared at the bear.

The Bigfoot guy spoke again. He said, "Throw him the satchel! He wants the fish!"

The old man nodded and haphazardly tossed the satchel at the bear's feet. The fish came half sliding out of the top, along with a cold pack he kept inside to keep the fish fresh.

The bear stared at the Bigfoot guy for a long second. Then it dropped to all fours and sniffed the fishtails and the satchel. Slobber came out of its mouth and over its massive lips. The bear opened its jaws and snatched up both the fishtails and the satchel in one bite and turned and ran off into the woods. It didn't stop. It never looked back.

They watched it run off with the old man's fish and satchel until it was gone from sight.

CHAPTER 4

Jack Widow had had enough. He'd spent the last several years sleeping in motel rooms and riding buses and hitchhiking, wherever necessary, across the United States. He had wandered aimlessly. Sometimes he had a general plan of action. Sometimes he had a simple notion of where to go to next, a destination, and sometimes he had nothing. Sometimes he simply went where the going took him. Widow was always moving, always living carefree. But no one on the face of the earth lived completely carefree. Everyone faced problems. Widow didn't run from them. He didn't cower to them. He solved them. Get a problem, solve a problem—simple.

Widow was a former SEAL. Navy SEALs were problem solvers with firearms. You can take the man out of the SEALs, but you can never take the SEAL out of the man.

Wandering and roaming aimlessly wasn't the thing he'd had enough of. He loved that part. The freedom, the choice, having no commitments, no taxes, no luggage, no dead-weight, no debt to anyone or anything—it was the driving force of his life. The thing that he had enough of was people.

Not a particular person. The problem was just people. He was sick of them.

The world seemed to be going crazy, and every year got worse, crazier and crazier, but this year seemed like the worst yet. The world was so interconnected now because of the Twitters and Facebooks and Instagrams and iPads and iPhones and the i-this and the i-that. He had simply had enough.

While riding on a bus out of Austin, Texas, about a month ago, he decided he'd had enough. That was the exact moment. It hit him like a ton of bricks. He needed a break. It wasn't a forever thing. He knew that. He wasn't going to live in a cabin in the woods for the rest of his life. He just felt like he needed a vacation. He was burnt out on people. He wanted some peace and quiet. Even a man who lives a life of leisure needs a break every once in a while. Right? Where was the perfect place to go? What was the last place in America he could find solace? Widow remembered being in Alaska about a year back with NCIS Agent Sonya Gray, a young NCIS cop who basically took his old job. She was new to Unit Ten, the secret undercover unit he'd helped pioneer. Widow had met many people on his nomadic odyssey, but none were harder to forget than Gray. Alaska wasn't the thing that Widow couldn't stop thinking about. It was Agent Gray. She was definitely a woman he would never forget.

The perfect place for him to escape the world for a while was Alaska, America's last frontier. It was the beginning of fall. It was what people farther south would call "sweater weather," only it was more like light coat weather. Right then, the temperature was a cool forty-five, not as good as summer, but better than freezing.

Widow wasn't wearing a sweater. He wore a comfortable outdoor coat, not anything overly dramatic, and a flannel underneath and a pair of comfortable blue jeans. There were hiking shoes on his feet. The coat was more a nighttime necessity than anything else because the days were warm enough, but the nights were a whole different story, depending on wind and rain.

Three weeks ago, Widow trekked up from Texas, mostly by bus, up over and through the Rocky Mountains, and on until he got to Seattle, Washington. The whole trip until then took him a few days of bus depots and bus transfers, including one bus breakdown, which happened in the northwestern corner of Colorado. From there, he hitched a couple of rides until he made it to another bus depot, where he bought a one-way ticket to Seattle. There, he booked a flight up to Anchorage. The airport had been fresh in his mind from the last time he was there with Gray. They had flown into and out of that same airport together. They sat on the plane together. They did a lot together.

Even though he hadn't seen her since they said their good-byes in Virginia, he still pictured her standing at the car rental counter, trying to get a sporty car to rent. The thought made him smile. It led him into other, more intimate memories of her—some with clothes on, some with clothes off. The thoughts put a smile on his face.

Widow liked Gray. After they got back to DC, he spent time with her. He stayed at her house. He slept in her bed. He walked her dog with her. She taught him some things about horticulture. She taught him about her Bonsai tree hobby.

With Gray, he felt something different than he had with other women. For once in his life, he understood why people get together and stay together. Once, he had viewed it as two people shacking up. Now his view had changed. He could see the appeal of having a home life. There was even a moment that it occurred to him what married life must be like.

He stayed with Gray longer than he had stayed with anyone else in years. He stayed nearly two weeks, a world record for him. She had taken some time off from Unit Ten and the NCIS. For two weeks, they lived their lives together like one of those happily married couples. She had taught him plenty, and he had taught her nothing. He couldn't. There was no skill that he had that she didn't already have. She knew how to throw a right hook. She knew how to shoot straight. She knew how to check for exits. She knew to check the corners of a room before clearing it. She knew criminal investigation. She knew undercover methods. There was nothing for him to add to her life, which made him feel a little lame, a little useless.

Widow hated three things with extreme prejudice. The first was injustice. He couldn't stand for wrong things to be overlooked. The second was being stuck. And the third was feeling obsolete, outmoded, and outdated—useless. There was nothing for him to add to her life. Nothing that he could see. For him, the writing was on the wall, as it usually was.

Gray was a fine woman and a fine investigator. She would do great in Unit Ten. No question. One day, when his old boss Rachel Cameron retired, Gray would make a fine choice to replace her as director.

Gray didn't need Widow. She didn't need anyone.

The only thing he did in his career that she couldn't do, not yet, was infiltrate the Navy SEALs as one of them. He did that and remained a SEAL for sixteen years. He was damn good at it. In most ways, he felt more like a SEAL than an NCIS agent. He went out on every mission and every assignment that was given to him. The other SEALs never knew who he really was. No one did. No one outside Unit Ten ever knew that he was a double agent. Even his friends inside the unit didn't really know him.

Unit Ten had assigned him to the SEALs. He was the only agent ever to pass all the obstacles that they threw at him. Once he was on a SEAL team, he became one of them, too. No question. He was more SEAL than undercover cop. He was always undercover, always taking on two imperatives at once. The SEALs gave him orders, and the NCIS gave him directives. He lived a lie. He was always juggling one lie over the other. He still completed both of his missions. He was a SEAL. But he also was their investigator.

The only way he could explain it to an outsider was to compare it to working in Internal Affairs in the NYPD. The scope of his larger obligation was to investigate crimes either committed by bad apples or around SEAL missions. Sometimes the culprits were foreign agents, and sometimes they were his teammates. Like an Internal Affairs agent, who was foremost a cop, Widow was a SEAL who was foremost a cop. Neither one ever really outweighed the other. Not in his mind. He swore an oath to the Constitution—twice, in two different ceremonies. One was out in the open, and one was in a room behind closed doors. Being an undercover agent for so long took a toll on him.

Then, one day, while he was in deep cover, his mom was shot in the head in a small town in Mississippi. She wasn't dead, but she was in bad shape. He was pulled off assignment and given leave to return home. She died holding his hand. After he found the responsible parties and brought his own brand of justice to them, he couldn't go back to his old life. He couldn't endure another sixteen years of living two lies. He wanted the one thing that he had never known—freedom. And nothing made him feel freer than the open road. In the same way that a caged bird covets the open sky, Widow coveted the open road. He was never going back. He would never give it up.

Gray was so tough that she probably would make it as a SEAL. No doubt about that. The SEALs had never had a woman. Not yet. Widow heard of a few women getting into Hell Week, but so far, none had made it into BUD/S, or Basic Underwater Demolition/SEAL training.

Widow knew Gray had what it took to make it. But that wasn't the issue. She would never make it because they wouldn't let her. The Navy brass liked to give the impression of being progressive without being progressive. No woman would ever make it into BUD/S as long as the old pointy-heads in Washington were still in power.

He didn't tell Gray any of this. He didn't need to. She knew it. Widow stayed out of all that stuff. He let the paper-pushers on the Navy side of the Pentagon deal with their own insecurities. Not his business. Not his fight. He'd served his country.

One day, two weeks after he first closed his eyes on Gray's pillow, he overstayed his welcome. He knew it. They both did. She was career-focused. He was forward-focused, not the same thing. She wanted a life of promotions and commendations and occupational achievements. She was an NCIS agent, a cog in the wheel, a taxpayer. He wasn't. He wanted no part of it. Therefore, he was no use to her. They had no future. Widow's future was paved in everlasting blacktop. Gray's was filled with more criminal busts, salary bumps, and rising through NCIS ranks.

There was no reason to kid themselves. One day, he didn't wait for her to ask him to leave. He simply showered, dressed, and said goodbye after coffee one morning. And that was that.

Nearly a year later, he was riding a bus near Austin, reading a paperback called *Into the Wild*, listening to a guy in a tie arguing on the phone with his parents about who they would vote for in the upcoming election. He listened to complaints about the state of the country, the economy, and the world. He thought the guy had some points. But it was a one-sided conversation for him because he couldn't hear the parents. He realized something in that moment. One-sidedness was rampant all over the world. He simply decided he needed a break.

The book he was reading gave him the perfect idea. What better place to get lost for a couple of weeks than Alaska? To add even more sense to his assessment, he thought, *Why not Kodiak Island?*

Now he was on an island that not only had a small population of people for him to deal with, but also, it was in Alaska to boot.

He spent two weeks camping; fishing for his dinner and bathing in rivers. And he loved it. He hadn't seen but a few people here and there. There were six days where he never even spoke. Not one word. He felt rested and reinvigorated and calm.

Everything was going fine until he felt lonely. Eventually, he missed the world, the people. Wasn't life funny? He'd come there to escape, which worked, but by the end of the two weeks, he missed the hustle and bustle of the world.

Widow had met several hunters and fishermen and campers in his two-week hiatus. All good people. All friendly. It was right there in the beginning that he met one young couple who shared a campfire with him. That's where he picked up a new interest and hobby. They were bird-watchers. They even gave him a pair of old binoculars with a strap and a little book on birds.

He was searching across the eastern part of the Karluk River for the Northern Shovelers when he heard a bear roar. And now he stood over a frightened old man who had nearly been breakfast for a huge bear.

The old man dusted himself off as best he could. He looked up at Widow and said, "Thank you. Thank you so much."

"You're welcome. You okay?" Widow said.

"Yeah. I'm whole."

Widow scanned the old guy. He stood maybe five eight, about a hundred and fifty pounds. He had gray stubble on his face and a mop of thick, gray-and-black hair. It blew in the wind even after he fixed it. He was dressed in a wader with typical outdoor-style clothing underneath. The old guy's face was amazing. There was a lot of life in his eyes. His face was symmetrical in all but one way. There was a long white scar down his right cheek. It went from his sideburn down his cheek. It was old and healed to a deep white. It looked like a knife scar. Widow would know. He had seen healed knife wounds before. He didn't ask about it.

There was something else about him. Something familiar. Widow recognized him from somewhere. It wasn't the scar. It was something around the guy's eyes. He had two big eye sockets, like a face designed to hold goggles on it without a strap.

Widow couldn't place him, but he felt he had seen his face once before.

"Sorry about your fish," Widow said.

"That's okay. I really wasn't out here for the fish. But that satchel, I loved."

"Sorry about your satchel."

"Better the satchel than my arm, I suppose."

Widow cracked a smile and said, "That's true. Although, I doubt the bear was interested in you."

"He seemed to be."

"Nah. He was just wanting the fish."

"He was pretty aggressive. More so than normal bears."

Widow shrugged and said, "You might've been fishing in his watering hole."

"Is that why he was so aggressive, you think?"

"Could be. Bears are territorial."

"Are they?"

"I think so. But I'm no expert."

"Well, he's gone now. Normally, I would've sprayed him with bear spray, but I left it back on my four-wheeler."

"Is that how you got out here?"

The old man looked at Widow sideways. "How else would you?"

"Lots of ways. By boat. Horseback maybe."

"You see a lot of horses around here?"

"There could be."

"You're not local. Are you?"

"What gave me away?"

To that, the old man didn't respond. He just gave a kind of sneer. Not intended to be rude. The old man reached his hand out and said, "My name's Bill Liddy."

Widow took the hand, tried not to crush it, and shook it. "Widow."

"Widow what?"

They stopped shaking hands.

Widow said, "Jack."

"Nice to meet you, Widow Jack."

"Not Widow Jack. It's Jack Widow."

"Oh. Why did you say your last name first?"

"That's what people call me. Always have."

"I see. Well, nice to meet you, Widow. Just call me Bill. That's what my friends call me."

Widow nodded and stayed quiet.

Liddy looked at Widow's rucksack. He knew there was a sleeping bag in it. That was obvious. He saw some basic camping gear. There was a cheap, retractable fishing pole. And he saw a tin coffee cup hanging from the backside of the rucksack.

He asked, "You camping?"

"Yeah. Pretty much."

"You get all that gear from Cutty's Fish and Tackle back in Kodiak?"

"I did. How did you know that?"

"It looks like his cheap shit," Liddy said, and he let out a cackle like old men do. Then he said, "He's always selling shit to the tourists. That's why his place is the first you'll see when you get to Kodiak on the other side of the island."

Kodiak was the largest and the closest thing to a city on Kodiak Island. They were about eighty miles away from it. Although there are plenty of waterways and people with boats all over the island, the fastest and most common way to get from one side to the other was by floatplane.

Widow smiled.

Liddy asked, "So, where is he?"

"I have no idea. Back at his shop. I guess."

"He didn't fly you over to this side of the island?"

"He flew me."

"And he left you?"

"Of course. I flew over here with him and another guy to Akhiok Airport. They went in one direction, and I went in another."

"Akhiok?"

Widow nodded.

"That's like thirty miles south from here? You rode a four-wheeler all the way here?"

"No four-wheeler."

"How did you get this far from them? Truck?"

"Can you get here by truck?"

"You'd need some serious off-road vehicles to do it. But sure. It's possible. I suppose."

Widow asked, "How many roads you got here?"

"Not many."

Widow stayed quiet.

Liddy said, "You didn't answer my question. How did you get this far?"

"I walked."

"How?"

"Cutty didn't bring me here just today or yesterday. I've been here for about two weeks."

"Doing what?"

Widow pointed down at the binoculars dangling from around his neck.

"Bird-watching."

"Bird-watching?"

"Yeah."

"You?"

Widow said, "Sure. Why not?"

"You just don't look like the bird-watching type. So you've been out here all by yourself for two weeks? Just bird-watching?"

"I'm camping too."

"Why?"

"I wanted to take a break from people. I needed some quiet time with just me and nature."

"What? Like Thoreau?"

"He lived in a log cabin, but sure. Similar."

Liddy looked around like he was looking for the bear again. He didn't see it. He lifted his hand and pointed north.

Suddenly, worry came over Liddy's face. He patted his pockets like he was searching for something. When he didn't find it, he spun around and scanned the ground. It was apparent that he had misplaced something.

"Oh no!" Liddy said.

Widow asked, "Everything okay?"

Liddy stopped patting his pockets and stopped searching the ground. He looked at Widow and said, "I need to get the satchel back."

"Why?"

"There's something important in it I need."

Widow asked, "What?"

"I can't tell you."

"Why not?"

Liddy didn't answer that. He said, "Can you help me?"

Widow said, "You want to hunt down a fifteen-hundred-pound hungry bear and take its fish from it?"

"No. Not the fish. I just need something from the satchel. Please! Help me! I can't do it without you."

"What's so important?"

Liddy paused a beat. He looked around like he was searching for spies in the trees. He said, "It's personal. It's sentimental."

Widow said, "If you want me to help you track down a bear, I think I'm entitled to know what for?"

"There's a photograph in it. It's important to me. Please, will you help me? I'll never find the bear on my own."

Widow asked, "You don't have a backup of the photo on your cell phone?"

"I don't have a cell phone."

Widow arched an eyebrow. He didn't have a cell phone either. He'd owned them in the past. The NCIS had issued him smartphones; usually, they were encrypted. He needed them for work purposes. But since he left years ago, he found them to be more of a nuisance. Smartphones are a little too smart for him. They come with GPS tracking chips inside them. Today's smartphones collect data on the user and report that data back to the mother ship corporation that designed the phone. He didn't like that. Widow liked to keep his digital footprint as small as possible, which wasn't easy these days. Even though he had no smartphone, he still needed to use money to get by. Cash money worked to keep his exact whereabouts and actions quiet, but he had to keep most of his money someplace. That place was a bank, which meant that he had to carry a bank card. Every time he withdrew money from an ATM, he was leaving a digital footprint of where he was. He tried to keep money withdrawals down to once or twice a month.

The other thing that was annoying was that a lot of motels only took credit or debit cards before they allowed someone to rent a room. They claimed it was for reclaiming damages left behind. But Widow just saw this as another means of tracking him. He only used locally owned motels. He found that most times, the person behind the counter was also the owner. They could be persuaded to overlook their own card-on-file policy.

Widow said, "I don't have a cell phone either. So I under-stand." He thought for a moment, and then he asked, "Why's this picture so important?"

Liddy looked down at his feet for a moment. A look of suspicion came over his face, like he was about to give away state secrets. Then he said, "It's of my daughter. It's the only one I have. We don't talk."

Widow nodded and stayed quiet.

Liddy said, "It's a long story."

Widow said, "No need to explain it. Not to me. I understand. I didn't speak to my own mother for seventeen years."

"Oh? Why not?" Liddy asked.

Widow shook his head and said, "That's for me alone."

"I'm sorry. None of my business."

Widow asked, "Which way is your four-wheeler?"

Liddy raised a hand and pointed in the direction he'd left it parked.

"Okay. Let's go there first."

Liddy asked, "Why?"

Widow said, "If we're going to track this bear, then we'll need that can of bear mace."

Liddy nodded and said, "Okay. This way." And he turned and walked away.

Widow followed.

The two men walked north, back to Liddy's four-wheeler. Liddy kept his head on a swivel. He looked every which way: into the tall grass, up and down the river as they crossed it, and behind every tree. He wanted to make sure the Kodiak bear wasn't lying in wait.

CHAPTER 5

They got lucky. It turned out they didn't have to track the bear down to retrieve Liddy's satchel. On the way back to the four-wheeler, Widow spotted the satchel just over the riverbank. It was sprawled out at the center of a large chunk of crushed grass. The bag was split in half like a torn phone book and nearly right down the center. Liddy stayed behind Widow as the two men walked over to it.

Widow pointed down at the chunk of crushed grass and said, "The bear must've sat down here to pull the fish out. He ripped your bag in half, took the fish out, ate one, and ran off with the others."

Widow pointed at a mess of fish guts, scales, and crushed bones peering out of the crater left behind in one of the bear's massive paw prints.

Liddy asked, "Why here? So close to us? Is he still around?"

Widow rotated his arm and pointed at bear-tracks that went off to the west. He said, "He's gone. You might've tired him out with all that running. He popped a squat here to get the fish out. He took the rest for later."

Liddy stepped out from behind Widow. He looked in all directions like he was crossing a dangerous intersection. He knelt on one knee and scooped up the bag. He clenched it close and examined the damage.

Liddy reached in and dug around the shredded contents of the bag. Finally, he pulled out the photograph. From the back, it looked like an old Polaroid with the black back and white frame casing around it. It was crumpled a bit. The corners were bent. One was torn clean off, but overall, the photograph looked intact.

Liddy brushed it off and straightened out the corners and the wrinkles. He inspected it. Widow shuffled and sidestepped and moved closer behind Liddy. He looked down and glimpsed the photo over Liddy's shoulder.

The picture was faded and a little too dark, like someone forgot to use the flash. But he could make it out, and once he had, he realized why it was too dark. It wasn't a picture of a little girl, like Widow had expected. It wasn't even a picture of a human being, not in the exact scientific definition of what a fully developed human being was supposed to look like. The photograph that Liddy was holding wasn't a Polaroid at all. It was an ultrasound from the nineties.

It was black and white. There was printed information along the left side. Widow could make out a somewhat-formed fetus. He was no expert, but he would guess it was maybe four months along.

Widow glimpsed the information on the left. He saw a name, maybe the name of the doctor. He saw technical information and numbers and arrows pointing out the head and other formed and forming baby parts.

Liddy caught Widow looking and hurried the ultrasound out of view. He put it in his inside coat pocket and rose off the ground onto his feet.

He sniffled and cleared his throat. Widow caught Liddy wiping away a tear from his eye. But he didn't ask about it. Like his own feelings and regrets about his mother, it was no one's business. Liddy's troubles were his own.

Instead, Widow knelt alongside Liddy and picked up the two halves of the satchel. He stacked them one on top of the other, and asked, "You're going to have this fixed?"

Liddy sniffled one last time and looked at the remains of his satchel and said, "Doubtful. But I'll take it back, anyway. I don't want to litter."

Widow nodded and said, "I'll carry it for you."

"Thank you," Liddy said. "Can you help me up?" Liddy reached up his empty hand to Widow.

Widow nodded and stepped up, grabbed Liddy's hand, then stepped back and pulled him to his feet.

Liddy thanked him and pointed north again. He said, "This way."

Liddy stepped away and walked out in front of Widow. He led the way back to his four-wheeler. Widow tucked the two halves of the satchel tight underneath one arm and followed. They traversed through high grass away from the bear's tracks and made it to a thick cluster of trees. After walking up a short hill and then back down the other side of it, Widow saw a narrow paved road in the distance. It looked like it was concreted long ago by locals. He doubted it was on any map that existed today.

Widow asked, "How old is this road?"

Liddy shrugged and said, "Who knows? It's old. Probably older than me. The island is full of old roads and paths like this. We've got lots of uncharted wilderness here. People didn't think to map a lot of this until a few decades ago. Hell, Alaska's only been a state for sixty years."

Widow said, "Sixty-one. Actually."

Liddy stopped and looked up at Widow. Something glinted back at Widow from his eye. It was weird, like a mirrored message at sea. It was like a person trapped inside of Liddy was there, and then he wasn't.

Widow shrugged it off, smiled, and said, "Alaska became the forty-ninth state in the Union in nineteen fifty-nine."

"You sure about that?"

"Yep. It's nearly sixty-two. In January, it'll be sixty-two years old."

Liddy said nothing to that. He continued to lead the way, and they stepped onto the road. The road was cracked and flawed and weathered, which told Widow Liddy was right. This road was cemented fifty years ago, maybe longer. Widow had seen old roads all over the world. In particular, he could recall roads in the Middle East and Africa and parts of Asia that were far older, and even those were in better shape.

The four-wheeler was right there, parked on the shoulder. Liddy got to it first. He patted the seat like he just wanted to feel the leather on the palm of his hand. He reached into a saddlebag and pulled out a can of bear spray.

He held it in his hand and said, "Here it is. Wish I would've brought it with me. I'd still have my bag in one piece."

Widow said, "And your dinner."

Liddy shrugged and said, "That's okay. The fish weren't important. I do it more for the sport of it. I got food at home."

"Where do you live?"

"There's a village that way," he said and pointed northeast. "It's called Bell Harbor. I got a place up there. Actually, I got places all over the state."

Widow asked, "Bell Harbor? I don't recall that on a map."

"You got a map?"

Widow pointed at his head and said, "I saw one before I came out here."

"Bell Harbor's not on any map. Like I said, a lot of the island is uncharted. Hell, much of Alaska is still unmapped. Bell Harbor is inside a small bay shaped like a bell. It's known among sports fishermen."

Widow stayed quiet.

Liddy looked up at him and asked, "So, you want a lift? Or are you still bird-watching?"

Widow paused a long beat. He glanced around, stared at the trees, the high grass, and the terrain. He contemplated with one simple question: *Am I done with my break from people?* He looked back over his shoulder and then back at Liddy. The answer was: *Yes*.

He said, "You know. I'll take you up on that."

Liddy asked, "Thought you were done with people? Doing the Thoreau thing and just wandering around the forests?"

"Are there a lot of people in Bell Harbor?"

"Nope. Maybe a few hundred residents, I think."

"Doesn't sound like a bustling city."

"It's not."

Widow said, "I've been out here for two weeks. I'm over it. It'll be nice to take a real shower again. I'm ready to go back to normal life."

Liddy said, "Besides, you're probably paying double, renting gear from Cutty."

"That's true. He forced me to use my bank card when I rented it."

"How long did you rent the gear for?"

"We left it open-ended."

"In that case, you better return it soon. He's probably got a clause in his terms and agreement saying that after so many days of not returning it, he'll charge you full price for it."

"I didn't sign any terms and agreement papers."

"You agreed to it when you swiped your card."

Widow raised one eyebrow and asked, "I did?"

"I'd bet my life savings on it."

Widow said, "I better get back then."

Liddy said, "When we get there, you can just call him, and he'll come pick you up. It'll cost you, of course."

"Of course. How much?"

Liddy shrugged and said, "A lot. Or we can arrange for you to get a ride back. I've got a plane."

Liddy smiled and took the two halves of his torn satchel from Widow. He stuffed them and the can of bear spray into the saddlebag and closed the flap. He climbed up onto the four-wheeler's saddle in drive position. He looked at Widow.

He said, "Hop on. Let's get."

Widow nodded and got on the rear saddle behind Liddy. The rear saddle was raised up a little higher so he could see over Liddy, which wasn't necessary for him, but that's how it was designed.

Widow planted his feet as best he could on the footrests behind Liddy's.

Liddy cranked the ATV to life and cycled the accelerator to get the engine revved up. Within seconds, they were off.

CHAPTER 6

Widow and Liddy rode to Bell Harbor on the four-wheeler, with little conversation over the rumble of the engine. Not that Liddy wasn't talking. He spoke here and there, but Widow half tuned out, half couldn't hear Liddy's mumbles over the hum of the ATV, which echoed between the rows and rows of black spruce trees.

They got there just in time to see storm clouds merge overhead. Thunder rumbled in the distance. Lightning crackled in the underbelly of the clouds. Liddy parked the ATV in a row of three others, all for rent, all battle-worn from hunters and fishermen. Widow hopped off the ATV first and Liddy second. Liddy killed the engine and took the keys out. He pocketed them and looked at the sky.

He said, "That don't look good."

Widow looked up and said, "It's been doing that on and off the entire two weeks I've been here. Glad Cutty's gear came with a rain slicker. Is the weather always like this?"

"Not all year round, but we're in the rainy season. The salmon season runs smack into the rainy season around here. You get more rain, thus more running rivers and faster salmon migration."

Widow stayed quiet. He scanned the dark clouds until his eyes met the treetops. He shifted his attention down, to Bell Harbor and the closest building. He saw that Liddy's name was mounted on a sign along the side of it. The building was a three-story wooden building painted white. It was up on thick stilts. He figured it was lifted in order in case of flooding. The building was parked right in front of the bay of Bell Harbor. The front of the building had a long wooden sign posted above the first floor. It read, "Liddy's Lodge."

Widow stared up at it.

"This your place?"

Liddy fished his torn satchel out of the saddlebag and frowned at it. Once again, Widow got a glimmer of a memory of the face that looked like Liddy's in his mind, only he didn't remember any scar. He would've remembered that distinguishing feature. No doubt. It was Liddy's eyes and his goggle sockets that flashed across his memory. But the face Widow remembered was different—younger and flat, like it wasn't three-dimensional. They were still the same eyes, the same goggle eye sockets. The memory was far, far away like a copy of a copy. Either it was a faint, distant memory, or his mind had suppressed it, or he was losing it. Widow didn't suppress memories or emotions. He faced them head-on. Losing his marbles was a possibility he couldn't rule out, because he had just spent two weeks out in nature.

Liddy said, "Yeah. It's mine. I got locations all over the island."

"Really? You must be pretty well known."

"Not really. I keep to myself—mostly. I've been running these lodges for a long time."

Widow asked, "You're the sole owner?"

"More or less. I mean I got a partner, but he doesn't come around much. He's more of the money side."

Widow nodded.

Liddy said, "You'd be surprised how much business I get. My lodges are always booked pretty close to full through fishing and hunting seasons."

Widow asked, "You from Alaska?"

A look came over Liddy's face. His goggle eye sockets furrowed his brows.

He said, "Oh, I'm not from Alaska. Not born here. I was born in Seattle, but I've been here for years. My father moved us to Anchorage in the sixties. Been nowhere else. Not that I remember. I can't remember much about Washington State."

Widow nodded along like he was just listening, but he couldn't help but have doubts about Liddy's sincerity. Widow had lied for a living in the Navy SEALs, undercover. He lied to the enemy. He lied to his friends. He lied to his commanding officers. He lied to his teammates. That was his job. He had to maintain cover all the time, at all costs. If he didn't lie, people's lives hung in the balance, including his own.

Widow knew liars. He knew lies. He knew how to spot them. But Liddy was genuine enough that he wasn't sure. Enough signs showed themselves for him to be suspicious, but not enough to be certain. None of it was conclusive.

Even if Liddy was lying to him, it meant nothing. Not really. Perhaps he was forgetting something. Perhaps he suffered from old age. He was an old man. Maybe he was lying. What difference did it make? It was none of Widow's business.

If Liddy wanted to tell a total stranger that he had been an astronaut who took part in a moonwalk, he could. Widow wasn't a cop anymore. No reason to expect every person he met to tell him the whole truth. No reason at all.

The conversation stopped, and the two men left the row of ATVs and walked to the rear of the lodge, to the open mouth of the bay. The water was dark. It sloshed up to the shore, calm and serene like a sleeping giant.

Liddy looked up at the sky and checked the weather. He gazed over the dark clouds. Widow did the same, and then he scanned what Liddy called Bell Harbor.

Widow saw immediately why it was called Bell Harbor. He imagined that from an aerial view, the whole bay looked church-bell-shaped. The mouth of the bay was narrow. Past that, the bay had a bulbous middle like a bell.

The small hamlet was spread out along the coastline. Most of the structures were on the water or near it. Widow saw small shops here and there. There was a grocery store, a church, and a huge bait shop. There were other competing lodges to Liddy's. Most buildings stood up on stilts. Rustic docks lined the shores here and there. Various sizes of boats floated alongside them. There were large fishing charters, schooners, and smaller private boats. Most were parked in an unorganized fashion. Foot traffic was everywhere. There were tourists, sport fishermen, and locals all over the docks and piers. There was plenty of space between everything. Dark green grass and trees took up the space between all the human constructs. There was a beach that outlined the shore around the bay. Children played down by the water. No swimsuits. It was too cold.

Liddy said, "Of course, we're pretty slow in the winter. Right now is the end of the busy season. We might have a couple more weeks, and that's it. It won't be dead but slow. We get *some* bookings. Many people ice fish, you know? Some guys just like the harsh winters. We even get birdwatchers out here. There's a big season for it. But most of my profits come in the summer."

Widow asked, "This is why you know Cutty so well? He's your main competition?"

"He is. I suppose. There are other lodges," Liddy said. He lifted a hand and pointed across the bay at other lodges. His fingers bounced from one to the next until he stopped on a larger one. It was Cutty's. Widow saw the name scribbled on a wooden sign hung out back by a chain.

Liddy continued, "But he and I are the biggest local boys. Cutty's got a shop right there."

Widow stayed quiet.

Liddy lowered his hand and said, "Let me give you a lift back to Kodiak? That way you can return your gear to Cutty. Believe me, you don't want to pay his overpriced late fees."

Liddy rotated at the waist and pointed to a red floatplane docked at the end of a pier out back of his lodge. It floated on the bay and drifted up and down.

Widow looked at it and asked, "Can't I return this stuff to his shop over there?"

Liddy shook his head.

"Nope. He won't take it at any other location. All his stuff must be returned to the port you rented it from."

"That's shady."

Liddy nodded and said, "It is, but that's Cutty. He's always out to make a buck. Not me. Here you can rent any of my equipment and return it to any location."

"Guess I'll take you up on that plane ride back to Kodiak. Thank you. I appreciate it."

"It's the least I can do. You saved my life after all."

Widow said, "I doubt it. I think the bear would've swiped the fish as soon as it had you pinned. Probably would've run away after. Statistically, you're more likely to get crushed underneath a fallen vending machine than killed by a bear."

Liddy shot Widow a sideways look. The eyes in Liddy's goggle eye sockets stared at Widow like a man trying to decipher a puzzle.

Liddy said, "No way. He would've swiped my guts open trying to get the fish. I could've been left there to bleed out before anyone would've found me."

Widow stayed quiet.

At the back of the lodge, there were several boats tied up all along the dock. Four huge local guys stood around in a circle, chatting. The conversation was loud and getting heated. Not like they were arguing. It was more like they were on the verge of being frantic like they lost something important.

The four guys instantly made Widow think of large corn-fed country boys. The kind you could find in the fields in Nebraska in places with spotty cell phone coverage. These guys were big enough to play professional football as long as it didn't require any running.

A second later, Widow saw another huge guy standing at the bottom of a thick wooden staircase that led up to the first floor of Liddy's Lodge. The guy was laser-focused on the deckhands on the pier. His back was toward Widow and

Liddy. He couldn't see them. They stood back behind the stairs, out of his line of sight. The guy stepped off the bottom step and marched over to the four workers like a field commander. He barked orders at them. His body posture told Widow he was used to barking orders and having those orders followed without question, without protest. But that wasn't happening. Instead, the four guys had all turned to their leader, but they stared past him, right at Liddy and Widow. The look on their faces was one of relief and confusion.

Their supervisor shouted, "Why aren't you moving?"

None of the guys spoke. But one of them lifted a heavy hand and pointed out the duo behind him. He kept his feet planted on one of the pier's wooden planks and turned his head and took a peek over his shoulder. He saw the two newcomers in his peripherals and turned around to face them. He stared at Liddy and then glanced over at Widow. He looked Widow up and then down. It reminded Widow of the Terminator movies. Good old Arnold's eyes registered people in a kind of digital vision. He had automatic targeting and threat assessments given in real time.

The Terminator guy marched over to them before the others budged from their formation. He was at the first plank that led onto the pier in seconds. Widow's primal brain noted the guy's speed. It was fast for a guy his size.

The Terminator guy stopped, ignored Liddy, and stared right at Widow. He looked Widow up and down like there actually was a robotic brain in his thick skull and the eyes were scanning Widow over, providing battlefield analysis right there—instant threat assessment.

The Terminator guy spoke to Liddy without glancing at him. He said, "Where've you been? Who the hell is this?"

Liddy put his hands up like he did with the bear. "Calm down, Peter."

The Terminator guy called Peter stood a little over six foot seven, three inches taller than Widow. Widow was a man with a towering frame, but Peter was something else entirely. The man was height and brawn. Peter's shoulders were so thick it looked like Bruce Banner right at that moment he was about to break out of his clothes, turn green, and morph into the Hulk.

An obvious vein on Peter's forehead turned purple. It looked on the verge of popping. His cheeks flushed red with anger. Clearly, the guy was upset. He almost looked betrayed.

Peter swiveled his head slow and stared down at Liddy. He repeated, "Where've you been? We've been searching all morning."

"Relax, Peter. Relax," Liddy said and reached a hand up and patted Peter on the chest. The pat made a sound that was like someone knocking on the side of a full oil drum.

"Where were you?!" he asked again. There was a certain tone in his voice. He spoke like he was entitled to know. He sounded like a jailer discovering one of his prisoners had stepped out for the night.

Liddy said, "Relax. I got up early and went fishing."

Peter looked Liddy up and down. He saw the disheveled hair, the torn satchel, and the dirt on his clothes and mud on his boots.

"He hurt you?" Peter asked.

"No. Of course not. Just relax. Take a breath, Peter," Liddy said.

Peter nodded slowly like he was powering down. He took a deep breath.

Liddy said, "This is Jack Widow. He saved my life."

Peter stared at Liddy's eyes. His expression went from adversarial to one of deep concern.

He asked, "Saved your life how?"

Liddy said, "It's not as dramatic as it sounds. I had a run-in with a bear. It chased after me."

"A bear?"

"Not that big a deal. It just wanted my fish," Liddy said and raised the torn satchel. "He shredded my bag to get at them."

Peter exhaled and relaxed a bit.

Liddy said, "I went fishing. That's it. See?" He showed Peter his satchel.

Peter took it in his hands and examined the two halves.

Liddy said, "It was just a hungry bear, that's all. Widow here scared him off, but not before he got my bag."

Peter asked, "Where's your bear mace?"

"I didn't have it."

Peter asked, "You snuck out without me and didn't take bear mace with you?"

"I took it. I just left it on the ATV. It was an accident."

Peter shook his head with disappointment and frustration. He said, "You mean carelessness. You were careless. You're not supposed to go out without one of us. You know that!"

"I wanted to be alone. Every man needs peace and quiet sometimes. Look, I'm back. All in one piece. Not a big deal."

With a hand that could palm a toaster, Peter reached out and shoved Liddy aside like he was nothing. It was gentle enough, far from assault, but firm. The whole spectacle confused Widow because he thought Liddy was the boss, and that Peter was some kind of hired right-hand man. Liddy's name was on the building and probably on Peter's paychecks. Widow couldn't imagine pushing one of his COs aside like that. Then again, civilians were different. Peter wasn't going to get court martialed for it. Maybe he was legitimately over-worried? Then again, maybe not. Liddy snuck off without his guys. He didn't tell anyone where he was going. He was old. And the forest here was no joke. They'd had a run-in with a bear.

Peter passed Liddy and walked straight up to Widow and stopped three feet out in front of him. He reached one of those toaster-gripping hands out to him, with a big reach. His palm was open. He offered it to Widow for a handshake, a peace offering.

Widow nodded and took it. They shook.

Peter said, "Thank you, Mr. Widow, for bringing Liddy back home in one piece for us. I'm in your debt."

Widow didn't know what to think. Not really. Peter's behavior was off-putting. It would've only made sense if there was an emotional connection between them, like a father and son, but Liddy didn't introduce Peter as a son or any other type of relative. The best Widow could figure it was that they had a father-son bond. Maybe they had worked together for years. A father-son relationship had formed. It happens.

There was a certain quality, a certain attitude in Peter's voice. It was his attempt at an apology for jumping to conclusions with the whole "He hurt you?" thing.

It reminded Widow of when he was a kid, and his mom made him apologize to one of the neighborhood kids for breaking the kid's Louisville Slugger in half over his knee. Widow broke the kid's bat out of anger. The truth was, the kid deserved it. He was picking on other kids, threatening them with the bat. Widow hated bullies. He took the kid's favorite bat and broke it right in front of him. It was all for dramatic effect. He wasn't really going to hurt the kid. He meant it as a sample of what he would do to the kid if he didn't stop picking on weaker kids. It was symbolic, like a warning shot. Of course, that's not how the kid told it to his parents. He told them that Widow was the bully, as bullies often do. Projection and blaming others are the key weapons of a bully.

The kid's parents called Widow's mother, who was the town sheriff. She forced Widow to march over to the kid's house and apologize to his face, which was embarrassing enough. Then she forced him to work all summer to pay her back for the replacement bat that she bought the kid. To this day, he wasn't sure what was worse: giving up his entire summer or apologizing to a bully who didn't deserve it. The whole time he apologized, he could see the look in the kid's eyes. The kid mocked him, all while keeping that look of innocent victim in front of his parents. It was a sham.

Peter's apology might've been a little fake, but his thanks seemed sincere. He was grateful that Widow was there to save his boss's life.

Widow said, "Not a problem."

Widow broke free of the handshake with Peter, who turned back to Liddy.

Peter said, "I'm grateful that Mr. Widow saved you, but you really shouldn't be talking to total strangers out in the wilderness."

Peter shot Widow a glance. He said, "No offense. It's just that there's no telling who you might run into out there."

Widow nodded and stayed quiet.

Liddy said, "Widow's not a stranger. Not now. He's our friend."

Peter nodded and said nothing.

Liddy said, "Widow, you're invited to stay with us. Free of charge, of course."

"No. I should really get back to Kodiak, turn in my gear, and be on my way."

"Okay. Let me buy you a beer first. Peter can get the plane ready. It's the least I can do. We have a bar inside. What kind of beer you like?"

"I'll take a coffee. Got any coffee?"

"Of course. The best on the island."

Widow smiled, and the two men went up the stairs to the lodge. They rounded some railing. Liddy led the way. They stopped at a pair of double doors. Liddy pulled one open and entered. Widow stayed behind him. Peter headed off to the plane.

The inside of the lodge had high ceilings. There was expensive leather furniture in the lobby, near a large rock fireplace. There was a stuffed grizzly bear in one corner. It was posed to look furious and intimidating.

Liddy pointed at it and said, "That one's smaller than the one we saw today."

Widow said, "I don't think so."

"Looked that way to me."

Liddy led Widow past the lobby furniture and over to a long countertop bar with a wall of liquors behind it. Widow slipped off his rented rucksack and set it down in a bar chair next to him. They both took seats at the bar. Widow had plenty of space between his head and the bar top, but Liddy was chest high to it. He couldn't set his elbows on it, not without it being awkward.

An employee in a white sweater with a name tag smiled at them.

Liddy said, "Tom, get me a Bud and my friend a fresh coffee."

The bartender named Tom asked, "Want sugar or cream?"

Widow shook his head before Tom finished the question. "Black is fine," he said.

Tom nodded and shuffled off to get the drinks. He returned pretty quickly, a seasoned employee. He had a smile on his face and a cold beer already poured into a pint glass for Liddy, like it was a common occurrence. He put a hot black coffee down in front of Widow.

Tom's eyes expanded wide, as did Liddy's, like two people who had been slapped in the face by something they saw. What they saw was the expression on Widow's face.

The moment the coffee hit the bar top, Widow slid two large fingers into the handle. They slid in with no space left between them. And this was no tiny, princess coffee mug. It was a large, white hole-in-the-wall-diner coffee mug.

Widow stared at the coffee steaming in the cup like a drug addict stares at a newfound bag of his favorite drugs.

Widow pulled the coffee mug to his lips. He didn't blow on it. He just took a pull from it. The heat. The stares. Strangers with him. Nothing was going to stop him from drinking the coffee.

Tom and Liddy stared for a long minute as Widow gulped down the entire cup, coffee grounds and all.

He put the cup back down and raised his eyes and stared back at Tom, then at Liddy. He realized they were staring at him.

He asked, "What?"

Liddy said, "You must really like coffee."

"I haven't had a cup in days. I ran out when I was out there."

Tom gestured at the cup and asked, "Want another?"

"Please."

Liddy said, "Wow. I ain't seen no one down coffee so fast."

Widow smiled and said, "It's my addiction. Some men deal in drugs, alcohol, sex, or gambling. I live for coffee. Can't help it. It's a genetic thing. Probably."

"Probably?"

"Never met my father. Think he might be patient zero."

Liddy was quiet a moment, and then he asked, "You got any kids?"

"No. I had a mom once. But she's gone."

"Me too. I had a mom once, but we had a falling out."

Widow said, "Sorry to hear that."

"Sorry yours died."

Widow said nothing to that.

Tom returned with a piping hot coffee refill and set it down in front of Widow.

Liddy asked, "Where are you from?"

"Mississippi."

"Really?"

"Yes."

"You don't have one of those accents."

"Not everyone from Mississippi talks like they're out of a Margaret Mitchell novel."

Liddy asked, "Who?"

"She wrote *Gone with the Wind*."

"I never saw it."

Widow said, "It's a book too. Movie's not far off."

Liddy drank his beer. They continued talking small talk over four full beers for Liddy and one more cup of coffee for Widow, which made three large mugs total for Widow.

Liddy seemed to hold his liquor like a champion. Widow couldn't help but notice.

He said, "I was in the Navy."

Liddy said, "Thank you for your service."

"Thanks. It was a long time ago. I've seen a lot of sailors drink. We're sort of known for it. I'd say you're doing good. Right up there with them. You must have an incredible metabolism."

Liddy put his glass down on the bar top. He stared at it for a long moment. Then he said, "No. It's nothing like that. The beer is nonalcoholic."

"Nonalcoholic?"

"Yeah. I used to have a drinking problem. It was a very long time ago," Liddy said, and he lifted the glass and took another pull. "I don't drink anymore. Not real beer. I only drink this crap."

"If you don't drink anymore, why drink nonalcoholic beer?"

"It quenches the need," Liddy said.

Widow nodded. He asked no more about it. He didn't need to.

Liddy said, "I bet you think I'm a hot mess? What reason would a guy like me have to be drinking so much?"

Widow stayed quiet.

Liddy said, "It was a long time ago."

Widow said, "I think nothing of it. What I said about there being a lot of drinking among sailors is true. It's an unspoken thing, but many service members turn into full-blown alcoholics by the time they get out. I've known some who have. Lives are ruined from addiction. No doubt about that."

Liddy asked, "Really?"

"Yep. Statistically, twenty-two American veterans take their own lives every day. I can only imagine the percentage of those that have a problem with drugs or alcohol."

Liddy added, "Or both."

Widow said, "Or both."

"It's probably ninety percent."

Widow said, "Maybe higher."

They went quiet for a long time after that. Widow drank another cup of coffee and got another refill. Liddy nursed the fifth beer a long time. People came in through the double doors to escape the weather. It was a trickle at first, but after the rain pounded for another hour, and the thunder rumbled every few minutes, and lightning crackled and lit up the sky outside, Liddy's guests entered through the double doors every few minutes until the bar was full. The leather furniture and tables filled up. More staff that Widow hadn't seen before appeared from the bowels of the lodge. They served guests here and there. Tom, the bartender, got so busy, another staff member hopped behind the bar to take care of guests.

Peter was nowhere to be seen. Liddy continued to sip his fifth beer. He didn't seem fazed by the busy lodge. Liddy seemed to only play the part of the owner and didn't seem to get involved in the operation side of things. Widow had known plenty of chiefs in the Navy who managed their commands the same way. *Let the underlings run around like a chicken with its head cut off* had been the attitude.

Sometimes this kind of management worked, and sometimes it didn't.

None of the staff bothered Liddy, and he didn't seem to want to be involved with them.

Widow broke the silence. "I gotta ask you. Have we ever met before?"

Liddy looked at him. He said, "We met today."

"No, I mean ever before? In the past? I feel like I've seen you before. You serve in the military?"

Liddy shook his head.

"Nope. No military on my résumé. I told you. I've been here most of my life. I've run these lodges for damn near thirty years now."

Widow nodded and said, "You've been here most of your life?"

"I told you. I haven't left Alaska in decades. Basically, I've always been here."

Widow nodded. He said, "Sorry. I just get that feeling that we've met before."

"Nope. Never met before. I don't think. Ever been to Alaska before?"

Widow said, "I was in Anchorage last year."

Widow had also been close to the Alaskan shores in a submarine before. But that was classified. He didn't mention it. Last year, Widow was in Alaska with Agent Gray. They had followed a string of clues in an investigation that led them to a local bad guy, a man who was famous in the state. Widow bet that if he had mentioned the name to Liddy, he probably would've recognized it. So he didn't mention it.

Liddy said, "Don't think I was there at all last year. I fly people all over the place, but you need special permission to land in Anchorage at the airport. And all I got is that floatplane."

"You look familiar. It's vague, like a distant memory. But I remember you."

"I don't think so. It wasn't me. I would've remembered you. You stand out. I just got one of those faces. I guess," Liddy said.

"Maybe I'm all wrong."

They continued talking for nearly two more hours and had lunch from the kitchen. Liddy had fried fish, even after losing his catch earlier. Widow had a double cheeseburger and fries. He ate it all so fast that Liddy offered him seconds, but he refused. He wasn't full, but the more food he ate, the less coffee he could stomach. With food versus coffee, Widow always went for coffee. When he was out there in the Kodiak wilderness, if he was given the choice between water and coffee, Widow would've gone with coffee. In Widow's opinion, coffee had all the ingredients a person needed—water and caffeine.

Once they finished their lunch, the lodge's double doors swung open. Cold air wafted across the dining room, lounge, bar top, and the back of Widow's head. He turned in his chair and saw Peter towering in the doorway. Behind him, Widow saw that the gray sky had gotten grayer. Thunder rumbled in the distance.

Liddy turned around after Widow. They both stared back at Peter.

CHAPTER 7

Peter entered the lobby. He was still dry, but he had put on a rain slicker like he was prepared for the worst. There was an eager look on his face. The heavy double doors closed behind him. He stepped down into the dining room area, passed through the lounge, and walked over to the bar. He stopped between Liddy and Widow. As soon as Peter got to the bar, the rain started pouring. They could hear it. In a flash, it pounded on the roof, the dirt outside, the sidewalk pavement, and the lodge's walls. It hit everything. More thunder rumbled. This time it was louder, more pronounced, like a concert of drums.

Liddy put down his latest pint of fake beer and asked, "Is that thunder outside?"

Peter looked at Widow and said, "Plane's ready. We better get going."

Liddy threw a hand up and said, "Hold on now, Peter. Sounds bad out there."

Peter said, "That's why we better go now."

Liddy said, "No. Come on, you can't fly to Kodiak in this." Liddy turned to Widow and said, "Widow, you gotta stay. Wait it out." Liddy looked at his watch and said, "It's only afternoon. If it slows up, then you can go. What's the rush?"

Widow shrugged and said, "Don't worry. I wasn't about to step on one of those little floatplanes. Not in this weather."

Peter's shoulders slumped like he was disappointed.

Liddy said, "Good. That settles it. Peter, go tend to the guests. We're fine here."

Peter said nothing. He turned and headed back out the way he came. Widow and Liddy returned to talking. Widow got another cup of coffee.

CHAPTER 8

Peter shuffled along, defeated in his quest to get rid of Widow. He zigzagged through the lodge's guests and back out the double doors. Once outside, he swung a right and walked along the sidewalk, which was mostly covered. It rained so much there that the covering was a no-brainer to invest in. Sports fishermen and hunters were everywhere, fleeing the rain, trying to return to their respective lodgings.

Peter pushed through the stragglers, trying to get inside, out of the rain, and looked around to make sure no one was paying attention to him.

He stepped into an uncovered alley between Liddy's Lodge and a neighboring business. He slipped the hood from the rain slicker over his head. The rain hammered on it. He took out his cell phone and made a second call to his boss. He had made the first call the moment Widow and Liddy went into the lodge.

That's when his boss told him to get rid of Widow.

Peter dialed the last number in his phone. It rang once, and a voice answered. The guy on the other line was not menacing but more matter-of-fact, like a journalist—not one of those nightly opinion anchors who spout their views of things, but one of the older, more respected TV broadcasters, a real newsman like Walter Cronkite.

The Broadcaster said, "You're not calling me from the air?"

"No, sir."

"Is the tourist gone?"

Peter swallowed and said, "Not yet."

"Why not?"

"It's raining here."

The Broadcaster said, "I know that. I'm still in Anchorage."

"It's bad. The old man won't let him go."

The Broadcaster was quiet a moment, and then he said, "Is he keeping him there on purpose?"

"I don't think it's anything sinister. I think he likes the guy, and it *is* raining."

The Broadcaster said, "If the rain doesn't let up, where will this tourist go?"

"I guess he'll stay the night. He saved the old man's life. I doubt he'll send him somewhere else where he'll have to pay for a room."

The Broadcaster said, "If he stays the night, just try to find out more about him. Found out why he's there."

Peter said, "I believe it's just an accident. He seems legit."

The Broadcaster said, "You believe that bear in the woods shit?"

"I don't know. It sounds plausible."

"Do I need to remind you about Kloss?"

"No."

The Broadcaster said, "Good. Someone sent Kloss here. This guy could be with him somehow. If he doesn't leave, find out more."

"Okay."

"Peter, remember when you got out of prison and no one wanted to help you. Do you remember that?"

Peter said, "I remember."

"How long has that been now?"

"Coming up on ten years, boss."

The Broadcaster said, "Ten years. That makes you the longest running caretaker I've had for Bill."

Peter said nothing.

The Broadcaster said, "You know, I can't remember the name of the last caretaker. Or the one before that. Or the one before that. You know why I can't remember their names?"

Peter said nothing.

The Broadcaster said, "Peter? Are you there? I'm asking you a question."

Peter swallowed and said, "I'm here."

"I can't remember their names because they were all replaceable. Is that you, Peter? Are you replaceable too?"

"No, boss. I'm good."

The Broadcaster said, "In the last two weeks, you've allowed one private investigator to get close to us and now a stranger."

Peter said nothing.

The Broadcaster said, "And you allowed Bill to escape you again. I need someone I can trust. Someone who isn't replaceable. I need someone who can take care of Bill. Keep him out of trouble. You've done good for the last ten years. But you know what?"

"What, boss?"

"That's in the past. I don't care about the past. I care about the present and the future. Can you handle the future?"

Peter said, "Yes, boss. I won't let you down again."

"Good. If you do, you will be replaced. Find out who this guy is. If he's nobody, get rid of him."

"Get rid of him, how?"

"If he's just a stranger, then send him on his way. If not, take care of it. Keep it clean," the Broadcaster said and clicked off the phone.

Peter was left listening to nothing but the rain and the shuffle of feet on wet concrete from the remaining stragglers trying to find shelter. The rain picked up, and the sky was so gray there was no telling where the sun was.

CHAPTER 9

Widow and Liddy talked through the afternoon. They were strangers, but they got along like two neighboring passengers stuck on a long flight. They were strangers passing the time. No sense in not being friendly.

Widow slowed down on the coffee at a certain point. His body was in sync with his caffeine needs and told him it was time to slow. There was one point where Liddy had left him alone at the bar for twenty-plus minutes while he went off to take a phone call. Widow stayed behind and turned in his seat and saw an empty bar table. He took his remaining coffee and moved over to it, left the two empty seats at the bar for others to use. Within a moment, both seats were filled by new patrons.

Widow took his paperback copy of *Into the Wild* out and picked up where he left off.

He sat facing the front door, leaving the bar at his back, which wasn't in his normal SOP, but he wasn't worried about the patrons at the bar or anyone else. He stared out a window at the front for a while. He watched the rain and lightning. He saw the tops of boat masts. He saw treetops across the shore and the roofs of buildings and the dark-gray sky. There was nothing else to see. It wasn't dark yet. He could still see, even if it was barely anything at all.

Because of the last two weeks out there in the Kodiak wilderness, Widow was familiar with Alaskan nights. They were cold. They were unrelenting. And they were dark. The darkness hadn't set in yet.

Widow turned his attention to the lobby and the lounge. He scanned the faces, the clothing, the gear some were wearing. Everyone appeared to be there for fishing, hunting, or just camping. They were all outdoorsy tourists. He noticed another thing about them. They all seemed wealthy. It was the way most of them carried themselves—the looks on their faces, the straight postures, and the demeanors.

He noticed another thing. They weren't all American. In fact, more than half of them seemed foreign. There was an obvious group of Russian businessmen that sat in a corner over by a massive stone fireplace. They smoked cigars, sipped on cognac from snifters, and spoke in Russian. They were laughing and having a nice time. Widow saw a similar group of Asian men, only they didn't have snifters. They had sake cups. And there was a group of Middle Easterners that looked like they could've been Saudi royal family.

Widow couldn't understand much of what anyone was saying. He picked up some Russian words and phrases here and there, but it was all elementary.

Liddy was doing well for himself to have patronage with such diversity and—Widow assumed—money. But why come to Alaska to sport-fish?

Widow thought about it for a moment, and it seemed plausible that Russians and Asians might come. Asia was right there. Technically, Russia was less than seven hundred and fifty miles away from Widow at that moment. Still, it was an impressive client list for a nobody businessman from Alaska.

Widow checked over his shoulder and looked back at the bar. He saw a clock on the wall behind the bar. It was ten past four in the afternoon. The sun would go down soon. Not that anyone could tell, because of how gray it was outside. He turned his attention back to the lounge and saw a woman walk in out of the rain. Her clothes were wet. Her hair was wet. She looked like a local. It was something about the way she came in. She dashed her shoes across the doormat and turned to the fireplace. She walked over to it and stood there, warming herself.

She was attractive but young—too young for Widow. She might've been old enough to drink, but that didn't make her old enough for his age range.

There was a tattoo across her hand. It snaked up the sleeve of her coat. She had two facial piercings. Nothing obscene or excessive. Widow had seen more piercings on former sailors.

Widow looked away and took a pull from his coffee. After a few seconds, he glanced back and watched the girl casually. She looked around the room and saw the Russians and walked over towards them. She stopped near them and looked them over. Her eyes scanned the faces like she was looking for one in particular. The Russians paid her no attention. She sauntered back over to the fireplace and stuck her hands out. She warmed herself and turned and smiled at them. She interrupted them and started talking with them in English. None of them paid her any mind at first. Two of them looked up at her with a quick once-over, like lazy security guards. There was also a hint of something else in their look. Widow saw judgment, like they knew her and didn't think highly of her.

She turned away and took off her coat and hung it on a coatrack. Without the coat, she looked like a different woman entirely. She wore a halter top that left little to the imagination. It was black, and her pants were also black, and they were shiny like leather, but fake leather. The tip of the tattoo that Widow had seen on her hand snaked up her whole left arm and vanished into her top. It was colorful but faded, like an original, centuries-old painting. She was pale white, had blond hair, and was tall. She was slender like young people often were—revved up metabolisms will do that. But Widow couldn't rule out drug use as being a contributing factor. Not that she looked like a street junkie or anything. She was a very attractive woman, just out of place.

She started talking with one of the Russians. Widow guessed he was the head of their outfit, whatever it was. The main Russian was the youngest in the group but was the best dressed. His hair was slicked back; he was clean-shaven. He looked like the son of someone important, but he also looked like he took a page out of every Russian gangster movie Widow had ever seen. Like the others, he'd hung his coat on the rack, and underneath, he wore a black dress shirt, black chinos, and polished boots. He sported a gold chain, visible because of the loose top buttons on his dress shirt. He wore gold rings and a watch that looked like it cost more than all of Liddy's four-wheelers. The other Russians were his entourage and were probably bodyguards, too. He looked like the kind of guy who gets messed with a lot—the kind that runs their mouth off so much he needs bodyguards.

One of the potential bodyguards took note that Widow was watching. He craned his neck, and the two made eye contact. Widow glanced away for a spell, like he was just casually watching the room. Then he came back to the girl and the Russians. The bodyguard had looked back to his associates.

They were out of earshot, but Widow caught the gist of it. She was flirting with them. A minute later, she was invited to join them. She sat between two of them. They laughed and talked. It wasn't long before she was sitting on one of their laps.

Between the drinks and laughter, the Russians and the girl seemed to have a good time.

Widow went back to his coffee.

CHAPTER 10

The rain settled down five minutes to eight o'clock in the evening. But it made no sense to return to Kodiak now, not by plane or any other method of travel. It was dark and cold and wet. Besides, the rain and the thunder could start back up at any point. Better not to risk it.

Widow was already comfortable in a bungalow.

A few hours earlier, Liddy returned to the lounge and told Widow they were throwing a party there later. Liddy had to get showered and attend the party himself. There was no way around it. It was expected of him, like it was some sort of corporate function, like a convention. New clients come to town, and the big boss has to be there to mingle, rub elbows, shake hands. It was that sort of thing.

He invited Widow to attend. Widow thanked him but declined the invitation. He still wasn't ready to mingle with people just yet. Liddy told him Peter couldn't fly him tonight. It would have to wait until morning because of the weather. Plus, Liddy didn't know where Peter was. Technically, he was off work and could be anywhere. Liddy said Peter was the only licensed pilot on the premises at that moment. It didn't matter. Widow was in no hurry to get going. Why would he be? He had nowhere to go to and all the time in the world to get there.

Liddy instructed a front desk attendant to set Widow up with a room. The desk attendant gave him a key to one of their bungalows, which was out of the main lodge and down the sidewalk, which turned to a footpath. The desk worker gave Widow instructions on how to get there. Widow thanked him and took his rucksack. He headed out the door and followed the path. It ran parallel with the shoreline and led Widow past a sequence of buildings, some on stilts, some not, until finally it veered to the left and went into a wooded area behind the main path. He followed it. The only things lighting the path were tiki torch–style lanterns here and there. He walked until he found the bungalow, which was nothing more than a one-story, two-room hut. He unlocked it with the key and entered.

The inside was pretty nice. There was expensive furniture and a wood-burning stove, a heater, modern amenities, and a huge bed. The hut reminded him more of a suite you might get on one of those island resorts in the Maldives or Aruba. The bed was made, and covered with a bearskin comforter. He knew it was fake, but it felt real.

The floors were wood, and the walls were brick tile. There was a small kitchen area in one corner, and a large bathroom. The bathroom was the second room. It was massive. There was some nice stonework inside the bathroom. There was a standup shower and a jet tub next to it.

Widow smiled at the tub. He couldn't remember the last time he had taken a bath with jets. Luckily, Liddy's Lodge provided toiletries already. There was a huge sink and vanity area. Stacked on a counter next to the sink was a tray with little bottles of soap, shampoo, conditioner, toothpaste, an unopened stack of two toilet paper rolls, and towels. There was even a little plastic toothbrush. It was small—palm-sized.

Widow entered the bungalow, shut and locked the door behind him. He placed his rucksack on a chair and went over to the heater. He clicked it on. Within fifteen minutes, the bungalow was pretty warm.

Widow hadn't showered in two weeks. He had been washing himself at rivers and streams across the Kodiak wilderness, which were always cold. He wanted a warm shower more than anything. He walked into the bathroom and reached into the shower stall and turned the water to hot. He ran his fingers under the spray. He waited and felt it go from cold to warm to warmer. He backed out and took his clothes off. He hung his coat on the back of the same chair with his rucksack even though there was a closet with hangers. He kicked off his hiking shoes and left them near the door. His socks, jeans, flannel, undershirt, and underwear all came off next. In his rucksack, he had two changes of underwear and two changes of socks. Two nights back, he washed the underwear and socks in the river and set them out to dry near a campfire. They were clean. The jeans and the undershirt and the flannel were more than two days dirty. He ran hot water in the bathroom sink, with the stopper set to keep the water from draining. He dumped some soap into the water and scrubbed his jeans over the sink until he was satisfied. Then he left the jeans in the sink to soak. He repeated the whole process with both the undershirt and the flannel.

Once he finished, he threw his worn underwear and socks in the trash in the kitchen area. He returned to the bathroom. The mirror was fogged up. The water out of the shower was good and hot. He adjusted the temperature to his satisfaction and showered.

Afterward, he stepped out of the shower, toweled dry, and tucked the towel around his waist. He stepped to the sink and brushed a hand across the mirror, wiping a streak across it so he could see himself. He pressed the stopper release, and the water in the sink drained.

Widow picked up his jeans and rinsed them out, and draped them over the shower to dry. He did the same with his under-shirt and flannel, making sure all three were hung out to dry and straighten themselves out.

He went back to the mirror, re-wiped a streak across it. He took the new disposable toothbrush out of its plastic. He added some toothpaste from the tube and brushed his teeth.

After, he returned to the main room and laid down on the bed, on top of the comforter. That's when he noticed the bungalow had no television, which was fine with Widow. He never watched TV unless it was playing on mute above a counter at a diner.

Widow stayed in his towel, on top of the bedcovers. The only lights on in the room were from the kitchen light and the bathroom. Widow left them on and got out his paperback book and dove into it. He read it until he drifted off to sleep.

CHAPTER 11

Widow woke up to a knock at the door. It was slight and small and meek, like the person was nervous to knock or nervous that they might disturb Widow.

Widow opened his eyes and looked up at the ceiling. His legs sprawled halfway out of his towel. He sat up and looked out a nearby window. The glass was spotless—clean enough to confuse and kill a bird. It faced out of the backside of the bungalow. Through it, he saw darkness and trees and nothing else. The leaves on the branches were wet. The wind blew the trees into a rhythmic sway. The branches waved up and down. The leaves danced around like candle flames. The rain had stopped.

Widow heard the slight knock again. He rubbed his eyes and got up off the bed. The towel nearly slid all the way off him. He caught it and adjusted it. He re-tucked the whole thing and made sure it was secure, and then headed to the door.

The person knocked on the door again. This time it was harder, louder, and more invasive.

"I'm coming," Widow said.

He walked past the end of the bed, the kitchen area, the open bathroom door, and the chair with his rucksack and coat. He stopped in front of the door. He was going to peek through the spyhole, but there wasn't one. There was no window next to the door, either. He only had two courses of action to choose from. He could open the door or not. There was no chain on the door either—only the one dead bolt. He unlocked it and opened the door all the way.

The tattooed girl from the lounge was standing on the bamboo welcome mat in front of the door. Her hair was damp and strung out like she had been standing out in the rain maybe thirty minutes earlier. She was in the same clothes— the same halter top under the same coat. The coat was opened up so that the halter top and her midriff showed either more of the same tattoo that Widow had seen earlier, or a whole different one.

The girl's eyes were glassy, and her breath smelled of alcohol.

She looked at Widow but didn't speak. She stared at his torso like she had never seen a man in a towel before. That wasn't why she stared at him. Widow's torso wasn't like the average man's. He had abs as hard as lava rocks. His pectoralis major was big and solid, like a breastplate forged for medieval armor. His shoulders were cut so broad the girl figured she and one of her friends could sit up there, one on each side, like on a ski lift.

Her eyes traced from the bottom of Widow's torso, up his arms, his chest, his shoulders, until finally she met his eyes.

Widow didn't know what to say. He didn't know what to think. He just stared down at her and said, "Are you lost?"

The tattooed girl looked at his arms, which were covered in sleeve tattoos, all meaning something to him. Some had deep meanings; others were from undercover operations. They were all reminders of his past life.

The tattooed girl reached in and gently touched Widow's left arm. She ran her fingers down his sleeve tattoos. She pushed her way past him and entered his bungalow. She walked in and looked around and spun once, slipping her coat off. She tossed it over his coat on the back of the chair.

Widow left the door open and spun around, following her with his eyes. He watched her do the whole thing.

He asked, "What are you doing?"

"I'm visiting you, honey."

Widow arched an eyebrow. This woman wasn't drunk. She walked straight enough, but she must've been tipsy enough to be confused.

He said, "I don't know you. This is my room."

"Well, I know that, honey," she said.

He asked, "Are you in some kind of trouble?"

Widow looked back out the door to see if someone was following her or intimidating her. But there was no one there. No one lingering back on the path. He saw no one.

Widow turned back to her and repeated his question. "Are you in trouble?"

She moved to his bed and dumped herself down. She said, "No. I just wanted to see you."

Widow was left standing in the open doorway. A breeze blew in and shifted his towel around a bit. He shut the door to close out the cold. He walked into the room and stepped past the chair, and stood in the middle of the room.

He asked, "Are you in trouble or something?"

She leaned back on the bed and leaned on her the palms of her hands. Widow noticed she had no purse, no bag.

The girl said, "I saw you at the lounge. Did you see me?"

Widow paused a beat. Normally, when he was in a situation that sparked his intuition, his mind would run tactical war games, calculating risks, giving him threat assessments, and telling him what to do. He couldn't help it. It was hammered into him during sixteen years of Navy and Special Operations life. But he wasn't getting that. His mind ran circles. It was confused.

He said, "I remember you. But what are you doing here? In my room?"

The girl sat up at the edge of the bed. She looked up at Widow and stared into his eyes. She said, "The name's Miley. Like the singer."

"Never heard of her."

"You don't know who Miley is?"

"No clue," Widow said. "Is there something I can help you with, Miley?"

"What's your name?"

Widow stayed quiet.

Miley edged off the bed and stood up. She sauntered over to him and paused a beat. She stared at his torso again and then his sleeve tattoos. She stopped on the American flags on both forearms.

"I like your tattoos," she said. She put her hand out and pointed to his left forearm. She stepped in—close—and brushed his arm up to his bicep. She tried to squeeze it, but it didn't squeeze. The muscle bounced back too fast, like it was counteracting the touch.

Widow stayed quiet.

"I like that too," she said. She lifted her other hand and brushed her fingers over his navel.

"I'm not looking for company."

Miley said, "A lonely roughneck like you? I bet you are. Roughnecks are always looking for company."

"I can't afford company," he said.

Miley paused a beat. The insinuation soaked into her brain a little slowly. Then she said, "I bet you can afford me."

"I'm not looking to pay for company, Miley. I don't find that sort of thing … company. I find it falls under goods and services. I'm not in the market," Widow said.

Miley stared at him. Her expression was blank. She kept touching him. She moved her hand from his navel down farther, to where the body part she was touching was way off from the navel.

Widow grabbed her hands, both of them, and jerked them up, slammed them together, and held them out in front of her like they were handcuffed. He kept them between their bodies for a long second. She stared at his eyes and struggled to get free.

"Hey! You're hurting me!" she said, but it didn't stop her. She kept on advancing.

"You need to leave, Miley."

She stopped struggling and inched forward, up on her tiptoes, and rubbed her pelvis on the front of his towel. She thrust once, twice. She nearly knocked the towel off him. She smiled and looked up at him.

She said, "I know you want me. Part of you definitely does. I can tell, honey."

Widow pinned her wrists together, one-handed, pulled her hands straight up, and moved her back like she was a slab of meat on a hook. He jerked her off her feet and shoved her off him, back toward the door—not hard, not enough for her to fall over and hit her head. He wasn't trying to damage her. He just wanted her to get the picture.

"Hey!" she shouted.

Widow followed her to the door. He scooped her coat up off the chair and shoved it into her arms, forcing her to carry it. He escorted her back to the entrance to the bungalow with one hand. He jerked open the door with the other.

He heaved her and her coat out into the night, not hard but enough to get the point across. Widow closed the door behind her and locked it.

Five minutes later, he was back in bed, only under the covers and without the towel this time. He closed his eyes and fell back asleep.

* * *

OUTSIDE WIDOW'S bungalow and back down the path, Miley was greeted by a looming figure from out of the gloom. She stopped cold and stared.

Peter stepped out of the darkness and walked right up to her. She shivered, just slightly. He put a hand on her shoulder.

He said, "That was fast."

She said nothing. She looked down at the ground.

Peter put a hand on her chin and pushed her face up so he could see her eyes. "Why so fast?"

"He's an asshole!"

"What happened?"

Miley said nothing.

Peter asked again, "What happened?"

"He didn't want me," she said.

"Why?"

"I don't know. He kicked me out."

"What did you do?" Peter asked.

"I did nothing. I did what you asked me," Miley said.

Peter stared intensely into her eyes.

She said, "I practically threw myself at him. I even sat on his bed. I touched him. He wasn't interested. He threw me out. I never had a man do that before."

Peter put his other hand on her other shoulder. He held her still and looked down at her. Miley shivered more.

Peter took a deep breath and asked, "So you left?"

"I told you he threw me out. I didn't have a choice. What else was I supposed to do?"

Peter squeezed her from shoulder to shoulder. He closed his eyes—tight. His cheeks turned red. She knew this look. He was angry.

She said, "I'm sorry."

Peter opened his eyes. He pulled her close. His arms wrapped around her like he was going to give her a bear hug and squeeze her to death. He could do it. Right there. No problem. She'd struggle and fight him, but it would be too late by then. By that point, she would already be in the trap.

Peter didn't bear hug her to death. He didn't try to kill her at all. He thought about it. She'd failed him. But he wouldn't kill her for that. It was a minor setback. That was all. He laid his hand on her head and stroked her hair like she was a pet.

He whispered, "Forget it. It's okay. I'll find out some other way."

CHAPTER 12

In the morning, Widow got up early and brushed his teeth one more time and dressed in clean underwear and socks and the same clothes from the day before. The jeans, the undershirt, and the flannel were all dry and wrinkle free. He dressed and double-checked the rucksack to make sure he had all of Cutty's rented items, and he left the bungalow. He left the key behind him on a table, where there was a sign that clearly laid out this procedure for "hassle-free checkouts."

The morning sun was warm, and Widow could see parts of a blue sky beyond the clouds. It was much better than the day before. The birds were out. People were up early. He saw fishermen on boats head out on the water. He saw a plane fly in and two couples get out. They weren't Liddy's guests. They headed to another lodge across the water.

Widow followed the path back to the main foot-traffic walkway, and followed it back to Liddy's Lodge.

Since he had much more available light, Widow could see more details of the buildings around Bell Harbor. Across, he saw a church and a building next to it that was possibly a school. He couldn't read the sign from there, but he saw a limited variety of playground equipment: a seesaw, a merry-go-round, and a swing set with an attached slide. It was all fenced in. There were no kids.

Widow saw the same large dockworkers from the day before and some new ones. Some worked for Liddy, and some didn't. They all ignored him and went about their daily tasks.

Widow made his way back to the bar and the lounge. He stood at the bar, kept the rucksack over one shoulder. There was a new bartender working behind the bar. It was a woman. She didn't know Widow from Adam. She asked for his order, and he told her coffee—black—and asked for a menu. He glanced over it and ordered scrambled eggs, toast, and bacon. She took up the menu. And ten minutes later, Widow was on his second coffee and starting his breakfast. He gobbled it up to where there was nothing left on the plate.

The bartender took his dish and asked him if he wanted anything else.

He said, "Are refills on coffee free?"

"They are," she replied.

"Then I'll take the check now."

She nodded, left, and returned with the bill. He looked at it and gasped. The cost for coffee and breakfast was twenty dollars.

Widow didn't protest. He had gotten a free room for the night, and he would get a free plane ride back to Kodiak later on. Twenty dollars was a steal if he factored in the value of the entire experience. He took out a wad of cash money and peeled off two ten-dollar bills to cover the twenty, and he stuck a third ten on top for the bartender's tip.

She saw it and said, "Thank you."

"Don't thank me. You'll earn it because I'll burn through the coffee refills."

She smiled and nodded and left him to sit and think.

Widow wasn't alone long because Liddy showed up and tapped him on the shoulder. They greeted each other. Liddy beckoned Widow to join him at one of the lounge tables. They moved to the table that Liddy probably sat at every morning he was in Bell Harbor. They talked a while. It was all morning pleasantries. Widow had a third refill of coffee. Liddy also had coffee.

Twenty minutes later, Peter walked in through the double doors. He entered right through the center and stood there for a moment. Sunlight beamed in past him. He made eye contact with Liddy and walked over.

"Good morning, Peter," Liddy said.

Peter nodded, but didn't smile. He just stared at Widow and said, "Plane's ready if you are. We better get going before the weather turns."

Widow paused a beat, and then he drained his cup. He stood up out of his chair and lifted the rucksack and slung it over one shoulder. He walked away and stopped and turned back. Liddy stayed in his chair and looked up at the two of them.

Widow asked, "You not coming along?"

"No. I better stay here," Liddy said and stood up halfway, keeping his legs under the table. He reached out a hand across the table to Widow.

Widow took it and shook it.

Liddy reached out his other hand and grabbed Widow by the bicep and patted him like they were old Navy buddies. He said, "Thank you for saving my life."

"Don't mention it. It was a pleasure meeting you. Thanks for the room. And the coffee."

"Likewise. Good luck to you, Jack Widow."

Widow nodded and turned away and walked past Peter back to the double doors.

Peter moved to one side and said something to Liddy. It was about when he would return. Peter moved away and walked past Widow, forcing him to step aside, like it was a contest of which of them would lead the other through the doors. But Peter didn't go through the doors first. He stopped and held a door open for Widow to pass through.

Widow exited the lodge and headed down the stairs. Peter walked down the stairs behind Widow and stepped off the bottom one. He crossed the walkways and stepped out in front of Widow, taking the lead.

"Follow me," Peter said. "You carry your own bag though."

Widow stayed quiet and followed Peter over the walkways and across the grass down to the pier. They stepped onto the dock and walked out to the plane. Along the way, they passed between the same four corn-fed-looking deckhands. None of them spoke. They just stared at him like he was a wandering gunfighter from the Old West who rode into a town run by a local gang, and they were watching him ride through every step of the way.

Widow stayed the course and said nothing. He didn't nod. He didn't smile.

At the plane, he reached out, grabbed a strut, stepped onto the float, opened the rear door, and jerked it open. He took off his rucksack and tossed it onto the back bench.

Peter sneered, but said nothing. Widow closed the back door and jerked the front open and dumped himself down in the front passenger seat. Peter got in the pilot seat. Two minutes later, Peter double-checked the meters and dials, and the corn-fed deckhands helped to push the plane off away from the pier.

A minute later, Widow bumped around in the seat a bit as they took off down the current toward the Gulf of Alaska. Widow put his seat belt on. They were in the air shortly after, and the bumping around stopped. The floatplane climbed higher and higher until it looped around toward the southeast, toward Kodiak. Once the nose faced the right direction and they were in a higher altitude, Peter straightened out the flight path.

After ten minutes of silence, Widow spoke first.

"How long does it take to fly to Kodiak?"

Peter kept his eyes straight and said, "Twenty minutes of airtime left."

He stayed quiet for another long minute, and then he spoke again. "You shouldn't come back."

"Why's that?" Widow asked, and looked over at Peter.

"You just shouldn't. Strangers aren't really welcome around here."

"Isn't that how you make your money?"

"How's that?"

"Tourists? I was under the impression that you worked at a lodge?"

"I do."

"So tourists, hunters, fishermen from out of town. That's your business. We're all strangers."

Peter didn't look up at him. He just continued to fly the plane.

They spent for the rest of the flight time in silence. Finally, Peter shuffled in his seat and looked down at the coastline. The town of Kodiak came into view.

"We're going to land," Peter said. He made the arrangements and the adjustments, and the floatplane's nose tilted down.

Widow looked out the window below. He saw low buildings and a few boats out on the water. He saw cars moving around the streets.

Peter maneuvered the plane out toward the Gulf of Alaska and down, and then looped it around and headed to the water.

They landed on the water and slowed a hundred yards from shore. Once the floats were settled on the water's surface, Peter moved the plane toward the shore. A couple of minutes later, they were headed for a pier. Widow saw five guys waiting along the dock. As they got closer, he realized they looked just like the four corn-fed deckhands.

Including Peter, the ten of them could've been from the same family. They might've been brothers or cousins. All looked like roughnecks who spent most of their lives at sea.

The floatplane pulled up alongside the pier, and Peter slowed it and killed the engine. The deckhands grabbed the plane by the struts and held it steady, and pulled it in close to the pier. Two of them roped it off, and one opened the door for Peter.

No one opened the door for Widow, and he was on the other side of the plane over the water.

He didn't wait for Peter or any of his guys. He reached back behind him, grabbed his rucksack, and got out of the plane. He stepped onto the float and grabbed part of the doorframe to haul himself out. He closed the door behind him, and maneuvered around the floatplane, somehow avoiding getting wet.

One of the guys helped Peter onto the pier, but they all ignored Widow. He made his way around the plane's tail and onto the pilot-side float and hopped onto the pier. None of the deckhands spoke to him, but he knew they were waiting for him to fall into the water. They were probably waiting for a good laugh. They never got it.

Widow was on the pier. He looked up and saw the five deck-hands all step into formation behind Peter. They lined up out of sequence, but somewhat in a basic wedge formation. It was amateurish and not military-trained. They probably saw it on TV.

It didn't bother Widow that they were forming up together to stare him down. What bothered him was that they were blocking his path forward up the pier and out of their lives. Behind him was the gulf. The only way to town was to go through them.

They stared at Widow, each of them, like they were waiting for him to react, to speak first. He didn't. He didn't panic or protest. He just stood there, rucksack on his back, hands down by his sides.

Peter stood at the front of the wedge. He looked into Widow's eyes. He said, "I appreciate what you did for Mr. Liddy. But we need you to go now."

"How am I supposed to do that when you're in the way?"

"I just need to make it very clear to you we don't know you. And we don't want to see you again."

"What is this?"

"Like I said, we just don't like strangers around Mr. Liddy."

Widow arched an eyebrow.

Peter asked, "You understand?"

Widow stared back. He asked, "You done?"

Peter stayed where he was for a long second, and then he stepped back and aside. He put his hand out and pointed the way up off the pier and into town.

"Goodbye, Mr. Widow," Peter said.

Widow didn't acknowledge him. He just picked up his feet and walked past Peter, through his boys, and up the pier back to Kodiak, back to civilization after two weeks in the wilderness alone.

CHAPTER 13

There was no need for Peter to follow directly behind Widow. Widow was only about a minute's walk ahead of him. Peter strolled up the pier into town, along the sidewalks, and headed east toward Cutty's store. That's where Widow would head first, he figured.

Peter didn't see Widow in front of him. He picked up his feet and moved at a fast walk. He veered through people, mostly citizens he had seen before. Not that Kodiak was a small village, but it was no metropolitan city. And the same people walked the docks daily.

Peter stopped on a hill for a brief second and saw Widow up ahead, who glanced back once before walking on. One hand was in his front pocket. The thumb of the other was tucked in front of him between the rucksack's strap and his chest.

Peter followed, but stayed far enough behind to not be made. He hoped.

Widow crossed a street and waved at a passerby in a car, who had started the exchange with a friendly hello, like the passerby knew Widow was a stranger. It was a small-town greeting.

Peter waited. He saw Cutty's store in front of Widow on a street corner. Widow entered the store.

Peter assumed that Widow had checked the pack and would return it with no damages. But that wasn't going to stop Cutty or one of his front store guys from following Cutty's standard procedure, which was to delay and inspect and ask about any little sign of damage from their use. They went through a whole orchestrated show, trying to get the client to admit they didn't notice that loose thread or that scratched buckle or that jammed zipper.

Widow wouldn't fall for any of it. Peter knew that. He figured the longest Widow would be in the store was ten minutes.

He took out his cell phone, walked back into a dark, shaded corner of a building, and dialed the last number in his call directory.

The Broadcaster said, "Peter. That was fast. Is he gone?"

Peter squeezed the phone. He wasn't the kind of man who feared anyone. He was a big guy himself. He had been in fights. He was a good fighter. He had never lost a fight. Not once. He was so good and so big and intimidating that he worked as street muscle for hire—once upon a time. He had been around the block.

But Peter feared the Broadcaster.

Peter said, "Not yet."

"What's taking so long?"

"We just landed in Kodiak. He's returning some gear he rented now."

"Is he leaving after that?"

"I think so."

The Broadcaster said, "It is your responsibility to get rid of him."

"I understand."

"Do I need to remind you what I can do to you?"

"No. You don't."

"Good."

Peter thought he better ask questions that feigned interest. He wanted to be a team player. He wanted the guy on the phone to know that he was dedicated to doing his part.

He asked, "Did you find anything out about him yet? Did you run his name through any databases yet?"

"I don't run names. I ask someone underneath me to do that."

"I meant—"

"I know what you meant." The Broadcaster interrupted Peter. "Nothing's shown up so far. But don't worry. We'll check all of them. This Jack Widow will show up."

The phone went silent for a long moment.

Peter said, "I get the feeling he's a cop."

"How do you mean?"

"Just the way he carries himself. I know cops. And this guy seems like a cop."

"A cop in the middle of the wilderness? Doesn't seem likely. Then again, an undercover cop who wanted an angle into our situation certainly could do it that way. But he'd have to have known Liddy would be out there by himself. Plus, the bear you mentioned. What, did this Widow guy get the bear to go along with it all? I doubt it."

Peter said, "Yeah. You're right."

The Broadcaster said, "Still, you did the right thing, calling me as soon as you did. We can't be too careful. Even now."

"Thanks, boss."

"I want you to know I don't overlook good work. You understand?"

"Of course."

"Just because I don't tolerate failure doesn't mean hard work won't be rewarded. You understand?"

"I do, boss."

"Good. Then you heard the part about not tolerating failure?"

Peter said nothing.

The Broadcaster said, "Never let Liddy leave without you again! The next time he ventures out and you're not with him, you're done."

Peter swallowed hard and said, "Okay. What do you want me to do about this Widow guy?"

"Make sure he leaves. Make sure he knows not to come back."

"Limitations?"

"Don't kill the guy. Don't put him in the hospital. We want him to walk away today. No questions asked. But we also don't want him coming back."

"You got it, boss."

The Broadcaster hung the phone up, and the call was gone.

Peter stared at the time on his phone's screen. He figured five more minutes at the most for Widow to return the rucksack and jump through Cutty's hoops and exit the store.

He shoved his hands into his coat pockets and waited.

CHAPTER 14

Widow spent ten minutes on an encounter with a store clerk named Edmond, a name that seemed out of place in the town of Kodiak. Making friendly banter, Widow asked the guy where he was from, to which he replied, "Here. Never been anywhere else."

The store clerk went through a whole inspection process with the returned rucksack. He laid it out on a glass counter like in a jewelry store and emptied the contents. It was all routine and mundane by design so that the customer would get bored and step away and browse the store's other items; the customer might buy something on impulse, or not pay attention to anything that Edmond might do to the rented equipment. It was a tactic used all over the world in shops by store owners and their employees. The act itself ranged from a little dishonest to a flat-out illegal. But it happened a million times a day.

It didn't work on Widow. He stayed right where he was and watched.

Edmond took out a clipboard with two stapled pages. It was typed with empty check boxes at the end of statements, like any rental inspection.

Edmond went down the list, pulling out items, inspecting them thoroughly, front and back, top and bottom of everything. He checked the boxes as he went along.

Widow watched him do it. He watched every item. The items all seemed in order and clean and intact and in the same condition he checked them out in. Every item but one.

Edmond stopped on a metal coffee mug that came standard with Cutty's Camper Pro package. This was the package Widow rented. He chose it because it came standard with the largest supply of coffee beans. It also came with a campfire percolator, which he would need to make coffee.

Edmond held the coffee cup up to the light and inspected the outside and then the inside. He arched an eyebrow and stared into the cup. He inspected it a long time. He looked like a guy staring into the barrel of a gun, checking to make sure it wasn't jammed.

Edmond made a sound like an over-rehearsed, overdramatic sigh, which Widow figured he had done a thousand times before.

Widow asked, "Problem?"

Edmond put the mug down and said, "No. It just looks far more worn than it did before."

"I drank a lot of coffee."

Edmond said nothing to that.

Widow said, "That's what it's for. Right?"

Edmond said, "Coffee stains are hard to get out. I'll have to mark this as 'Needs cleaning.'"

"That gonna be an issue?"

"No. But I'll have to take the fee out of your deposit."

Widow stared back at him in disbelief but stayed quiet.

Edmond returned to inspecting the other items, and then he checked out the interior of the rucksack. He checked the buttons, snaps, buckles, and zippers. Everything was in order.

Finally, Edmond returned all the items to the rucksack and set it down behind the counter. He signed the bottom of the inspection report and reversed it and slid the clipboard over to Widow. He handed Widow the pen.

"Sign the bottom, please," Edmond said.

Widow took the pen and signed on the line. He set the pen on top and slid the clipboard back to Edmond.

Edmond left it there and stepped over to a cash register behind the counter and pressed some buttons, and the drawer popped open. He reached in and came out with a short manila envelope. He closed the drawer. He opened the envelope and pulled out a wad of cash. Widow recognized it. It was a hundred dollars, in four twenty-dollar bills and a ten and two fives. It was his money, the original bills he deposited to rent the gear.

Edmond peeled off one of the fives and returned the rest to Widow.

Widow took it and stared at him. He said, "The cleaning fee for a stained coffee tin is five dollars?"

"That's right."

Widow stared at him in such a way that the guy sensed his life might be in danger. Which it wasn't, but the thought crossed Widow's mind.

No sense lingering on about it or loitering there over five dollars. So Widow pocketed the remainder and shoved his hands into his pockets. He spun around and walked to the door to leave.

Edmond called out behind him. "Don't you want your receipt?"

Widow stopped at the door and shrugged, back turned to the clerk. He walked out and back onto the street.

Widow looked left and looked right, but stopped on movement across the street on the opposite corner. There was a series of shops across the street. At one of them, a bakery's front door was slowly closing behind a figure that darted inside. The figure had darted fast like he was hiding from someone. It was impulsive, for sure. Widow stared, but he couldn't see the figure. So he ignored it.

At the same second, a car horn honked in the distance, and a motorcycle engine roared to life down the block.

Widow left Cutty's and headed west. He zigzagged a few streets and rounded a curve that led him over a hill. He was looking for the ferry that went back to the mainland. He remembered it was down by the docks but far from where Peter had given him the warning goodbye.

He passed by shoppers, and people just out for a morning stroll. There were plenty of guys in fishing gear, and some in hunting gear, walking the streets. A beautiful woman crossed out in front of him, talking on her cell phone as she walked. She was dressed like she didn't belong there. She was in heels and a skirt. There was a shopping bag under her arm. She talked on her phone and paid Widow no attention.

She didn't look like anyone he knew. It was just that she was attractive, which made him think of Sonya Gray.

Suddenly, he wondered about Gray. They had been in Alaska together just last year. She would be surprised that he was here again.

What was she up to? Was she working a new case? Was she thinking of him?

Widow glanced right and saw a post office. And a thought occurred to him. Maybe he should get a postcard for Gray? When's the last time he did that? He couldn't remember.

Widow smiled and crossed the street over to the post office. It was a tiny white building with a deep-red door and glass windows everywhere. He stepped inside.

The interior was small. There was a single countertop with those blue and white colors all over the place. There were chest-high aisles with rows of envelopes and package boxes of various sizes.

Behind the counter was enough space for two post office workers, but there was only one. A short woman of about late forties sat behind the counter. She had dark skin. She looked to be of direct native descent, perhaps Sun'aq, which was the dominant native tribe originally from the island. She had big, happy eyes and a smile on her face to match.

Above her was a long plastic display lit up by a backlight. The US Postal Service seal was on it along with information about pricing for shipping and mailing.

She looked at Widow and spoke almost as cheerfully as her smile.

"Hello. Welcome, sir. Can I help you with something?"

Widow walked up to the counter and laid a hand on top. He smiled back at her and realized that he had been wrong. She wasn't seated. She was standing. She was just that short. She might've been five foot zero, maybe.

He said, "I'm thinking about getting a postcard for a friend of mine."

"Oh, cool!" she said. The smile didn't budge.

"What's that cost from here?"

"Where does he live?"

"It's for a she. And she lives in Washington, DC."

"A postcard is thirty-five cents for inside the US."

Widow asked, "From here?"

"As long as it's going from inside the US to anywhere inside the US, it's the same price."

"Really?"

"Yep. Among the fifty states."

"Good to know."

She asked, "What kind of postcard are you looking for?"

"What kind do you have?"

The postal woman pointed to a far corner behind Widow. She came out from behind the counter, pointed behind Widow, and said, "The postcards are over there near that aisle. But we have some holiday cards in the back."

He asked, "Holiday?"

She stared up at him. She had to crane her head way back to look into his face.

She said, "You know, for the Christmas season."

"This early?"

"We get the cards this early so we can put them out next month."

"You guys put out Christmas-themed postcards in October?"

"No Christmas themed. We can't just endorse a religion like that. We do 'Seasons Greetings' and winter holiday–themed cards. You know? No Santa Claus on a card, but some of them have snowmen or snowy scenery."

Widow nodded, and said, "I need nothing like that."

The postal woman walked Widow back to the corner where there was a spinning rack filled with postcards.

She asked, "What's the nature of your relationship with this woman?"

Widow thought for a hard moment. "Friend."

"Okay. Well, here there are generic postcards," she said and pointed at a row from top to bottom of postcards. "They'll all work for a friend."

She spun the rack and stopped and gestured again from top to bottom.

"Here's a variety of types of cards. Parents. Siblings. Children. Some are humorous. Some are regular."

"Okay. Thank you."

The postal woman said, "My name is Uki. If you need anything."

Widow smiled and said, "Thank you, Uki. I'll let you know."

She nodded and spun around and walked back to her post at the counter.

Widow turned to the cards and started going through them. He thought about Gray. What kind of postcard should he get her? He sifted through the cards, spending too much time reading over them. Some had words. Most were just pictures of Alaska.

He spent some time in the humor section. He laughed out loud twice, but in the end, he chose a colorful postcard with two Kodiak bears on it. They stared off into the sunset over the mountains. Most of the card was bright and chirpy and jovial. Even though Gray and Widow had been in Alaska working a deadly investigation, he regarded his time with her as intimate and romantic.

He picked up the card and walked back down the aisle. He looked at Uki, who stood ready behind the counter to ring him up. A foot before he stopped walking, he glanced to his left at an old corkboard on the wall. It was nearly buried behind post office posters and advertisements.

Widow stopped and set the postcard down on the countertop. But he kept his attention on the corkboard.

"Will this be all for you?" Uki asked.

Widow said, "Give me a second."

"Sure. Take your time."

Widow left her at her post and slid down the counter to the end. He stopped dead in front of the corkboard on the wall. He stared at it.

On the corkboard were a bunch of community advertisements. Some looked professional. Some looked like they were created at someone's kitchen table with construction paper and a black sharpie. There were ads for work needed and work wanted. There were ads for roommates wanted and roommates needing a place to live. There was one about a missing dog with pictures of the dog and a bunch of torn pieces of paper off the bottom, which was the owner's personal phone number. There was a thousand-dollar reward for finding and returning this dog. There were ads for automobiles and snowmobiles and fishing equipment. There was one ad with a photo of a homely-looking woman who was "seeking a man"—exact words.

None of these ads interested Widow. What stopped him in his tracks was something he hadn't seen in years. It was an eight-by-ten poster that read, "FBI's Top Ten Most Wanted," at the top. Underneath, there were ten black-and-white photographs of men. Each with a name, age, description, last-seen report, and the crimes they were wanted for.

Widow stared at it a long minute like a moth at a bug zapper. He was entranced by it. It was like he was staring at an important puzzle piece, and his cop brain was telling him something, but he couldn't connect the dots.

Uki asked, "Everything okay?"

Widow looked up and saw she had moved off the counter. He asked, "You guys still put out the FBI's Top Ten Most Wanted list?"

"We do. Although, it's mainly digital now. We mostly do it out of tradition. We're big on law and order here. Alaska is more of a red state, you know?"

Widow nodded and returned to the counter. He went back to the postcard and slid it over to her side of the counter.

"I'll take this."

"Do you want me to mail it for you?" Uki asked.

"Yes. That would be great."

Uki looked down and reached her hand under the counter and came out with a pen. She set it down in front of Widow.

"Fill it out, and I'll drop it in the mail for you today."

Widow took the pen and filled out the postcard. He closed his eyes and pictured Gray and her little house with the Bonsai trees and her dog and her view of the Potomac River. He pictured the address on the mailbox.

He opened his eyes and filled out the information on the back of the postcard. Then he froze. He didn't know what to write to her.

Miss you was what he wanted to write, but he didn't. *Thinking of you* was another accurate impulse, but he didn't write that either. *Wish you were here* was also a true statement, but he didn't write that either.

Widow stood there for a long moment, pen in hand, ready to write, but what? He couldn't think of the right thing to put.

Uki said, "Maybe you should take it with you. Something good will come to you. Just drop it in any public mailbox along your travels."

Widow said, "You're right. Let me pay for the postcard."

He handed the postcard and the pen back to Uki and smiled.

She took them and looked over the postcard.

Uki set the postcard and pen down and stroked some keys on a computer beneath the counter. Uki typed up the card on the keyboard and gave Widow the price.

Widow pulled out his cash money and peeled off the remaining five and handed it to her. She stroked some more keys, and a cash drawer popped open. She inserted the money and came out with his change and dropped it in his hand. He returned the money to his wad and pocketed the loose change and then the wad of cash.

Widow took the postcard and slipped it into his pocket.

Uki asked, "Anything else I can help you with?"

"Where's the ferry dock at?"

"Leaving Kodiak Island?"

"Headed back to civilization."

Uki raised a hand and pointed behind Widow. She said, "Head down that street, take a left and a right …" She trailed off like she was counting in her head and said, "At the first stoplight. That'll take you to the car entrance."

Widow looked at a digital clock on the wall. It was still early. Earlier than he thought. The time was eight thirty in the morning.

"Know when the ferry counter opens?"

Uki didn't turn to look at the clock. She checked the time on her wristwatch. "The counter is open now, but the first boat has already left. It left at eight."

"When's the next one?"

"There's a couple more. Usually, one around lunchtime and then again around six tonight."

Widow nodded and thanked her, and walked out of the post office. He followed her instructions and went up the street and took the left, and then the right at the light. After nine minutes on his feet, he came to the end of the road that led to the ferryboat boarding area. But there was no boat there.

There was a large parking lot with a line of cars on one row, and a loading zone, but the rest of the lot was empty. There were people here and there, waiting near or in their cars for the next boat. Seabirds cawed overhead. There were fishing trawlers on the horizon. Some headed into harbor. Some headed out to sea.

Widow walked towards a hut built out of wood. There was a sliding glass window. The window was open. A young man sat back on a chair playing on his phone. The sign above the hut indicated it was where Widow would have to purchase his ticket for passage on the ferry.

He walked to the hut and stopped in front of the window. He cleared his throat so the kid would acknowledge him. The guy put the phone down on a ledge and smiled at Widow. He said nothing.

Widow said, "When's the next ferry?"

The young guy said, "It's at noon."

"That's the next one?"

"Yep."

"Give me one ticket."

"Can't."

"Why?"

"It's booked solid."

Widow glanced over his shoulder at the parking lot.

He asked, "It is? But there's no one here?"

"Most people buy their tickets online. Today's Friday."

"And?"

"Most of the locals have a half day of work today."

"And?"

"There's a big music festival in Homer tonight. Everyone's going to be there. They're taking their cars. A bunch of locals will head over at noon and stay the night. Come back tomorrow."

Not everyone, Widow thought. He said, "So the noon is booked up?"

"Yep. All the car space is gone."

"I don't have a car. Can't I just book passage just for me?"

"No can do. Occupancy is all booked too."

"Okay. What's the next ferry?"

"Next one is around six p.m."

Widow asked, "That late?"

"There's a final one. It leaves at nine. If you would rather take that one?"

"I'll take the six."

"Okay."

The kid told him the price, and Widow pulled out his wad of cash money again and paid for the ticket. The kid rang it up on a calculator and put the money into a cash drawer without a register to slide into. The wind blew, and the bills shuffled at the tips but stayed in the drawer because they were pinched down by metal clasps.

The kid stared at the calculator and pulled out Widow's change in ones and handed it to him. Then he tore a ticket off a roll, out of several colored rolls, and gave it to Widow too. The colors designated the time for the ferry. Widow pocketed the ticket and nodded a goodbye to the kid, who immediately returned to his phone.

Widow pulled the lip of his collar up to keep his neck warm. The wind was still blowing. The temperature dropped a few degrees. It was getting colder.

With time to kill, Widow did what he always did. He went hunting for coffee.

* * *

ACROSS THE STREET, standing behind trees, Peter watched Widow buy a ferry ticket, which was good. But then he saw Widow turn around and head back into town, which was bad.

He pulled out his cell phone and texted a message to someone. It wasn't the Broadcaster. It was to someone else. Someone below him on the chain of command. It was an attack order. He issued it to one guy, who would relay the order to several guys.

The guy responded in the affirmative.

Peter couldn't keep following Widow around all day. He had to get back. He had to keep eyes on Liddy. That was his first responsibility. Plus, he didn't want Widow to make him. He might need plausible deniability later on.

He texted one last thing to the guy below him in the chain of command: "Make sure he doesn't return. Tell me when it's done."

Peter pocketed his phone and returned to the floatplane.

CHAPTER 15

Widow walked the streets through the port side of Kodiak, looking in store windows, nodding hello to passersby, and staying vigilant on hunting down a place to get coffee. He hoped for a coffee-house or café or an establishment with a dedicated coffee countertop, something that said, *We take coffee seriously*. Establishments that are devoted to coffee offer the best brews, in Widow's opinion.

Widow rounded a street corner and his brain target-locked on a store window at the corner of a tan brick building along a row of connected shops and offices with various awnings over the windows. A sidewalk sandwich board stood out front of the main entrance. It was decorated with a hand-drawn cartoon coffee cup, two different sandwiches, a cup of espresso with steam rising out of it, and a coffee cake. All of it was drawn in different colored chalk, color-coordinated in such a way that the illustrator must've had a bachelor's degree in marketing. From the top down, there was a hand-written list of the daily specials—all of it neat, all of it tidy, all of it written with care and affection.

The store was a local coffeehouse called Kodiak Espresso. The name was posted on a sign above the door. It looked promising. It was the kind of coffeehouse Widow preferred, like a diamond in the rough. It was a local business—small but not a stop-and-go. It was not a get-your-order-and-get-rushed-out type of place. It appeared quaint and cozy, like many of the hamlets on Kodiak Island.

Widow walked over and entered the coffeehouse as a local woman was coming out. She held the door open for him. He thanked her with a "Ma'am" on the end, like the Navy never left him, and he walked through the door.

Inside, there was sizeable seating area with multiple levels. There were six heavy, dark wood tables spread about and a rock fireplace and two sets of living-room furniture, one near the fireplace, giving it a similar welcoming feeling as Liddy's Lodge. The other was pushed into a back wall. Shag area rugs covered concrete floors. Off to one corner, there was a "Wet Floor" sign near a set of public bathrooms.

There were board games, and paperback books—all with bent spines—scattered across shelves and coffee tables. Some books were old. Some were older. There was an old man in a tweed outfit playing a game of chess with a younger man near the fireplace. The two men bore a striking resemblance to each other. One was bearded and one was not. They were both grayed, but at different levels. The older man was grayed through and through. The younger had gray at his temples. They looked like two generations of the same family. They were probably father and son or brothers nearly a generation apart, which was improbable but not impossible.

There was no fire in the fireplace. But the heat was on. It was warm inside, but not hot. *Toasty* was the right word for it. Widow soft-clapped his hands together quietly and rubbed them like two sticks to amplify the warmth. He turned a forty-five degree angle and approached the counter. There was no line. He ordered from a young female barista. She could've just been out of high school. It was hard to tell. Widow noticed as he got older that young people looked younger and younger to where guessing their age became difficult. Everyone under twenty-five seemed to look the same age to him.

While he ordered from the young barista, a second barista stepped out from behind a white wall with warm plates of food in both hands like he came out of a back kitchen area. The second barista was male. His hair was clipped short on one side. The other side of his haircut was long and draped over his ear. If Widow were to guess, he'd guess that the second barista was in an aspiring garage band. And he would be correct. A single customer stood at the end of the counter waiting for the food in the band-haircut barista's hands. Widow watched the food trade hands. The customer nodded at the band-haircut barista, and the barista nodded back without words. It appeared to be a daily ritual, like they were being friendly but also saying, *See you tomorrow.*

A third barista, another female, appeared out from behind the same back wall. She carried a tray of warm rolls. Steam rose off them. The smell enticed Widow like a siren to a sailor at sea. Only instead of crashing into rocks, the only danger was weight gain, something Widow had never worried about since he spent most of his time on his feet, moving.

At the counter, the first barista asked what she could get for him. He nearly ordered black coffee, but he thought of the place's name and got a quad shot of espresso instead, thinking it was their specialty. He ordered it black, no cream, no cube, no peel. Before he paid, the smell of rolls seduced him, and he ordered two of them and paid for all of it with cash.

He left a five-dollar tip for the girls. The first one took it and dropped it into a glass tip jar. The other returned with the rolls and set them down on a thin plate. Widow scooped up the rolls and waited at the end of the counter for one of the other baristas to make his espresso. He ate one roll right there.

One of the baristas told him the espresso would be a few minutes. He nodded and strolled back to the entrance and stood at a counter by the window, pulled his paperback out of his pocket, and read it. He ate the last roll over the plate as he read. He only got through two pages, but progress was progress.

After he was done with the roll, he closed the book, pocketed it again, and set the plate down in a bus tub set out near the door. It had a few other plates and two coffee mugs already inside. Then he threw away the napkin at a trash station on the other side of the door.

Widow glanced out the window and saw a large guy, another of those dock-roughneck types, standing across the street. At first, he thought nothing of it, until another one—the same roughneck look, the same fisherman clothes—came from around the corner and joined him. The first one pointed at the coffeehouse, and they both stared at it. They couldn't see Widow staring back at them because the outside glass was tinted, and the sun was at their backs beaming down on the window. The sunlight glimmered back at them like from a mirror.

Widow never read comic books in his life. But he knew who Spider-Man was. Who didn't? He also knew what Spidey sense was. He never called it that, but that's what he felt at that moment. His primal brain was telling him something was up with these guys. Of course, Widow lived in a civilized society. Although he was more analogous to a savage who had woken up in a block of ice, his brain did what anyone's brain does. It second-guessed his instincts.

Skepticism kicked in and told him he was wrong. But then a third roughneck-type guy came around the corner. He was followed by two more. They came from all directions like they were in five different places, meeting up right there across the street like a roughneck convention. That happens. Friends, coworkers, colleagues meet up for a late breakfast every day of the week all across the world. Maybe their favorite breakfast place was Kodiak Espresso.

The thing was, they weren't coming in. They stayed standing across the street like they were waiting for someone to come out. Their intentions didn't seem friendly. Not because it wasn't possible, but because they were all bowing up, talking to each other, clenching their fists. They looked to be scheming, planning something. They looked like a group of gorillas in the distance, warming each other up before raiding a rival gorilla population.

Widow looked around the room. The only customer that made any sense for them to be waiting for was him.

The evidence wasn't conclusive. Maybe they were just meeting there, waiting for a sixth friend to show up before their late breakfast. But that didn't fit either. Why the peacocking? Why the firing each other up?

Maybe they weren't paying attention to the coffeehouse at all. Maybe they were about to go into the storefront behind them. The only thing about that theory was the storefront behind them was a bank. Looking at them, Widow doubted they would go into the bank, not unless they were planning to rob it. No, they were up to something. Widow had been a part of enough ops to know that the moment before it began was a moment of hyping each other up.

Widow heard the barista call out his completed espresso order, and he turned and went over to get it. He scooped up the espresso, thanked the baristas, and took a swig. It was hot, fresh, and caffeinated, the three things he looked for in an espresso.

Widow walked to the entrance and opened the door. He glanced at the roughnecks across the street. Quickly, they all turned their heads away or at each other like they weren't staring at the door, waiting for him to come out. It was the saddest display of tradecraft he had ever seen in his life. These guys were like two sets of Three Stooges minus one Curly tailing someone. He stayed in front of the coffee shop and took a pull from the espresso.

Widow looked left and looked right. No cars came from either direction. He crossed the street straight to the five guys and realized they were the same five from the dock. At least some of them were. One of them had a mustache. He was pretty sure that none of the roughnecks from Peter's dock had a moustache. Then again, he had paid little attention to their faces. He had noticed they were all big guys, same as these five. He clocked a tattoo on one arm that seemed familiar. His best guess—it was them or some of them. They were definitely connected to Peter.

Widow stepped out into the road and stopped a little past center. He stayed back about four yards.

He said, "Hey. Any of you guys got the time?"

All five roughnecks looked at him, confused. One of them looked at his wristwatch, which looked more water beaten than the side of a boat. He gave Widow the time.

One of his partners gave him the stink eye, like he was saying, *What the hell are you doing?*

Widow nodded and thanked him, took a slow sip from his espresso, and turned and walked back up the road to the east. The roughnecks followed but stayed back, like they were still trying to maintain a sense of cover.

Widow stayed in plain sight for a long time. He had plenty of time to kill before he had to be on the ferry. He had some fun with the roughnecks. He walked a mile in one direction and turned left and then right, heading down one street to the other, all of it random. None of it made any sense to the roughnecks. He did it for another mile and then repeated the process, only he circled back around and headed right back in the same direction they had come.

The whole affair killed half an hour.

Widow glanced in store windows, using the reflection to make sure they were still following him. He used windshields on passing cars to do the same.

On the way back, he tried to stay with the sun at his back so he could catch glimpses of their long shadows on the streets.

One reason for him to head back toward the ferry was to wait for his ride out of there. But the main reason he turned around and led them back was that he had one last shot of espresso left. He wanted another. It was a damn good espresso—best on the island, he figured. It was an issue worth fighting for.

Widow took a final left and ended up between two neighboring buildings. There was about twenty feet of space between them. The path was straight, with plenty of dark shadow on one side. It was a paved alleyway. Long, jagged cracks allowed overgrown grass to cover much of it in sporadic spurts, like weeds.

Widow walked to the middle of the alley, still thinking that the five roughnecks were on his tail, but they weren't. Not all of them.

Right then, three of the five roughnecks came from around the corner and stepped in Widow's path. They must've run around the buildings. The other two weren't with them.

Widow stopped. He stayed where he was. He glanced at their hands. A common mistake when a potential street fight is about to break out is that people don't check the hands of their opponents. The second guy had empty hands, but the first had his stuffed in the pockets of his coat. He was the one to watch. Could be anything concealed inside the coat. The worst-case scenario was a gun. The best case was nothing. Widow saw the third guy had a pair of brass knuckle-dusters on his left hand. He saw little skull engravings on the knuckles.

Cute, he thought.

The three roughnecks stepped up and stopped at different distances from him, but all stayed more than ten feet away. They spanned out in front of him from eleven to one on the clockface.

Widow took a deep breath and said, "I wondered when you boys would make yourselves known."

One of them spoke. He asked, "What?"

One of the others asked, "What're you talking about?"

Widow took a last pull of the espresso, knelt at the knees, and set the empty cup on the ground. He got back up on his feet. He stood tall, shoulders straight, like he had with the Kodiak bear. The only difference was he didn't wave his hands up in the air.

The third one said, "Hey boy. We don't appreciate litter around here."

"I'm not littering," Widow said.

The second one pointed at the empty paper cup on the ground. He asked, "What do you call that?"

Widow said, "I'm setting it down. I'll pick it up after I break bones—your bones."

The three roughnecks kept their eyes forward and chuckled.

The first said, "Really? You think you can take us?"

Widow changed gears and said, "You boys have been following me all over downtown."

The three roughnecks stared at each other. Eyes glanced back and forth. None of them looked behind him, like they were trying to hide their numbers from Widow. He knew the other two were around.

The last of the three in front of him repeated a question. "What are you talking about?" he asked. "You saw us?"

Widow said, "Of course, I saw you. You boys stick out like—"

"What you gonna say? A sore thumb?" the first one said, interrupting him.

Widow said, "No. I was going to say like five dumbasses."

The three roughnecks repeated the same glances at each other —three dumbfounded looks on three dumbfounded faces, like they were rehearsing for a skit.

One asked, "Five?"

The third one said, "You not too good at counting? There's three of us."

Widow breathed in and breathed out. He kept his hands down by his sides, visible and in plain view, like a magician before a trick. He said, "There's five of you."

All three of the roughnecks' eyes turned from their empty glances at each other to stare directly at Widow. Then they all glanced behind him like they couldn't help it. It was a colossal mistake. They gave away their drinking buddies. Not that it mattered. Widow had seen them already. He had no problem counting to five.

Before any of them knew it, Widow exploded at the hips. He stepped forward on his left foot and back on his right. He pivoted and angled, and his left arm reared back like a spring-controlled mechanism, and his hand fired forward like it was rocket-fueled and someone slammed on the ignition switch. He sent a gigantic open-handed palm strike right into a fourth guy's neck, like an automated machine-arm slamming into a car part and bolting it together in a factory somewhere.

Widow moved with robotic precision.

The guy had been trying to sneak up behind Widow. He was smart enough to stay in the shadow of one of the buildings, but dumb enough to think it would work.

Widow's palm strike slammed into the guy's jugular with tremendous force. The impact into his neck was hard enough to put him in the hospital for a week. It might've killed the guy had Widow applied a little more torque to it. Widow had intended to hit the guy in the chin, but he misjudged the guy's height. This one was taller than he thought by a few inches. It was a simple mistake. He almost felt bad about it, until the fourth roughneck dropped a two-foot-long piece of rebar from God knows where. The rebar bounced twice on the grassy concrete, resonating and echoing between the buildings like a guitar's tuning fork.

The fourth guy slumped to the ground like a puppet with the strings cut. He wheezed and grabbed at his neck. He was in pain. No doubt about that. Widow listened to his wheezing for a long second, keeping part of his attention on the others. He didn't want to lose track of them, but he also didn't want the fourth guy to die.

Widow wasn't a cop, not anymore, but he knew enough to know that if he killed a local guy, intentional or not, self-defense or not, the local police would detain him. How long they might detain him could be days, weeks, months, or hell, even years. The US Constitution guaranteed that every American got the right to a speedy and public trial—the Sixth Amendment. But Widow had heard of people getting arrested and being kept without trial for years. It happened, even in a democracy. The system wasn't perfect. And for a nobody like him—a drifter, a stranger—the local justice system might be more forgetful that he's in custody. Widow had no plans to go to jail for murder.

Unfortunately, the guy looked bad. Widow wasn't a doctor, but he had enough training and experience to know the guy could breathe—barely—but at least he was getting air. The guy wheezed in and out. If Widow wanted to kill the guy, all he had to do was take a step forward and stomp on the guy's neck while he was down. That would've ended it right there. But there was no reason for that. Tactical assessment didn't call for it, and if he wanted to avoid cops and handcuffs and charges and long investigations, it was best to move on to the others.

Widow didn't have to turn back or to look far for another one. The fifth roughneck stood right there to Widow's right. He was a little farther than the fourth guy had been, a little out of reach. He stood there, frozen in fear. He stared at Widow. The look on his face looked like someone slammed the brakes on a truck, and it just stopped inches from killing him. He was in utter shock that he and his friend's plan of attack was foiled so quickly and violently.

The fifth guy also had a long deadly piece of rebar.

Widow asked, "That meant for me?"

The fifth guy stared down at Widow and then glanced down at his wheezing friend. He looked back up at Widow. For a split second, Widow saw horror in the fifth guy's eyes. In that second, Widow thought the fifth guy might drop the rebar and turn away and run as fast as he could, but he didn't. He stayed there for a long second, still frozen, still lost on what course of action to take. Widow gave him the chance to run. He didn't attack. He could have. But he didn't. He gave the guy a long second to make his mind up. Widow kept the other three on his radar. In the end, the fifth guy decided. It was obvious because the look in his eyes turned from terror to retribution and anger.

Widow didn't wait for the guy to retaliate. Widow stepped up to the fifth guy fast, pivoted on his left foot, and threw a right hook. This time, he didn't hold back on the use of force. He saw the guy clear as day. No need to worry about missing his target. Plus, the guys were armed. Widow was not. This was enough to justify the use of deadly force. The rules of engagement were clear. But Widow wasn't looking to kill anyone.

Widow's fist slammed into the guy's right cheek like a freight train. It was a colossal blow. The fifth roughneck stumbled back off his feet. His body dangled in the air in slow motion, like a KO scene from a boxing movie.

Widow turned back to the others before the fifth guy hit the ground. And he hit the ground—hard. They all heard it. It was a loud *thud* of the guy's body landing on concrete. It sounded like a two-hundred-pound bag of coffee beans thrown from a second-floor window. The fifth guy was out cold. Widow didn't to turn back to look. He knew it. They all knew it.

Widow stood with both feet planted on the ground. He stayed in an athletic position like he was ready for the next guy. He faced the same three roughnecks that he started out facing. But Widow hadn't been the only one who had been moving. Once he was fully stopped, he saw the first rough-neck pull a weapon out from a place of concealment, and it wasn't another piece of rebar. It was a gun—a Springfield XD-S, which was a reliable handgun. Ask a cop what his preferred choice of firearm to carry is, and the old-timers will talk about the models they grew up with. The word "Glock" will get thrown around. You might even hear "Beretta." But with the new generations of cops, the Springfield XD-S was a brand you'd hear often enough. In the consumer market, it was a completely underrated firearm; cheaper than a Glock but similar enough.

The one in front of Widow wore desert camo like the guy got it serving a tour in the Middle East, which he didn't—clearly. It had been picked up online or at a gun show or special-ordered from a gun store, he figured.

Widow hated the type of guy who liked to dress up and pretend to be in the service. It was called "stealing valor." And it's a great insult to service members of all branches. It didn't matter which branch they were in. No one put up with it.

Typically, the kind of guy who stole valor was the kind of military reject who couldn't hack it. By the looks of it, the closest this guy ever got to military service was the day he was rejected at his local Army recruiter's office.

Widow knew the type. There were multiple indicators, but the one that stuck out, the one that was big and obvious, was the fact that the gun shook in his hand. His whole hand trembled like he had just climbed out of freezing cold water naked. It shook because he had never pointed it at a living target before, not a human target anyway.

Maybe the guy had been hunting before. Being that he lived on Kodiak Island in Alaska, that seemed like a reasonable deduction. But hunting animals and murdering people weren't the same thing. There are several key differences.

Holding a rifle isn't the same as a handgun. Pointing a rifle at a helpless Sitka black-tailed deer wasn't the same as pointing it at a living, breathing man. Maybe the guy had hunted bear. Kodiak Island had a bear-hunting season, but hunters rarely incite the bear's rage before killing it. They kill it from high in a tree stand, from a distance, with a scope and rifle. They don't shoot it up close and personal with a handgun. It's a whole different thing.

Widow was no grizzly bear, but he was just as dangerous.

The first guy said, "You hold it right there."

Widow stayed where he was and stared into the guy's eyes. The distance was too far for him to outrun a bullet, but close enough to leap at the guy if he missed, which he might. The best option was to not get shot, but in case the guy tried, Widow wanted to make sure he missed. The thinking part of Widow's brain calculated his chances of dodging and reaching the guy before he could fire a second round. He guessed fifty-fifty, which wasn't great odds when talking about a bullet. Of course, there were a lot of unknown factors, like how good of a shot was the guy?

The distance was about twelve feet between them. Which meant the first guy would have to be blind to miss Widow. But that's only if Widow stayed still. Moving targets were harder to hit. That fact alone didn't increase Widow's odds much, but when he factored in the guy's inexperience shooting a man, his hesitation, the trembling hand, Widow thought fifty-fifty was about right.

Those odds went from fifty-fifty to zero chance the guy would shoot him because the second guy stepped in and took charge of the situation like he was their leader, only it was odd. It was a bit off. It felt more like he wasn't their leader, but the next rung down the ladder. They had no leader. None present. Clearly.

The second guy stepped closer to his friend and reached out and clamped a hand over the first guy's wrist. He moved the gun down and away so that the muzzle was no longer pointing straight at Widow.

Widow's first instinct was to bum-rush them while they were distracted, but that would leave the chance open of someone getting shot. So he waited.

The second roughneck said, "No! Johnny, put the gun away! We can't shoot him!"

Widow stayed quiet.

Johnny said, "But, Eddie, he could've killed Carl."

"Put it away!" Eddie shouted.

The one called Johnny looked at Widow, anger in his eyes. His cheeks flushed like he was boiling over. But he did as Eddie had ordered him to do. He put the gun away. He tucked it back into a concealed holster at his hip under his shirt, tucked inside his waistband. Widow watched him do it. He kept his eyes on the weapon until it was out of sight, until it was rendered a non-threat—for now.

Widow said, "You boys should walk away now. Take your friend to the hospital. He sounds bad."

Widow stopped and twisted at the hip and looked back at the one called Carl.

Carl was still wheezing, still hacking, but he was breathing. He laid on his back, tossing and turning, struggling to get back to normal. He reached a hand out to Johnny from far away like he was drowning and begging Johnny to jump in and save him.

Widow said, "I'm not a doctor, but he doesn't look good. He needs medical attention. Any of you guys doctors?"

No one spoke.

Widow looked back at the one called Johnny. He looked at Johnny's face and expression. He watched the cheeks flush more and a vein on his forehead throb like it might pop. Johnny's anger intensified. Under pressure, Johnny would be the one to snap first. Widow had seen it a million times before. It was the guys like Johnny who always seemed like they were the most dangerous, but in reality, they were usually the weakest link in the chain. Guys like Johnny were always the ones to squeal in interrogations first. The right amount of pressure and anyone will crack. For guys like Johnny, any pressure will do.

Widow tried a new tactic. He taunted the guy, to take ahold of Johnny's exposed nerve and apply pressure. Guys like Johnny are terrified. Under the surface, guys like Johnny are cowards. They are the furthest thing from honorable. They're fake. Guys like Johnny are often afraid of anyone different. They're often racists and homophobic. They're the kind of guys who hate the smallest implication of homosexuality, especially directed at them.

Perhaps exploiting this weakness with this tactic was less than civil, less than genteel. Widow was no gentlemen. It didn't matter what Widow believed in. All that mattered was getting the job done, using any means necessary. Widow never fought according to any kind of gentlemen's rules. In a gentlemen's duel, Widow would've shot his opponent the moment he got a pistol in hand. He would've never turned his back on him. He never would've lined up back to back. He never would've walked twenty paces and turned and then fired. Why would he? Widow never understood that kind of British-Renaissance philosophy. Graveyards are full of gentlemen who fought by gentlemen's rules.

Widow said, "You seem really protective of your friend. What's he to you? Your boyfriend?"

Johnny stared back at Widow. His face turned more flushed than it had before. If that was possible. Eddie released Johnny's wrist and turned back and faced Widow.

Johnny said, "He's my brother."

Widow said, "I guess that explains his stupidity. Is that a family thing?"

Johnny's lips quivered. His eyebrow fluttered. His cheeks looked like they were going to explode. He couldn't contain himself any longer. Impulse was always a mistake in a fight with an experienced fighter because an experienced fighter wasn't fighting on impulse. An experienced fighter was playing chess, thinking several moves ahead.

Johnny exploded into action, but on impulse. He shoved Eddie aside and took several big strides forward, cleared the distance between him and Widow. He lunged at Widow bare-knuckled. Widow's eyes caught sight of the third guy. The knuckle-dusters glimmered on his hand like the little skull engravings were diamond encrusted. Only they weren't, at least not with real diamonds. They were encrusted with tiny fake diamonds. They were probably some kind of cubic zirconia.

Johnny lunged with a fist aimed at Widow's face. Unlike Johnny, Widow was an experienced fighter. Before Johnny took a step forward, Widow's tactical brain plotted several moves ahead. Widow's brain laid the plans, and Widow's feet did the work.

In an explosion of raw power, Widow sidestepped to the left. Johnny's momentum and weight and amateur fighting style carried him right past Widow. Widow planted a foot in his path, which tripped Johnny up. He stumbled forward and off his feet and fell. He slammed face first into the concrete. There was no rest for Widow, because Eddie wasn't as dumb as Johnny. He recovered from being shoved aside and scrambled around and ran at Widow. The third guy followed alongside him, lagging, but only by a few feet.

Eddie raised his fists, followed by the third guy. Widow threw his hands up in a boxing position, hoping that these guys would follow suit because they had probably seen too many boxing matches on TV. Widow was right because both of them threw their fists up like boxers in a ring. Both the one called Eddie and the third guy took up boxer's stances to match their fists.

Widow smiled. He saw imitators, not trained professionals.

Widow danced farther to the left, forcing Eddie to turn his back to the third guy. Widow kept them both in a straight line in front of him. Every time one of them straggled out of line, he parried by dancing to the right or to the left, whichever was required to get them back in line. He wanted to keep them that way. He didn't want them circling around him. He didn't want those knuckle-dusters getting behind him and out of his line of sight. He wanted to keep them in plain view.

Widow moved his fists up and down, randomly, which made it seem like he was gearing up to throw a punch. He stood in an upright stance, which was another move a boxer might do. He wanted them thinking that's what he was up to, that he was trying to box with them.

Eddie did the same, mimicking Widow. He put his fists up in a defensive boxer pose like he was ready to guard his face with one hand and throw a punch with the other. All of it was exactly what Widow wanted him to do.

Unlike these clowns, Widow was a trained boxer. He had been trained in everything. Navy SEALs don't practice one form of combat. They practice everything. In a straight-on, fair boxing match with Muhammad Ali back in 1960, Widow would've gotten his ass handed to him by "The Greatest." No question about it. But Widow wasn't fighting Ali. And it wasn't a straight-on, fair boxing match.

The secret to boxing wasn't in the hands at all. That's a common amateur mistake. It's all in the feet. Boxing was a sport of skilled eye-feet coordination as much as it was about eye-hand coordination. Defense came from the feet. Punches came from the feet. The power came from the feet and resonated up through the hips and the body until a blow was delivered with the fists. Widow knew this. These two didn't.

The other thing about boxing is that it comes with rules. Street brawling has no rules. In a boxing match, there are referees and time-outs and rounds and a bell and judges and penalties and rules.

In boxing, all punching was done above the belt. The blows are all to the face or body. Widow wasn't above breaking rules, especially when there were none. He shuffled his hands again and telegraphed that he was going to throw a right hook at Eddie, using his shoulders. Like a lot of boxers and boxing spectators, Eddie watched the shoulder. He knew enough to know that. He saw Widow's movement and prepared to defend against a right hook. The only thing was that Widow never delivered that right hook. Instead, he came up off his right foot, stood on his left, and fired the right foot forward at a dizzying speed like an NFL kicker going for the goal post. The top of Widow's hiking shoe slammed into Eddie's groin like a wrecking ball. The damage was immediate and immense.

Eddie let out a squeal that was somewhere in the vocal range of alto to soprano. He folded over, dropped both fists, and cupped his groin. He dropped to his knees. He looked straight up at Widow. The pain on his face was unmistakable. It was the worst pain he'd ever felt in his life. Eddie's eyes rolled back a little. His face flushed over. Widow came at him again. This time he used a right hook. Widow bashed his right hook straight into Eddie's cheek. The guy toppled over without a squeal or a whimper because he hit the concrete and was out cold.

Widow turned his attention to the third and last guy. The third guy came at him. He punched with the fist that had the knuckle-duster first. Widow slapped it away with his right hand. He came back at the guy and smashed the elbow from his right arm into the guy's gut. He followed it with the same elbow to the guy's chin. It was a one-two strike, like it had been printed with stick figures in a diagram of a book on hand-to-hand combat.

One. Two. And the guy stumbled backward.

Widow grabbed the knuckle-duster as the guy fell back on his ass. He ripped it off the guy's hand and slipped the knuckle-duster on his right hand and smashed a straight jab into the guy's forehead—knuckle-duster and all. It was instant good-night. The third guy sprawled out on his back and didn't move. He joined his friend Eddie in dreamland.

Widow slid the knuckle-duster off his fingers and tossed it off into a cropping of weeds and grass. He walked away, but he forgot one thing. It was a momentary mistake anyone could've made. He actually forgot about Johnny for a split second.

Widow heard shoes scuffling on concrete behind him, and he spun around. Johnny was back on his feet. He had his Springfield XD-S out again, and it was pointed right at Widow's face…again.

Widow saw Johnny's eye lined up right over the sight. It stared at him. Johnny's hand trembled again, but not like before. This time was different. He was different. This time, there was a look in his eyes. He intended to pull the trigger— first time or not. The look in his eyes told Widow all he needed to know. Johnny was dead set on shooting him.

"You stay right where you are!" Johnny said. He stood about five feet away from Widow, close enough to lunge at but far enough to make it a risky move.

Widow stood his ground. He raised both hands up in the air like he was surrendering. His palms open. He showed them to Johnny and stayed quiet.

Carl coughed and gagged behind Johnny. But Johnny didn't turn around to check on him. He called back to his brother but didn't take his eye off Widow.

"Carl, you hang in there. I'm coming to get you."

"You better hurry. He really needs a doctor," Widow said.

Johnny inched closer, stuck the gun closer to Widow's face. His arm was stretched out all the way. He held the gun one-handed, waved it at Widow.

"Shut up! You shut up!"

Widow stayed where he was. He didn't move. Didn't flinch.

Widow said, "Seriously, he's turning blue. The damage to his throat could cause lasting effects."

"Shut up!" Johnny said and inched closer.

Widow said, "If he doesn't get medical attention soon enough, the damage might be irreversible. He might need one of those holes in his throat to help him breathe. You ever seen one of those before?"

Johnny stepped closer, and this time, he was going to pull the trigger. Widow knew it. Widow counted on it.

Johnny stepped in. It was the final time. He was going to shoot Widow in the face. He knew it. Widow knew it. No backing down now. He didn't care about repercussions or consequences or jail time. It was time to pop his cherry. Widow was going to die.

But Johnny made two mistakes. The first was the same mistake he made minutes earlier. He pulled a gun on Widow. That was the first mistake.

The second mistake was that he did something all novice shooters did. Not that he was a novice. Not firing a weapon. But he was a novice at killing a man. The second mistake Johnny made, which Widow counted on, was he closed his eyes before pulling the trigger. Johnny stepped forward, gun out, aimed, shut his eyes—briefly like a flutter of a butterfly wing—and pulled the trigger.

Widow waited for that butterfly flutter. He was counting on it. It was a hunch that Johnny would do it, but it was a hunch formulated from sixteen years of combat and cop experience. Widow took a final step closer and exploded from his feet like all great boxers. He danced right and turned himself to the side so that his target profile was much thinner. Johnny pulled the trigger with his eyes closed. But by that second, Widow wasn't standing in the same place. The bullet flew out of the muzzle and blind-fired into open air. The bullet slammed into the brick of one of the nearby buildings. A burst of dust and gravel from the brick exploded into the air, leaving a cloud of white smoke.

Widow clamped a hand down on the gun and wrenched the other all the way back and punched Johnny square in the nose, shattering it. Blood gushed out in all directions like a loose firehose. The nose *cracked* in a violent, deafening sound like someone slamming a drum set with a sledgehammer.

Johnny released the weapon completely and clawed at his broken nose. He was desperate to stop the bleeding, to stop the intense pain. He pawed and scraped at his face. There was so much blood. In seconds, he was blinded by the red blood that gushed from multiple holes in his nose.

He tried calling out in pain, but blood rushed into his mouth.

Widow watched him for a long second. Johnny stumbled back several paces. He was dazed, and blinded by the blood. He couldn't see where he was going. He couldn't see where Widow was.

Widow delivered another painful blow. Not that he had to. Johnny was immobilized, mostly. But the guy had tried to shoot him in the face.

Widow took several strides forward and lined Johnny up like he had Eddie. And Widow drove another powerful kick, right into the guy's groin.

Johnny's hands grabbed at his groin in horror, and he collapsed to the concrete. His mouth hung open like he was screaming in pain, only there was no sound. He couldn't speak.

Widow stepped past him and took the gun with him. He walked over to Carl, bent down, and checked him out. The guy looked up at him in terror.

Widow reached down and moved Carl's hand out of the way. Carl tried to swat him away but couldn't.

Widow said, "Relax. I want to see."

Carl didn't relax, but he didn't fight back either. He was too afraid to anger Widow. Widow inspected the guy's neck wound. He felt genuinely bad about that.

Widow said, "Keep your head up. You got a phone?"

Carl nodded and patted the left-hand pocket of his coat. Widow fished into it and pulled out a cell phone. It was one of those cheap flip phones from ten or fifteen years in the past. Widow flipped it open. There was no passcode or thumbprint scanner or facial recognition on it. It worked just like an old landline phone—ready for use.

Widow dialed nine-one-one and asked for a paramedic. He told the operator there was a medical emergency and informed her about Carl, about the damage to his windpipe, and gave her their location. He also told her about the four other guys who were all unconscious. But the moment she asked for his name, he clicked off the phone, folded it, and returned it to Carl's pocket.

Widow stood up and pocketed the gun. He walked away from them. Leaving the scene of the whole incident was probably illegal in Alaska. He didn't know for sure. But he wasn't interested in sticking around to be questioned by local police. He also had a real fear of a place like Kodiak having what he knew in the South as "good ole boy" syndrome. Which was where local police in rural or small-town communities often sided with locals over strangers. This was especially true when local police were drinking, hunting, or fishing buddies with the local boys.

Widow had no proof that Johnny and his friends had even known any local cops, but he didn't want to stick around to find out. Widow had had enough of Kodiak.

He walked away, out of the alley, and out of suspicion—so he hoped.

CHAPTER 16

Widow knew nothing about the local police in Kodiak. He wasn't sure about their capabilities, infrastructure, force size, or jurisdiction. He wasn't sure if the township of Kodiak had a police force or if the whole island was under the jurisdiction of a sheriff's office, like the county he grew up in. He knew none of it. He didn't know the police response time or their procedures for shots-fired scenarios. He figured on an island as vast as Kodiak Island but with a population of only thirteen thousand people, give or take, that there was most likely only one police force. Probably with wings of solo officers stationed in hamlets across the island. Maybe Bell Harbor had one of its own?

Of course, Widow was wrong. Not completely. There were two law enforcement entities on the island. Kodiak had a police force with a chief and captains and desk sergeants and patrolmen and watch commanders and so on, like a regular police structure. But it wasn't the only law enforcement unit on Kodiak Island. Also, there was the US Coast Guard, which had its own police presence in Kodiak. That jurisdiction encompassed the waters, the coastline, anything off the land,

and all property which belonged to the USCG, which included all the service members. Like the Army and the Navy, coastguardsmen are GI, government issue, or government property. Once you sign the dotted line, your ass belongs to Uncle Sam.

Widow ended up back at the place he knew, Kodiak Espresso. He walked in and discovered the baristas had rotated. This time, he ordered his espresso from the kid with the band haircut. It was just as good as the first. He took it to go and headed back down to the docks, where the ferry would leave. He thought it best to wait there until the six o'clock ferry boarded.

Widow popped the collar on his jacket to help fight off gusts of sea breeze. He perched himself on a concrete wall, stayed away from the sight line of the entrance to the parking lot, and sipped his espresso and cracked open his paperback book. He read for a couple of hours without interruption.

Later on, the sky was too overcast to find the exact location of the sun. But he knew it was sometime after noon. He didn't need a watch to know when it was time to board his ferry. In a few hours, it would be there waiting, plain as day.

Suddenly, Widow saw what he was hoping to avoid. A white police car rolled up into the parking lot. It came up over a dip at the entrance and stopped. The back tires were still on the main road. Widow saw the side of the vehicle had "POLICE" written in block font, with the word "Kodiak" underneath in a smaller font, less intimidating. The car was a Ford sedan with the Police Interceptor package. There was a black metal ram on the front grille. The windows were tinted, but Widow figured the officers inside were probably looking straight at him. He was a stranger, seated all alone, waiting for his ticket off the island.

Widow crossed his fingers and hoped that the patrol car would roll on, but it didn't. He knew it wouldn't. He didn't have luck that good.

The patrol car turned and came into the parking lot, off the main road completely, and stopped near the first line of parking spaces. There were cars parked in some of the spaces. There was one cluster of three cars right in the middle distance between Widow's perch and the patrol car. The rest were scattered in different spaces all over the lot.

The Kodiak Police car stayed where it was. The engine idled, and a plume of exhaust came out of the tailpipe. The car's heater was running. With the low sunlight, Widow couldn't see through the tinted windows. He took a sip of his espresso and just stayed where he was. He wasn't going anywhere. If they were looking for him, they'd found him, and he wouldn't run. Widow never ran, not from the police. Although the thought crossed his mind. But that wasn't the right answer. If they were looking for him, the worst thing he could do was run.

The patrol car stayed there in the center of the aisle under a streetlight, which was off. Widow continued to sip his espresso, hoping for the best, planning for the worst.

A minute later, another Kodiak patrol car drifted into the lot. It went forward and turned down the next aisle. The second patrol car was the same model, same interceptor package, and it had the same tinted windows. The second car pulled up halfway down the aisle and stopped. The engine idled like the first one, and exhaust plumed out of the tailpipe, same as the first.

The chances that these cops were gearing up to confront Widow were probably ninety-five percent. That changed when a third police vehicle skipped the dip at the entrance and drove up into the lot. This one was an SUV, same tinted windows, same ramming bar on the front. It seemed to be the leader of the pack. It drove slowly past the first row and then past the second, and pulled into a third row of empty parking spaces and moved past the second car. The SUV pulled right up to the end of the third row and turned and headed straight for Widow.

The cops driving the two patrol cars behind the SUV released the brakes and followed on a slow roll behind. Widow stared at them. They were there for him. Had to be. There wasn't anyone else around him, only the seabirds marching around the lot near a public trash can. As the SUV pulled up and stopped just ten yards from Widow, the seabirds took off and scattered and circled above like confused scavengers.

Widow took the lid off his espresso and chugged the rest of it, thinking he may not be able to finish it if these guys put him in handcuffs.

The SUV's driver door opened, and a jarhead police officer stepped out. He had ten years on Widow in age. He was short but thick with a barrel chest. Besides the jarhead buzz cut on his head, his whole demeanor and look screamed *Marine Corps*, which made Widow wonder why he was here and not on a Marine station somewhere. Maybe he was already retired. A lot of guys figured that out early. You sign up right out of high school, work twenty years, and retire. It's a pretty good way to have a steady retirement income early on and still be young enough to start a whole new career. Widow had almost made it. He had stayed in for sixteen years.

The jarhead cop stepped away from the vehicle and left his door open. No one got out the other side. There was no passenger. The other two patrol cars followed suit, like they probably rehearsed in arrest drills involving a three-car formation around a suspect. Widow knew all the moves, all the drills. He had run drills in Quantico on vehicle maneuvers and arrests, with the world's very best FBI and NCIS instructors. Plus, Widow had gone through SEAL training and operations. So he knew the maneuvers—no question.

The two rear officers stepped out of the other two patrol cars, right out of the driver's side doors, same as the jarhead cop. They left their doors wide open, same as the jarhead cop. They took positions behind his trajectory, which was targeted right at Widow.

The officer from the first car was a man, brown hair cut short, and clean-shaven, but not former military like the jarhead cop. The officer from the first car had that civilian look on his face. The officer from the second car was a woman. She was shorter, maybe five foot one. She may have served in the military somewhere before. She held herself with the right professional confidence. But Widow couldn't be sure. The bulletproof vest under her uniform shirt puffed her torso up and made her look about two sizes bigger than she actually was underneath. All three had vests under their shirts. All three had serious looks on their faces. And all three had their hands resting on the butts of their service weapons like they were ready to draw at a moment's notice and put Widow in the ground.

The jarhead cop stepped out and around the nose of his SUV. He walked up to the curb and stepped onto the sidewalk. Widow sat on the perch over the water. He had one leg dangling off over the water and the other on the parking lot side. He straddled the wall and watched the cops. He glanced at a trash can and gently tossed the empty espresso cup into it. He didn't want to litter. The earth had been good to Widow. He wanted to be good back.

All three cops watched him do it. He knew they would, that's why he did it slow. He didn't want them thinking he was ditching evidence or some other action that could be taken as a threat. Two of the cops didn't react. But the rear male, the clean-cut one, reacted. He drew his weapon and left it down by his side. Widow saw it.

It was a Glock 19. They all had Glocks, same model. They must've been department issue. This one fit neatly in his hand. He held it down by his side, ready to go, but he didn't point it at Widow. It was likely he drew it as an overreaction to Widow tossing the paper cup into the trash can, but he had it out now. No sense in putting it back.

The clean-cut cop said nothing.

The jarhead cop stepped to the middle of the sidewalk, about fifteen feet from Widow, and stopped. The two other cops moved in closer and stopped at seven and five o'clock positions at his back. They both stayed about ten feet behind him.

Widow looked at them, made eye contact, and stopped on the jarhead cop. Widow spoke, and maybe he was a little sarcastic, but these moments are always awkward. What should he have said?

Widow said, "Something on your mind, guys?"

The jarhead cop was all business. He asked, "You got an ID, sir?"

Widow said, "Why?"

"Sir, I'm a Kodiak police officer, and I'm asking for your identification."

"I can see that. But I'm asking you what for? I'm not operating a vehicle. I'm not loitering. I'm in a public place minding my own business."

"Sir, I'm asking for your driver's license. Do you have it on you?"

Widow thought for a quick moment and said, "I don't have a driver's license."

"Sir, do you have a form of ID on your person?"

Widow glanced over the jarhead cop's shoulders, once at the female cop, and then at the clean-cut cop. The female was cool, calm, and collected. Next to the jarhead cop, she appeared to be the most professional. She wore a pair of aviator sunglasses. Widow could see a tiny blip in their reflection that he thought might've been him.

He could turn right, fall over the edge, dive into the water below, and swim down deep. He probably could swim beneath the wharf. They would have to regroup, call in divers and boats and the Coast Guard. He might get away. Maybe. But he didn't do any of that.

He said, "I got a passport."

The jarhead cop said, "Where is it?"

Widow said, "Back pocket."

He knew that was exactly where the cops didn't want it to be because it meant they would have to ask him to stand up and reach behind to grab it and pull it out. They didn't want him to say it was there because that's where he would also keep a gun. If he had one, which he didn't.

The jarhead cop said, "Stand up for me please, sir. Slow."

Widow looked at him again, glanced at the other two, glanced at the clean-cut cop's un-holstered weapon. He thought about going over the side again. He could make it. He was a good swimmer. Being a former SEAL, that was a given. But he couldn't out-swim bullets at his back, and Widow had experienced being shot in the back before. He never wanted to feel that again. So he turned back toward the police. He lifted his right leg that had been dangling over the wharf side of the wall and swept it over, then planted his foot on the concrete. He stood.

The jarhead cop held one hand up, palm facing Widow. It was his left hand, the hand that wasn't resting on his gun. It wasn't his gun-drawing hand. He said, "Move slow, please."

Widow slowed down his pace and stood up on both feet. He kept one eye on the clean-cut cop's weapon.

The jarhead cop said, "Hold up."

Widow froze, his hand halfway back to grab his passport out of his pocket.

The jarhead cop asked, "You got any weapons on you?"

Widow paused a beat. He remembered once stabbing a guy with a toothbrush. But he wasn't carrying a toothbrush, not today. He had used one back at Liddy's place, and he left it there sitting on the sink.

Widow said, "No weapons."

"Okay. Get your ID out."

Widow continued reaching behind him. He kept his other hand out, palm out, and visible for the officers to see it was empty. Widow fished around in his back pocket and pulled out his passport, and reached it out in front of him for the jarhead cop to take it. The jarhead cop looked Widow in the eyes with a stare that looked like it came from years of working as a drill instructor in the Corps. Maybe the guy had done that very thing. He moved his gun hand away from the butt of his Glock and stepped forward. His boot went up on the curb and the sidewalk, followed by his other one. He kept his eyes on Widow's and stopped walking at arm's length. Widow moved his hand up and extended the passport out. The jarhead cop took it and inspected it.

The passport's cover was crinkled and worn. The interior wasn't much better.

The way the jarhead cop flipped the pages, he accidentally started from the rear and worked his way all the way to the front, passing up dozens and dozens of stamped locations that Widow had traveled to.

The jarhead cop didn't ask about all the country stamps. He flipped until a bald eagle stared at him along with the Preamble to the US Constitution: "We the People." He looked down at the photo in the passport. He held it up, a little high because of Widow's height, and out in front of his face until Widow could only see half the guy's face.

The jarhead cop cocked his eyes over to the photo and then over to Widow, and back to the photo. He followed this action by doing it a few more times. The eyes darted to Widow's face, back to the photo, back to his face, and so on.

The jarhead cop lowered the passport and inspected the information. He read out loud. "Jack Widow?"

"That's right."

"It says here, your passport has expired."

"It has?" Widow asked.

"Yep."

"That doesn't nullify it though. Not as an ID."

The jarhead cop looked up at Widow and said, "I didn't say it did."

Widow stayed quiet.

The jarhead cop asked, "You former military?"

"Navy."

"What rank?"

"I got out at Commander."

The jarhead cop nodded. He held the passport closed with his index finger jammed into it, bookmarking Widow's photo. He looked Widow up and down.

Widow tried to be polite by smiling and asking a counter question to show interest in the guy. It was a long shot, but sometimes that old military comradery is planted down deep in a man. Sometimes it was down in the core, making it harder to ignore. Widow tried to be tactful, to bond with the guy.

So, with a smile on his face, he asked the most obvious question of obvious questions. Widow asked, "You were a jarhead?"

It worked—sort of. The jarhead cop grinned half a smile and said, "What gave me away?"

Widow nodded and asked, "What rank?"

"I retired at master sergeant."

"That's impressive. You did twenty years?"

"I did. How long were you in?"

Widow said, "I was in sixteen years."

Although that wasn't technically true. He did four years at Annapolis, worked in the Navy for a while before the NCIS tapped him. Then he went to school in Quantico and was recruited into Unit Ten, where he went right back into the Navy undercover and through BUD/S, SEAL training. The rest of his time was as a SEAL, but really, he worked undercover for Unit Ten.

The jarhead cop said, "I was in twenty years. I would still be in if I could."

"What happened?"

The jarhead cop reached down and patted his right leg, top of his thigh. He said, "I got shot in the leg. I can walk and jog and all. But I had to go through months of physical therapy. It was nearly a year before I could walk without a cane."

"You look good now. No one would even know."

The jarhead cop said, "I still look funny running."

Widow cracked a smile and stayed quiet.

The jarhead cop said, "Listen, you don't have any weapons on you, right?"

"I already told you no."

"I'm going to ask you to turn around and face away, keep your hands up," the jarhead cop said.

Widow furrowed an eyebrow involuntary. He looked at the three cops, one by one again, and then he asked, "What for?"

"Just comply please, Mr. Widow. I'll explain, but first we need to check you for weapons."

Widow frowned, but in the end, what choice did he have? Resisting would just make matters worse. So he did as the jarhead cop asked. He lifted his hands up over his head and turned around slow.

The jarhead cop said, "Put your hands on top your head."

Widow put his hands on top of his head slow.

"Interlock your fingers," the jarhead cop said.

Widow did as he was told. The jarhead cop moved in closer and pocketed Widow's passport. Widow could sense the other two cops moving in closer and circling around to the ten and three clockface positions from him. He confirmed it with his peripheral vision. He saw both of them from one side of his line of sight and then the other. He kept his head as straight as he could.

The jarhead cop put both hands on him and patted him down. He checked Widow's pockets, waistband, both arms, both legs. He stopped in the front and was more reluctant to pat Widow down in his groin. The jarhead cop was so reluctant Widow could've smuggled a firearm in his underwear, in the front, and the jarhead cop would've missed it. Of course, Widow wouldn't have done that. It's the dumbest place to conceal-carry. Forget about the obvious dangers to a man. It's not practical or tactical. You can't draw a gun quickly from your underwear. That takes time. He'd have to undo his belt, unbuckle his pants, and pull them down just to reach in there to pull out a gun.

Once the jarhead cop was done with his search, he stepped back and tapped Widow on the shoulder. He said, "You can put your hands down and turn back around now."

Widow kept moving, slowly. He let his arms lower down to his sides, kept his palms out, and he turned around. He stared at the jarhead cop and glanced at the female and then the clean-cut cop. He looked back at the jarhead cop and asked, "Satisfied?"

"Yes. You are unarmed."

"I told you that."

The jarhead cop said, "I had to be sure."

Widow asked, "Wanna tell me what this is all about?"

"Were you over near Lucky's about an hour ago?"

Widow said, "I have no idea what Lucky's is?"

"It's a sports bar. It's over in a plaza. Were you behind it in the alley between other buildings … downtown?"

Widow said, "I don't remember seeing any bar."

"Were you in an alley downtown an hour ago?"

"I might've been."

"Did you have an altercation with some local boys?"

Widow thought for a moment. He didn't want to give the guy more information than necessary, but he also didn't want to lie. Lying to police is a whole other set of charges that he might already be facing. So he told the truth but kept it simple.

He said, "They attacked me. I defended myself."

The jarhead cop asked, "You beat up five guys?"

Widow stayed quiet.

The jarhead cop asked, "By yourself?"

Widow stayed quiet.

The jarhead cop said, "So there was a firearm discharged. The bar staff heard it, and we located the bullet."

"That was quick."

"It slammed into the back of a laundromat. Luckily, the building is made of brick. The owner was in the back office when the bullet hit the exterior wall near his head. If it had been siding or wood, then he might be dead."

Widow stayed quiet.

The jarhead cop said, "Where do you keep your gun?"

"I don't own a gun."

"Did you shoot that gun?"

"I don't own a gun."

The jarhead cop said, "You were there?"

Widow stayed quiet.

"Are you refusing to answer my question?" the jarhead cop asked.

Widow didn't want to lie, but he didn't want to admit the truth either. Impasse. So instead, he reverted to a time-tested measure—the Socratic method.

He asked, "You think I was there?"

The jarhead cop said, "We know you were there."

Widow searched his memory banks for a security camera. Maybe he had been seen on one back at the alley? But he was pretty sure there were no cameras and no witnesses, except for the guys he left in a heap on the ground.

"How do you know that?"

The jarhead cop raised his hand and pointed at the trash can. Where Widow had discarded his empty espresso cup and said, "You left behind a paper espresso cup. I'm sure if we pulled the prints, yours would come back. Plus, one of the guys told us they were attacked by a man who …"

He trailed off before finishing his sentence and smiled.

Widow asked, "What?"

"One of them called you Captain America."

"What?"

"He said you were like Captain America. You know? A muscle-bound pretty boy who beat the shit out of five big guys like you were a super soldier from a science experiment."

"Pretty boy?" Widow asked. He had been called a lot of things in his life, but never that.

The jarhead cop said, "Yeah. That's you. Gotta be."

Just then, the female cop spoke for the first time. She stood to Widow's left. The tips of her boots were about fifteen feet away from the tips of his shoes. She said, "It's him."

The jarhead cop said, "Did you fire the gun?"

Widow said, "I don't own a gun."

The jarhead cop said, "One guy is in the hospital, you know?"

Widow stayed quiet.

The jarhead cop said, "He likely won't breathe right again. He might need medical assistance for the rest of his life. You know what that means?"

Widow stayed quiet.

The jarhead cop said, "It means he might need a device around his throat to help him inhale and exhale correctly."

Widow stayed quiet.

The jarhead cop asked, "You do that to him?"

"They attacked me. Five of them. They had weapons. I was unarmed. They had rebars and a gun."

The jarhead cop reached to his belt and pulled a set of hand-cuffs out of a leather pouch. He held the cuffs by one side, and the other side dropped and dangled from his hand like a metal noose.

Widow stared at them. He was no kind of gymnast, but he could move fast, faster than people often thought, because of his stature. He could tuck his head in, fold his body inward so that he was a smaller target, and he could turn right, run, and dive off the wharf. He could still make his water escape. At least there, he would be free from handcuffs and cops and interviews and paperwork and possibly a trial. But Widow had done nothing wrong. That's the inevitable dilemma of a fair and equal justice system. It punishes the guilty and frees the innocent, but it takes its sweet time doing it.

The jarhead cop said, "We have to take you in. Come peacefully, and we'll get this all straightened out."

In the end, Widow put his hands out, palms up, and offered his wrists to the jarhead cop. Technically, the jarhead cop should've cuffed Widow from behind, but he didn't. Probably because of Widow's cooperation or his military record, or their comradery, or all of that, the jarhead cop cuffed Widow in the front, and they led him over to the back of the female's patrol car. He went in the back seat.

The clean-cut cop had his Glock out the whole time until Widow was secure in the back seat of the female cop's car. Then he holstered it.

CHAPTER 17

Nervous and a little uneasy, Peter sat in a pickup parked across the street from where Widow was being arrested. The truck belonged to Liddy's company. It was unmarked, low miles. The interior was a burnt-orange leather. The truck was matte black on the outside. The dashboard had all the bells and whistles of a new truck, only it wasn't new. It was five years old. The odometer showed just over twenty-three thousand. The vehicle didn't get driven much. It was unmarked on the outside because it was for company use, which meant it was used to transport guests from the Kodiak Airport or their hotels in city of Kodiak to the dock, where they would board the same seaplane that Peter had flown Widow in, unless the number of guests was larger than four.

If there were more than four, then Peter took them in Liddy's larger seaplane. The larger plane was parked on another part of the island. They used it more to transport different guests together to one of the other islands in the Kodiak Archipelago, all depending on what package they purchased. The hunters were put together in hunting parties, all based on what the game was, the hunters' country of origin, the time slots they preferred, and the dollar amount on the package's purchase price. The more money they spent, the better time they had. The same system went for the sports fishermen. It was all standard operational procedures. It was all standard practice among Alaska's largest gaming companies and lodging services.

The Kodiak Archipelago contains roughly 5,360 square miles of land when combined. There are numerous islands. Kodiak is the largest. And there are forty smaller glaciers that can be traversed by foot.

Peter looked at himself in the rearview mirror and wiped his face dry with his hand, as if that would calm him down. He was about to deliver his boss the bad news. His boss wasn't Bill Liddy. Peter was Bill Liddy's keeper.

Peter picked his cell phone up off the seat and looked at the screen, and unlocked the phone. He scrolled until he saw the number and dialed it. The phone rang once, twice, three times. On the fourth ring, he prayed for voicemail. He didn't get it. Instead, he got the Broadcaster.

The Broadcaster said, "Yes?"

"I have bad news."

"I'm listening."

Peter said, "They got him."

"Who? They have who? And who are they?"

"The stranger. The new guy. Jack Widow. They arrested him."

The Broadcaster asked, "Who arrested him? The cops?"

"Yes. KPD. They have him in custody. They just arrested him."

"Peter, you were supposed to get rid of him. You're proving to be quite useless. You know nothing about this stranger. You let Liddy get away from you. I told you to get rid of this guy, and you couldn't even do that. Now you telling me he's staying longer because he's in lockup?"

Peter said, "Not yet. They're arresting him right now. At the ferry. He was going to leave. I swear. I'm watching the whole thing. He bought a ticket. He was waiting for the next boat."

"How did this happen? What did he do?"

"He's not the only one. My guys are already in jail."

The Broadcaster asked, "What? How?"

"I sent them to give Widow a message. To expedite his departure."

"And?"

"He beat them up."

"What?"

"Yeah! He put one in the hospital. Carl. I don't know if he'll be able to work for months. Widow smashed his windpipe, or damn close to it. I don't have the details. He'll be seeing a surgeon later today to repair the damage."

The Broadcaster asked, "Forget about Carl! I don't care about your crew! They're all replaceable!"

Peter said, "I'm sorry. It's not my fault."

"Then whose fault is it?"

Peter paused a beat, like he was having second thoughts about saying something. He said it anyway. He said, "One of my guys brought a gun. He pulled it on Widow."

"So that's why one of them is in the hospital. This guy is a little better than just some nobody."

Peter said, "He beat up five of my best guys though."

"That's nothing. Any of my guys could do that. Hell, you could do that. Those roughnecks don't have two brain cells they could rub together to make a fire."

Peter said nothing to that.

The Broadcaster stayed quiet for a long moment. Then he said, "This Widow guy. He'll be in lockup soon. Unless you have a plan to get the cops to let him go?"

Peter said, "No. I don't."

The Broadcaster said, "Tell your guy to fess up to it."

Peter interrupted and said, "But they'll charge him. He'll probably do time."

"Since he's the one who messed up to begin with, it's time for him to take one for the team. Or he could rat. Remind him what will happen to his family, to people he cares about if he does."

Peter said, "Yes, sir."

The Broadcaster said, "This Widow guy sounds like trouble. More than we thought. Do you think he's with Kloss?"

Peter said, "No. I don't think so. He's just a stranger. Kloss is gone. Nothing to worry about."

"We want this Widow out of here. If he's just a passerby, then let him pass by before he gets curious and starts more trouble. How long will they hold him?"

"If Johnny confesses to everything, I imagine they'll let him go. But"—Peter paused a beat and looked at his watch—"it'll probably be overnight. By the time they book him and all that, it'll be after hours."

The Broadcaster said, "Fine. In the morning, I want him gone. Call a lawyer. Get your guy to fess up, and get this prick out of here for good."

The Broadcaster hung the phone up without another word.

CHAPTER 18

The Kodiak Police Station and Jail was this monstrous twenty-eight-thousand-square-foot complex built with serious money behind it. The builders had to excavate and backfill the grounds before laying down even one inch of concrete for the slab. They used two hundred and twenty-five steel pilings plus more structural steel-braced frames before they poured concrete for the foundation. The builders insulated the roof with a ridiculously built-up asphalt roofing assemblage. The station's exterior walls integrated over-elaborate stonework with metallic panels to give the outer design a masonry facade like something out of an architectural trade magazine that you might find in the waiting room of a fancy dentist's office. Widow didn't like it. It was all overblown, over-budgeted, and overdone.

The interior spaces weren't much different. There was everything they needed but over-expensed. There was a massive public lobby area, administrative offices, an emergency operations command center, enormous evidence storage, police locker rooms, vehicle bays, and support offices. Because the station doubled as a jail, the security systems for the building included intruder detection, video surveillance, alarm panels, double-layered access control, audio threshold alarms, secure visitor communication, and video and audio recording systems for the police interview rooms.

Widow saw the vehicle bay where the female cop, whose nameplate read: "Qaunak," had driven him into. She waited for the jarhead cop to arrive, and the two of them escorted Widow out of the bay, past parked patrol cars, and through a cop entrance. Then they led him down corridors and into the processing center. The station's interior was more of the same modern art nonsense as the exterior. It was like being arrested and processed inside a spaceship.

Widow stayed quiet the whole time. When he sat in Qaunak's cruiser, the only time she spoke was to read him his Miranda rights. She only looked at him in the rearview mirror. She never turned around—not once. She never took her aviators off—not once. Not even when they entered the underground vehicle bay. Not even when she and the jarhead cop escorted Widow to be processed.

On the way to the booking desk, Widow saw the jarhead cop's name was Wayne, which made Widow wonder if his first name was John, making him Officer John Wayne. That would be a humorous gag to play on your son. He could imagine all the Waynes born into the Wayne family tree since the actor died. John was a common name. He could imagine how many parents skipped it so their kid wouldn't grow up with that name haunting them. He figured by now it was okay to name your kid John Wayne. Although John Wayne was still famous, it had been forty-plus years since he died. He died before the cell phone. He died before social media became a thing. Hell, he died before the World Wide Web was worldwide at all.

Widow didn't ask Wayne's first name. He kept his eyes forward.

They brought Widow to processing, where they handed him off to the two biggest officers on duty in the room and probably in the whole building. The two new officers were gym big and not cake-fed big. They were like Widow: lean in the waist, broad shoulders, covered in muscle. The difference being that they got all of it from lifting things and pushing things and pulling things. Widow got it from a hearty road diet and coffee and walking everywhere. It made him think that if he had a desk job or a job sitting ninety percent of the day away inside a patrol car, he'd have to go to the gym two hours a day, five days a week just to achieve what nature and an active nomadic lifestyle had blessed him with.

The two officers tried to hold Widow by the triceps, but it was like palming a basketball.

The two big officers took Widow the rest of his journey, through processing, booking, and all of it. They made him do the whole song and dance. First, they took him to a station and searched him. One of the big cops stood back and watched, his arms folded like a bouncer at a club. The second searched him from top to bottom and back up to top again, a double pass over. The cop searching him set all of his belongings on a countertop. There was his passport, fifty dollars in cash money, two quarters, two nickels, pocket lint, a paperback copy of *Into the Wild* with a cracked spine, and the postcard he bought for Gray.

The officer at the desk inspected all the belongings, showed them to Widow, and wrote his name down on a large plastic ziplock bag in the space for labeling. She took his name from his passport, never asked him directly. Once she was finished writing his name legibly, she placed all of his belongings into the ziplock bag and sealed it. She showed it to him for his approval. It was the only time during their interaction that she made eye contact with Widow. He nodded, and she took his stuff and vanished into another room.

The two big cops took him to another station, where one officer asked him a bunch of questions. He exercised his Miranda rights and stayed silent through all of her questions. This frustrated her. She kept making all kinds of faces. It was like she forgot about his right to remain silent, like she was used to prisoners doing the complete opposite. In the end, she marked down *Prisoner refused to answer* in all the blank spaces on a piece of paper on a clipboard. Then Widow got his mug shot taken by a bony cop with a camera on a tripod. Finally, he ended up at the last station and got fingerprinted. They had to take his handcuffs off. He didn't resist them, but the officer who operated the fingerprint station looked at Widow's size and asked one of the big cops to do it for him.

Widow's prints went onto a page with ten boxes for the prints. His prints took up damn near the entire spaces.

Widow stayed quiet through all the processes from beginning to end. He never spoke. Never complained. Never resisted.

The whole process seemed to take forever, and it was quite lengthy. In his experience, in a small community like Kodiak Island, this process should've been thirty minutes, tops. But it took about an hour. There were other new inmates ahead of him. Which surprised him. The cops seemed to make their arrest quotas and then some.

At the end of all of it, they took him to a long white corridor and stopped at a white phone on the wall. They looked at him. One of the big cops asked him a question.

"Do you want your phone call now?"

Widow thought for a long moment. He looked around the room and didn't see what he was looking for. So he finally spoke. He asked, "What time is it?"

One of the big cops took his hand off Widow's triceps and dug his hand into his pants pocket, fishing around for his cell phone. He found it, took it out, and looked at the screen.

He said, "It's seven thirty."

Widow thought of Gray. He could call her. She could get him out of this mess. She would too. She would do whatever necessary to help him out of a jam. He had no doubt about it. But right then, Gray would be at home in Quantico, Virginia. It was four hours ahead of Widow. It would be eleven thirty at night there. Gray worked tomorrow. She was a good agent. She'd already be in bed, probably snuggled up with her little dog, probably fast asleep. She'd probably been asleep for hours.

Widow thought he could call her. She'd answer. Maybe she'd sound gruff and sleepy, but she would take his call.

The big cop put the cell phone back in his front pocket. He stared at Widow. Impatience flooded his face. He asked, "Well? What's it gonna be?"

Widow said, "No phone call. Later."

"Suit yourself," the cop said.

The two big cops took Widow by both triceps again and hauled him off to the holding cells.

CHAPTER 19

Widow woke up in a holding cell with four other guys. He had fallen asleep on a cot that might as well have been the floor because it was as stiff as concrete. It was okay because he had slept in worse places on worse beds before. He was amazed that he could sleep at all. They had the whole place lit up with blinding white lights. The ceilings were high, too high for anyone to reach the bulbs. He supposed anyone could have thrown a shoe up at the lights and smashed them if they weren't guarded by plastic covers. Of course, those could've been smashed too.

The holding cell itself was a large concrete block. The room was large enough to park a fleet of cars in, but small enough to fit inside a baseball diamond. The walls, the ceiling, the floor, all of it, was painted white, amplified by the bright lights. It smelled like alcohol and fresh paint.

Widow sat up and put his feet on the floor. He stared forward and looked around the room. The other four prisoners were all male, all still asleep. Three of them were snoring. As large as the holding cell was, Widow was on one wall, and the other four inmates were huddled closer together on the opposite wall. They had moved as far away from him as possible. He figured they were afraid of him, he guessed because of how he looked. He got up and moved around the cell. Instead of bars, the cell had one large window of glass so that the guards could see straight in. There was a door cut out of it on one side. It was mostly glass and steel.

Widow stared out across from the holding cell and saw another cell. In that one, he recognized four of the guys. They were the ones he beat up. Only now, they had black eyes and bruised faces. One of them was the guy called Johnny. They were all asleep as well. They must've told the guys in his cell what he had done to them. That's why his cellmates were less than eager to share a cell with him.

Widow wondered what the time was. He figured it was early morning, probably first light. He could use that phone call now. Gray would be awake. On the East Coast, the day would've been well into the morning hours.

Widow stood up slowly and stretched his arms all the way out and turned his head from side to side, cracking the bones and ligaments. Next, he cracked his knuckles. Once he was satisfied, he moved to the glass.

He looked out across the hall, over at the guys he'd beaten up. The only one missing was the one called Carl. He was probably at the hospital.

Widow leaned into the window and looked left, saw a guard station. He was about to rap on the glass when he saw a male guard coming from around a corner. He was huge, bigger than the two cops that escorted Widow the night before. He came around the corner and locked eyes with Widow. He walked straight for Widow's cell. He stopped in front of the glass. He moved over to the door.

At eye level, there were holes cut through the glass for talking. The guard looked at Widow and asked, "Jack Widow?"

Widow said, "That's me."

The huge guard pulled on a security badge that ran from a thin cable to a retractor on his belt. He stepped to a card reader near the door and swiped the card. There was a buzzing sound, and he opened the cell door.

"Step out," he said.

Widow didn't protest. He stepped out of the cell. The huge guard let the door shut behind him and waited for an audible clicking sound that confirmed it was locked.

The guard said, "Follow me." And he walked back the way he came. Widow followed.

They went back through corridors and back past the fingerprint and mug-shot stations and the rest of processing. They didn't go to the vehicle bay. Instead, they took a left down a corridor that Widow hadn't been through. They went to the interview rooms.

The guard took Widow to a green door marked "Interview Room G." The guard opened it and led Widow inside.

"Have a seat," the guard said.

Widow entered the room. Inside, there was a metal table and two metal chairs. The whole space was painted green—the floor, walls, and ceiling, all of it.

Widow glanced up to one corner and stared at a security camera. It went to the video and audio recording systems center Widow had already passed by. There was no two-way mirror, like in the movies.

The guard said, "Have a seat."

Widow asked, "What am I doing in here?"

"I was told to bring you here. Have a seat."

Widow stayed standing.

The guard said nothing and retreated out in the hall. He closed the door behind him. Widow was left in the interview room, wondering what the hell he was doing in there.

Widow stayed standing. He had been sleeping all night and didn't need to sit down. He waited for around fifteen minutes, then he leaned against the back wall and folded his arms across his chest. The door opened right then. The huge guard stood in the doorway for a long second and then stepped back into the hall. A woman carrying a thick navy-blue folder stuffed under her arm stepped into the doorway past him. She wore enough makeup to cause her to appear older than she was at first glance. The problem with her strategy was no one took just a first glance at her. Widow guessed she was aiming to look in her early thirties, but she was probably closer to twenty-five than she was thirty-five.

The woman was taller than most women Widow encountered. Widow estimated she was about five foot eleven, but an inch and a half of that was because of molded block heels on a pair of black Rockport dress shoes she wore with her outfit. She wore black dress pants, a leather belt, and a black V-neck sweater under a black leather jacket. There was a gold badge clipped to her belt. She looked tough but with a dash of deer-in-headlights look. Widow couldn't put his finger on it, but she didn't quite fit in, like she was in the wrong room or something.

She came into the room and glanced at Widow. Her eyebrow arched like she was just now realizing why they sent her in with the huge guard. It was for her protection.

Even though Widow saw slight fear in her eyes—fear that he was used to seeing on people when they first encountered him—he thought she was a little too attractive to be a detective. It wasn't an intentional line of thinking, just a gut reaction. She had shoulder-length blond hair. But her eyes. They didn't fit. Her eyes were a large, intoxicating, and a vivid Caribbean blue. They belonged on a billboard in Times Square, not in a little known island in Alaska.

She entered the room despite feeling intimidated. She walked over to one side of the table, took the folder out from under her arm, set it down on the table, and pulled out a chair. She looked at Widow and spoke.

"Good morning, Mr. Widow. Would you like to have a seat?"

Widow looked at her. He glanced at a SIG Sauer P226 under her jacket in a hip holster clipped onto her belt, her right-hand side. The SIG Sauer P226 was a firearm he knew well. It's one of the regular weapons carried by SEALs. This one was chambered for the nine-millimeter parabellums.

Widow said, "Sure."

He moved across from her and pulled out the other metal chair. He dumped himself down on it. It was just as he suspected—uncomfortable, like all metal chairs everywhere since the beginning of time. Widow put his hands out in front of him on the tabletop. He knitted his fingers together like he was planning to pray.

The woman sat down across from him. She asked, "Would you like coffee or soda or something?" She must've seen the flicker in his eye at the mention of coffee because she said, "Coffee, is it?"

"Sure," he said, trying not to make it seem like she had won him over.

The woman turned and called out the guard's name and asked him for two coffees, black. He nodded and left, and about five minutes later, he returned with two coffees in paper cups. Neither was hot. They were both lukewarm, which Widow figured. Cops never give inmates scalding hot coffee that can be used as liquid grenades.

Widow didn't complain. He drank it anyway.

The woman put her hand on top of the folder and said, "Mr. Widow, my name is Chelsea Keagan—Ensign Keagan. I'm here—"

"Ensign?" Widow asked. He looked up from his coffee, lowered it away from his face, and hovered it over the metal table.

"Yes. I'm a junior officer. That's my rank."

"Rank? You're not a detective?"

She said, "No. I'm with the CGIS. I'm an investigator."

"CGIS? Coast Guard?"

"Coast Guard Investigative Services."

Widow asked, "Why are you talking to me? Where's a detective?"

"This isn't about what you were arrested for."

Widow set the coffee down on the table and folded his arms across his chest. He asked, "What is this about? I've never been in the Coast Guard."

"I know. I pulled your Navy file," she said and opened the file in front of her.

Widow saw an old photo of himself. It was upside down to him and black and white, like the whole file was faxed over, or she printed it herself. But it was him. It was his graduation picture from the United States Naval Academy in Annapolis, a long time ago. He was in his dress whites. Technically, he was a midshipman right then in that photo. It was taken the day before he actually received his diploma. A sea of memories came washing over him, and a smile cracked across his face, remembering some of them.

She had his file. No question about it.

Keagan said, "Well, I pulled what I could get my hands on anyway. I know you were NCIS and Navy SEALs. But the time lapses are all blacked out. Most of your file is redacted, which tells me you used to be somebody important."

"I'm surprised you were able to get any of my file."

"It wasn't easy. I had to ask a favor from someone high up the chain, and I really do hate to owe anyone anything. But he said it was an interesting file."

"And you agreed to those terms?" Widow asked.

She said, "I did. Should I not have?"

"I'd ask for my money back. The file is mostly redacted. What do you think?"

"I think I got something good here, but I may never know what."

Widow stayed quiet.

Keagan looked down at the open file and flipped pages like she was skimming it. She said, "I can follow some of the thread here. Some of it I can piece together. It's not rocket science. Most of it, I can only speculate."

"Oh yeah? What do you speculate?"

"I can assume the blacked out parts are black ops, right?"

Widow stayed quiet.

"That's what I'm guessing," Keagan said, and she flipped the pages until she got to the next-to-last page. She stared at it and looked up at Widow. They were both seated across from each other, but she had to look up to see into his eyes.

She said, "Something that bothers me, I can't figure out, is that you're a commander in the Navy SEALs. I can see that. There's no record of your departure. No dismissal records. No discharge procedures followed. Nothing. But there's also no arrest warrant for you either. So you didn't go AWOL. It's like you simply disappeared. How is that possible?"

Widow thought back to the death of his mother, her last moments of life, her last words to him.

I raised you to do the right thing, she had said. He always tried to do the right thing. He tried to live his life by it.

Keagan stared at him like he was somewhere else in his head off in a daydream.

She repeated, "How is that possible?"

Widow stared back her. They made eye contact. He shrugged.

She took that as a nonresponse, and she moved on. She looked back down at the file and flipped over to the last pages. These pages differed from all the rest. They were three pages stapled together, like they came from a different source. There was another picture on the top of one of the first pages. It was black and white. It was Widow, older and different from the first photo. His head was shaved down to stubble. The hair on his face was also stubble, like he hadn't shaved his face in a week. He looked pissed off in the photo. There were two photos of him. The first was straight on, and the second was a profile shot. They were mug shots. He didn't even remember them. He couldn't recall where they were taken, the year, or the circumstances.

Keagan stared down at the mug shots for a long second and then back up at Widow like she was comparing the mug shot to his face right then—the real thing versus the past. She looked back down at the page. Her blue eyes followed the words below the mug shot. Widow looked at them too. There were dates and locations and brief descriptions.

She said, "Wow. You've been arrested a lot since you left the Navy."

Widow looked down at the paper. The last pages were a record of all the times he'd been arrested since he left.

Keagan put her index finger on the page and passed it over each section, counting to herself, but her lips moved as she went along. At the last post, she looked up at him and asked, "You've been arrested six times?"

Widow said, "Technically, eight times if you count the times I was in handcuffs but never booked."

"Eight times?"

Widow stayed quiet.

Keagan asked, "You've been arrested eight times, booked and processed six times?"

"Since I left the Navy. Not in my entire life. I've been arrested more times than you've got written there."

Keagan stared at him. She asked, "How is it you've been arrested eight times, booked six, and not one conviction? These arrests either had no charges filed, or they were dropped, or there was never a trial? How is that possible?"

Widow shrugged and said, "I'm misunderstood."

"I have a theory."

Widow watched her, looked into her eyes. It was easy to get lost in them, like clinging to dear life on a raft right in the middle of the bluest ocean. He could see how, one day, she could get information from any man with a brain. But today, she seemed to be under-prepared. In his opinion, so far, she had the right stuff. She had the eyes. She had the file. She'd done the legwork, but she was nervous. He saw that. It was like it was her first time. But why was she here? Alone? And with him?

He said, "I'm all ears."

"I think you weren't really enlisted in the Navy. Not when you quit. I think your enlistment was fake."

Widow stayed quiet.

She said, "I dug as much as I could, and I couldn't find what happened to you when you were in NCIS and then a SEAL? Why? I'm in the CGIS, and I know that we have some civilians and some enlisted. But the NCIS doesn't work that way. It's ninety-five percent civilian and five percent military. When I tried to find out why five percent were military, I came up cold. So here's my theory. I think you were part of undercover operations. That's why your file is redacted. It's probably filled with classified operations—both SEAL and criminal investigations. Am I close?"

Widow said nothing.

Keagan said, "I think you were deep cover. I think a man who would live a life like that must have an obsession with justice. I don't know why you live like a drifter, but I can see from these arrests what it looks like. I can see from a little digging that every time you've been arrested, you helped solve an unsolvable crime. It looks like you've been going around the country, playing caped crusader. Is that what it is?"

Widow thought, *Captain America and now Batman*. It was true, though. He had put no thought to it, but he had been a silent avenger—uninterested in glory, unimpressed by commendations, unmotivated by recognition.

Widow said, "I don't like injustice. I don't like to see good people destroyed by bad people."

Keagan stared into Widow's eyes. If someone else had been inside the room with them, staring at them from a side profile, they would see her Caribbean-blue eyes in a staring match with his ice-blue eyes.

Keagan asked, "It's that simple?"

"It's that simple."

"I've got one last question for you."

Widow stayed quiet.

Keagan said, "Matt Tyler?"

Widow stared at her blankly. He said, "The name's familiar."

"You don't remember him?"

"I can't place the name with the face, no."

"What about Alaska Rower?"

Widow paused a long beat. Not because he didn't recognize the name, but because he did. He closed his eyes and pictured Rower in his mind. He saw her bomber jacket. He saw her short, brown hair. He saw life in her. He saw a lot of happiness and pride in her accomplishments. He opened his eyes and said, "Alaska Rower was an FBI special agent. She worked out of Minneapolis. No partner. She was a damn good agent. And she was my friend."

Keagan asked, "She *was* your friend?"

"She was shot. Killed in the line of duty. In South Dakota. She's dead."

Right then, it dawned on Widow. Keagan didn't have to remind him, but she did. She said, "Matt Tyler was an FBI Agent. Right here from Alaska. He's dead too."

"I know. I can match the name to the face now. It was last year."

"That's right. Last year. North of Anchorage. He was also shot to death."

"Shotgun blast to his abdomen. It wasn't pretty."

Keagan asked, "Why?"

"Why what?"

"Why are two FBI agents dead? Two that you knew? Two that it looks like you were helping on different cases?"

Widow broke her gaze and looked away. He stared at the wall for a long second. He saw Rower's face in his mind. He took a deep breath and looked back at her. He said, "Those are not my fault."

Keagan paused a beat like she was mulling over the answer, evaluating and calculating and gauging something. It looked like a major decision, like she was about to go out on a limb. She studied Widow's face like she was looking to see if he was telling her the truth. She mulled it over some more, whatever was on her mind. Finally, she closed the file, looked at Widow, and said, "In that case, I need your help."

CHAPTER 20

The ice in Widow's blue eyes seemed to melt away, and he appeared to be deep in thought and waiting for more information from Keagan. She watched him and paused after she told him she needed his help because of that look on his face, like he was struck by a distant memory.

Widow wasn't struck by a distant memory so much as a face —Rower's face. That was the first, and then came a flood of all the other good people he'd known who died because of his failures.

Keagan said, "Widow?"

The look on his face faded away, and he was suddenly present again. He said, "Yes?"

"I need your help. Did you hear me?"

"What for? I thought I was here to talk about a fight I was in yesterday? A gun went off. I thought the Kodiak Police were gonna try to pin it on me."

Keagan said, "So about that. The case against you has been dropped."

"Dropped?"

"Yeah. One of the other guys admitted he brought the gun. He fired it. You had nothing to do with that."

"What about the guy in the hospital?"

"I know nothing about his condition, but they all agreed that they attacked you. Including the guy in the hospital, so he must be stable. You acted in self-defense."

Widow asked, "So, I can leave?"

"Yes. You're free to go. But what about my question? Can you help me?"

Widow thought for a moment. He could get up and walk out now. But he knew he could never live with himself. If he could help a fellow service member and investigator with a problem, he had to do it.

He said, "What's the problem? Why me?"

Keagan stood up and scooped up the file and put it under her arm. She walked over to the door and looked back over her shoulder at him. She said, "Follow me. I'll show you."

Widow got up from the metal chair and table and met her at the door. Keagan opened the door and looked at the huge guard. He eyeballed Widow being so close to her proximity and without restraints on.

Keagan looked at Widow, and asked, "You got any stuff here?"

"Yes. They took some items from me last night."

Keagan looked at the huge guard and asked, "Would you grab Mr. Widow's belongings and meet us at the morgue?"

At the morgue? Widow thought.

The huge guard looked at her and then at Widow with disdain in his eyes, like he hated two things in this world: the first, inmates; the second, being ordered around. But he did as he was told.

Keagan didn't wait for him to go about it. She walked on, leading Widow down hallways and past stations he recognized and some he didn't. She led him through groups of cops and past civilian workers with security badges. He was uncuffed and unguarded the whole time. He felt police eyes lock on him like he could be a potential security threat.

Eventually, they took an elevator down to the ground floor, and Keagan led him down two more hallways and around one corner until the station looked more like a hospital. The hall was white all over. The floor was white linoleum, mopped to a polished shine. Everything had a sterile look. They entered through a pair of double doors and came into another section and went through a door to the morgue.

The morgue was cold. The floor was concrete. There were two drains on either side of the room. There were eight thick metal doors on one wall that opened to drawers for the corpses. There were two large metal tables in the room with bright lights overhead. On one of the tables was a corpse. On the other table was an apparatus, worn and torn by weather and ocean water.

There was a man standing in the middle of the room. He wore a lab coat and plain clothes underneath—button shirt, tie, black chinos, and black shoes. The man was in his late fifties with a gray beard and bald head. He wasn't wearing glasses, but had a pair of goggles on his face, which made Widow think of goggled eye sockets and Liddy.

Keagan turned and looked at Widow. She said, "This is Dr. Bowen. He's the coroner here."

Widow nodded but stayed quiet.

Keagan shook the doctor's hand and said, "Show him."

Bowen went around the table with the dead body and stood over it like a blackjack dealer at a card table in Las Vegas. He stood over it like he was proud of his work.

Widow stepped up to the other side of the table, and so did Keagan. She stood close to him. They both stayed back a couple of feet, and both for the same reason. The doctor wore goggles, which told them to stay back a safe splatter distance. What for, they had no idea.

Widow looked at the corpse. The body had already been autopsied and sewn back together. He saw the stitching.

Bowen snatched up a pair of surgical gloves from a box of throwaway ones and pulled them on. Afterward, he clapped his gloved hands together and asked, "Where to start?"

"Tells us what you know. From the start, like you haven't told me yet," Keagan said.

"Okay," Bowen said. He laid his hands out over the body like he was presenting it to them. He said, "Here we have a dead white male, sixty-eight years old and only by a month. His name was Gary Kloss."

Bowen looked up at Keagan and then at Widow. He said, "We know his name by his dental records. And it's been confirmed with the FBI."

FBI? Widow thought.

Bowen said, "The body washed up near shore three days ago. A fisherman discovered it floating. It had been in the water for four days, give or take."

Keagan asked, "What state was it in? Did it decompose yet?"

Bowen said, "It's at the beginning of decomposition. Decomposition in water depends on the water temperature. In cold ocean water, bacterial action, which causes a corpse to become gassy and bloat, can be slowed."

Keagan asked, "Shouldn't the skin be peeling off from being submerged in water?"

Bowen said, "A corpse's skin will absorb water and peel away from the underlying tissues, but that takes about a week. That's when the fun starts. The ocean's creatures—you know, fish, crabs, and even sea lice—will come around and start nibbling at the corpse's flesh.

Widow said, "The decomposition can also be slowed by adipocere."

Both Bowen and Keagan looked at Widow. Bowen looked at Widow sideways, like he could've been startled either by Widow's knowledge or the fact that he spoke.

Bowen said, "The ocean water is cold right now. It always is this far north. And cold water encourages the process of adipocere."

Keagan asked, "What is adipocere?"

Widow said, "Adipocere is like a grayish, waxy, soapy substance. It happens when you slap the beginning of decomposition and moisture together."

Bowen said, "It's formed from the fat in the human body. It's actually meant to protect the corpse from decomposition."

Keagan said, "Weird."

Widow wasn't sure if she was talking about the process of adipocere, or that Widow knew what it was.

Bowen moved his hands down to the corpse's knees. He said, "The victim had two broken legs, and they were broken before he died. His kneecaps were shattered by blunt force trauma. Very blunt and very traumatic and full of force. And see here?"

Bowen pointed at Kloss's face, which was missing part of his eye. He said, "See how the face is bruised?"

Keagan said, "I see his eye was removed."

Bowen said, "No. Not that. The eye wasn't removed. It's partially eaten. That's postmortem. It happened when he was in the ocean. I'm talking about the bruises here and here. See the swelling around the eye cavity?"

Keagan nodded.

Bowen said, "He was beaten about the face."

Widow asked, "He was tortured?"

Bowen said, "Yes. Badly. Someone beat him nearly to death and then stopped."

Widow asked, "How did he die? Did he drown?"

"Yes. That's the weird part," Bowen said and looked at Keagan like he was seeking her permission to say more.

Keagan said, "Show him."

Bowen stepped back and away from the table and turned to the other table. He went around it so he faced Widow and Keagan over the table. He took the pose of a blackjack dealer again.

Widow and Keagan stepped over to the other table.

"What's this?" Widow asked.

Bowen started to speak, but Keagan put her hand up for him to stay silent. She asked, "What do you think it is?"

Widow examined a heap of a man-made contraption. There was metal mesh, and straps, and more metal. Some of it was painted a bright red color.

He asked, "Can I touch it?"

Bowen said, "That's okay. There's no trace evidence on it. It was submerged with the body for four days."

Widow touched it. He felt the metal mesh, and he pulled on the loose straps. He took his hand away and said, "It looks like a gurney from a rescue helicopter."

Keagan said, "That's exactly what it is. It's called a litter. They hang from a winch on our rescue helicopters."

Widow stayed quiet for a long moment, and then he said, "This guy was beaten, tortured, and then hauled out to sea hanging from a rescue helicopter?"

Keagan said, "It appears he was hung from a helicopter in a litter and dropped into the ocean, where he drowned."

Widow asked, "And he couldn't have escaped because his legs were broken, and he was strapped into this thing. He probably couldn't even have moved his arms."

Bowen said, "He was found with one arm free. That was probably before he drowned. He probably exerted all the oxygen he had in his lungs just fighting to free one hand."

Widow asked, "Did he sink to the bottom? He didn't float?"

Keagan said, "Whoever did this to him probably tied him to an anchor or something. We didn't find that."

Widow looked at her and then Bowen. He said, "You said he was FBI?"

Keagan said, "He was FBI. He retired. After, he worked as a private investigator."

Widow asked, "And the Feds know?"

"They know," Keagan said, and she turned to the doctor and said, "Thank you. That's all we need for now."

She took Widow by his forearm, which caught him off guard. She led him back out the double doors and back to the elevator. The elevator doors snapped open just as they were getting there. The huge guard was inside the elevator. He held Widow's belongings in the same plastic bag from before. He also held a clipboard with papers.

The huge guard stepped off the elevator and explained to them that Widow had to sign his release papers before he could leave or before he could accept his belongings. Widow took the clipboard and looked over the paperwork. It was all standard. There was a section that said he agreed that all of his belongings were returned to him, like the inspection check at Cutty's. Only this was inventory—his inventory. He looked over the plastic bag in the huge guard's hand and counted his belongings. It was easy. He didn't have much. He saw it all there with a quick glance. He signed the paperwork and returned it to the guard, and took the plastic bag. He opened it and pocketed his belongings: his cash money, his passport, his paperback copy of *Into the Wild*, and the postcard he had bought for Gray.

Widow didn't thank the guard, but he gave him the empty plastic bag. The guard took it and pressed the elevator button to return to where he came from.

Keagan took Widow by the forearm and pulled him along. "This way," she said.

After long minutes of more corridors and finally a fire stairwell, where they went up a flight, they were outside the building. Keagan led Widow across a catwalk. She released his forearm and motioned for him to follow her. She acted like she was in a hurry.

They crossed the catwalk and entered a parking garage. She led him around through parked cars until they came to a crew-cab pickup truck. It was painted white with "US Coast Guard" printed on the front doors. There was a light bar with large bulbs on top. The truck bed was covered with a utility box and cover. The tires were big and thick. They'd seen plenty of action. The truck was a four-by-four, which made sense because the only land the Coast Guard had jurisdiction over was usually rocky, sandy terrain and coastlines.

They got into the pickup—Keagan in the driver's seat and Widow on the passenger side.

Inside, Keagan set the navy-blue folder containing Widow's life in a briefcase on the back seat. Then she unclipped her weapon and holster from her belt so she could sit more comfortably. She did this instantly and automatically, like she did it every time she got into a vehicle. She went to place the gun in the cupholder in a center console. But she looked at Widow like she forgot he was there, and she was hit with second thoughts. She recovered and set the weapon on her lap instead.

Widow said nothing about it.

Keagan fished a set of keys out of her jacket pocket and started up the truck. She turned the heater on and let the vehicle warm itself up.

She turned to Widow as if to speak, but said nothing.

He said, "Don't take offense, but are you brand new at this?"

Keagan said, "I'm a good cop!"

"I meant are you new to this department? Are you new to this post?"

Keagan said, "I've got five years in law enforcement and four in the Coast Guard."

"What did you do in law enforcement?"

Keagan paused a beat and said, "Here's the thing. I was a patrolman."

"A patrolman?"

"Okay, a patrolwoman, whatever."

Widow was turned sideways in his seat, his back against the doorframe. He stared at her. He said, "You were a beat cop outside of the Coast Guard?"

"Yes. I was a cop in Freeport."

"Maine?"

"No. It's in Kansas."

"I never heard of it."

"It's a small town."

Widow said, "I like small towns."

"You've never heard of this one. Trust me. It's got a gas station and a stoplight. That's it."

"Sounds amazing," he said.

She said, "So the thing is, I'm new here. I just graduated OCS."

"Officer Candidate School? When?"

"I know you went to Annapolis, but we can't all be so smart."

Widow asked, "How long have you been out?"

"Six months."

He said, "Okay. That's not such a big deal. Congratulations on getting a murder case so soon. But where's your partner?"

"So here's the thing," she said again, like she was nervous. "I just got here to Base Kodiak. This is my first case."

"Not alone?"

"I'm the only one left on base."

"Only what left?"

Keagan said, "I'm the only member left of the investigators."

"So, you're on this case all by yourself? For your first assignment?"

"I'm not the only person on it, but I'm the only one who's still looking at it."

Widow looked at her, confused.

Keagan said, "So the FBI is on it. Obviously, they're interested in one of their own being murdered. And the local cops are on it, but they've all closed the case."

"Closed the case?"

"Yeah, they think they have the suspects in custody. The FBI and Kodiak Police have four guys in custody already. They've confiscated a Sikorsky MH-60 Jayhawk—*our* Jayhawk. The US Coast Guard's, I mean."

Widow said, "I don't understand."

"The four guys they arrested are the other four members of my department here."

"What?"

"Yeah, so apparently my boss and three others from CGIS here on the island took a Jayhawk out the other night without permission. At first, they lied and said it was a practice mission. But then that guy was found dead, and now they claim they went out drinking, horsing around on one of the abandoned islands, seven nights ago."

"Are they telling the truth?"

Keagan said, "I think so."

"How well do you know this CO?"

"Not very. I know him from our interview and phone conversations."

"Interview?" Widow asked, "How long did you say you've been stationed here?"

"I started three mornings ago. This is my fourth day."

Widow said, "So you started on the same day that your whole department was arrested?"

"Yes."

"And you believe they're innocent? That they didn't abduct some retiree, beat him half to death, and take him out to sea, where they dangled him from a cable and drowned him?"

"I do. Why would they?"

Widow thought for a moment, and then he said, "So, you need me to help you prove them innocent?"

"I'm just asking you to help me look into it. I know there's more going on. These guys have families. I know they went out horsing around, and they should get punished for that, but not framed for murder."

"What about the basket from the Jayhawk they took out?" Widow asked. "Is it missing?"

"It's called a litter, and yes, it's missing. But they claim it's from horsing around, not from them killing a guy they don't know."

Widow went quiet.

Keagan said, "Please, Widow. I read your file. I know you can help me. I want to exonerate them."

"Why did the cops let you take me away so easy?"

"The Coast Guard called them."

Widow asked, "Who called them?"

"Chief Bell."

"Chief Bell?"

Keagan said, "Master Chief Corey Bell. He's third in command at Kodiak Station."

"Bell? I never heard of him."

"He's how I got your file. I was looking for other suspects, to show doubt about my guys being involved."

Widow said, "So you found me locked up and thought I was interesting as a suspect?"

"Actually, you're quite the godsend. I feel lucky to have you right here to help. Looking at your record, if anyone can help, it's you."

"Okay. You don't need to blow smoke, Ensign. I'll help. But here's a question."

Keagan said, "Sure. What is it?"

"Does the FBI know about me?"

She paused a beat and said, "They warned us to leave you alone."

Widow nodded and asked, "That's how you found out about Rower and Tyler?"

"Yes. They said you were trouble. But of course they would."

He looked right into her Caribbean-blue eyes and asked, "What do you think? Am I trouble?"

"Maybe. But the good trouble. I can see from your past that you're a man who tries to do the right thing, even if that means doing wrong to correct things so that they are right."

Widow nodded and turned in his seat to face the windshield. He asked, "These guys they got—your guys—are they good men?"

"Yes. They're rowdy and were unaccounted for during the night of the murder. But like I said, they took a Jayhawk out for what they called "a beer run," which they explained was just them flying it to an island out there on the ocean and getting wasted and then flying back. One of them is an idiot, but the others seem solid. They're not killers. And certainly, they wouldn't have been so sloppy about it."

Widow said, "In that part, I agree with you. This guy Kloss was tortured, so he had information that somebody wanted. My guess is once they got it, they cut him loose."

Keagan nodded along.

Widow asked, "Any other Jayhawks unaccounted for?"

"No. Just the one."

"Then we're looking for someone who has a Jayhawk or access to one. Do you know of any place else like that?"

"Not for hundreds of miles. All the Jayhawks are a part of the Coast Guard."

"There's gotta be one somewhere."

Keagan said, "I doubt it. But I suppose it's possible for decommissioned models to be around. Or for customer versions to be out there."

"Do you have a support staff?"

"I do."

"Call them up and see if they can track down any possible Jayhawks within six hundred miles."

Keagan asked, "Six hundred miles?"

"Jayhawks can fly three hundred miles without refueling."

"So why six hundred?"

"In case it refueled," Widow said.

Keagan took out her cell phone and started dialing her office. She put the phone to her ear and waited for an answer.

Widow said, "And ask them to account for all the litters on all the aircraft on base. Make sure none are missing except for the one they claim to have lost."

Keagan nodded. She was still waiting for an answer. She got a voice on the other line.

Widow interrupted one last time. He said, "What about Kloss's room?"

Keagan said hello and the name of the staff member who answered the phone, identified herself, and asked him to hold for a second. She looked at Widow and asked, "Kloss's room?"

"Yeah, you said he was a private investigator. That means he was probably here investigating something, which means he's not local. So, where was he staying? We need a hotel and room number. Ask them if the FBI or police have already looked into it. If they haven't, then we can do it for them."

CHAPTER 21

There weren't that many hotels on Kodiak Island to begin with. Widow and Keagan started visiting the ones in the city of Kodiak, and her support staff started calling around to others, asking about Kloss. Keagan stayed in touch with her guys by phone and text messages. There wasn't anything in Kloss's pockets to indicate a hotel key card or where he might've stayed. Keagan had suggested checking his bank statements, but Widow shot that down. His thinking was if Kloss was a retired FBI agent and an experienced PI, then he wouldn't pay for his hotel with a debit card. He would use cash, or a prepaid card, which was plausible because he could use the same card for the deposit file that most hotels required.

In the city of Kodiak, there were more than thirty hotels where he could've stayed. Not to mention that he may have stayed in an Airbnb or a lodge, like Widow had. Although Widow doubted a PI would shell out the money to stay in one of those expensive places. Besides, he knew Liddy sold his rooms and huts in a hunting or fishing package.

So they started with the most popular hotels in town and worked their way down to the more out-of-the-way ones. They drove around for hours, asking inside at each front desk with no luck. The early morning hours turned into midmorning, which turned into early lunchtime when they checked in with Keagan's support staff again, and they had all came up with nothing.

They finally came to a hotel on the far side of town near the farthest side of the docks from Peter's plane. They parked and went in.

The hotel was a three-story building with a few single bedrooms. All the singles had full-sized beds. There was no sharing allowed. Keagan and Widow knew that because of a handwritten sign on paper that hung behind the desk on a corkboard.

The hotel had an old sign on the road with a logo similar to Smokey the Bear, only without the hat and shovel, just enough to avoid copyright infringement. It was just a face of a bear. However, they were pushing their luck because the name of the hotel was Smokey's Inn.

The front desk was in a small, cramped office with two hard wooden chairs in the lobby. There was a squirrelly guy behind the counter. He was the morning worker. He made that clear. He had jitters, which he blamed on too much coffee the moment that Keagan showed him her badge.

Widow stayed back and crossed his arms, and Keagan did all the asking. She leaned on the counter and asked the guy questions like she was a crack detective on a case. Which she might've been. The jury was still out on that in Widow's mind. So far, she had been pretty good, but she was nervous and green. He knew that, but he only knew that because he was more experienced than she was. Not everyone they encountered would notice it. In fact, most probably wouldn't notice. She carried herself confidently and professionally.

Keagan stared at the jittery front desk guy and took out her cell phone and showed him a picture of Gary Kloss from his FBI badge. The bureau had sent it to her. It was all in the case file. She asked, "Have you seen this guy?"

The jittery front desk guy looked at the phone screen and said, "Maybe. Should I know him?"

She said, "He's dead. We're investigating his death. We believe he might've stayed here. Can you find out for us?"

"I don't recognize him."

Keagan said, "Can you look him up on your computer?"

The jittery front desk guy said, "Okay. But I don't recognize him."

The jittery front desk guy clicked a mouse in front of him to wake up a computer that was asleep. Keagan and Widow couldn't see the screen. The jittery front desk guy moved his fingers to a keyboard that was down and out of sight behind the counter. He asked, "What's the name?"

"Gary Kloss," Keagan said.

The jittery front desk guy tapped away on his keyboard and waited for the computer to search, and then he looked up and said, "No one here by that name."

Keagan said, "Check in the last two weeks?"

The jittery front desk guy looked back at the screen and tapped away on the keys again. Then he looked back up and said, "No one by that name for the entire last month."

Keagan asked, "Anyone have a room here last week and not check out yet? Or not come back to their room yet?"

The jittery front desk guy tapped away again and said, "Everyone who checked in last week has already checked out."

Widow stepped up and asked, "Check if anyone prepaid for a room for an extended period that hasn't checked out yet."

The jittery front desk guy stared up at Widow. He jittered a little harder, a little more aggressive, like it wasn't the jitters at all but fear. Widow knew the difference.

Fear or not, the jittery front desk guy didn't budge.

Keagan said, "Do as he asks, please."

The jittery front desk guy said, "I saw your badge, but I didn't see yours." He was talking about Widow.

Keagan said, "I showed you mine, and I'm asking you to do as he requested."

The jittery front desk guy nodded and tapped away on his keys again. He said, "I have two names here. Both men. I suppose."

Keagan asked, "Are there drivers' licenses with the names? Don't you guys photocopy them?"

The jittery front desk guy said, "Our guests prefer we don't keep their IDs with their, um, real home addresses on file."

Keagan said, "Okay. So who are the two guests that prepaid for extended periods of time but haven't checked out yet?"

The jittery front desk guy paused and said, "Not sure I should share that information."

Widow looked at Keagan and nodded a slight head nod, nothing dramatic. She returned the same and took out her phone and stared at the screen. She said, "Oh, I gotta take this phone call. It's important. I'll be right back."

She winked at Widow and walked away, back down the hall and out the front door to the parking lot they came from. Widow turned to the jittery front desk guy and smiled. He placed both of his hands down on the countertop and fanned out his fingers. His hands were enormous. He stretched out his torso to elongate it, to make him look taller and wider than he was normally. It was all the same tactic he did with the grizzly bear two days before, with Liddy in the woods. He stood over the jittery front desk guy, menacing and terrifying.

He said, "Give me the names of the two guests. And before you say no, I won't ask twice."

The jittery front desk guy stared at Widow's hands and up his torso and into his eyes. He said, "Come and look."

Widow stepped around the counter into the jittery front desk guy's space and put his hands on the guy's shoulders. He squeezed just enough to give the guy the impression that he could snap him like a twig, which was true.

The jittery front desk guy pointed at the screen. There were two names. Widow knew immediately which was Kloss. He pointed at one of the names on the screen and said, "Give me the room key for that guy's room."

The jittery front desk guy didn't fight back. He didn't resist. He did as requested. He went over to a cabinet that hung on a wall. He opened it and found the spare key for the Kloss's room and handed it over to Widow.

The jittery front desk guy said, "Please, bring it back when you're done."

Widow took the key and thanked the guy for his help, and reminded him to keep his mouth shut. Then he met Keagan out in the parking lot. She was leaning against the grille of the US Coast Guard truck.

"Did you get it?" she asked.

"I got it."

"How do you know it's his?"

Widow said, "The name he checked in with is Eureka Hoover."

"Who's that?"

"Hoover and Eureka are both popular vacuum cleaner companies."

Keagan asked, "Why pick those names?"

Widow shrugged and said, "Maybe he tried ex-presidents for a while, and maybe he ran out, so he combined Herbert Hoover and Eureka."

Keagan said, "Whatever. Let's go check out the room."

Widow led Keagan around a corner and up a flight of stairs that clanged as they climbed them. The room was on the second floor. Keagan knocked on the door, identified herself as a federal agent, and waited. No answer. Widow inserted the key, and Keagan put her hand on her gun, ready to draw if necessary. Widow unlocked the door to the room, and he shoved it open and stepped back. Keagan readied herself to draw her gun. But there was no need. The room was clearly empty. It was tiny. It was a twelve-by-twelve space. There was a made bed, blue carpet, a single cushioned chair in one corner, a vanity, a closet, and a bathroom. Everything was clean and tidy.

They entered the room and switched on the lights. Keagan opened the curtains and moved the blinds to let in as much light as possible.

Widow moved around the room. He looked at the carpet, at the bed, at the vanity. He moved his fingers over the vanity's top and inspected his fingers.

Keagan said, "Be careful not to touch anything else. The Feds might want to have a look here."

Widow said, "It won't matter. They won't find anything."

Keagan said, "Why do you say that?"

Widow didn't answer her. He stared at a phone in a cradle near the bed. Then he moved on and went to the closet and opened it. Inside, he found Kloss's clothes. He said, "Look here. Everything's neat and tidy. The clothes are all ironed and pressed and hung up."

Keagan came over and looked. She asked, "What's wrong with that?"

Widow knelt and inspected a pair of loafers. They matched both of Kloss's suits, which were hung up. He picked up one of the shoes by pinching his index and middle finger inside around the lip of the hole for a foot. He picked it up and got back on his feet and went over to the vanity. He placed the shoe on top the vanity. He stared at it.

Keagan said, "What are you doing?"

Widow stepped into the bathroom, turned on the light, and came back out with a clean towel off the rack. He went over to the vanity and started going through the drawers, using the towel. He opened them all, one at a time. He left them opened and stared into each. He reached in and shifted around Kloss's clothes. He was careful not to mess it up too much in case he was wrong about the FBI using forensics inside the room.

He used the towel to shift around Kloss's clothes, checking under items, looking for something. He moved the underwear, the socks, the folded T-shirts. He found nothing. He went over to the bed and looked under the pillows, under the bed. He found Kloss's suitcases. He pulled them out. There were two. They were pushed under the bed. He opened them, using the towel from the bathroom to touch the handles and the zippers. He set them open and looked inside. He sifted through all the compartments and the pockets and didn't find what he was looking for. He found Kloss's passport. He set that on the bed.

He said, "We can confirm that this is Kloss's room."

Keagan looked at the passport and nodded.

Widow continued his search like he was looking for something in particular. He checked everything from inside a microwave in a little kitchenette to under the sink to the medicine cabinet to behind the mirror over the sink in the bathroom to the toilet tank itself. He couldn't find what he was looking for.

Keagan followed him the whole way. She didn't pester him to answer her; she just followed along.

Finally, Widow was done with his search, and he stood in the middle of the room and looked out over all of it.

Keagan asked, "What are you looking for?"

Widow said, "Notice anything strange about this room?"

Keagan said, "No. Not really."

Widow said, "Okay. Let's put that aside for now. Kloss was an FBI agent. Right?"

"Yes?"

Widow said, "Was he any good?"

Keagan said, "I don't really know. The Feds haven't shared that with me."

Widow said, "Speculate. A lot of your job is to imagine."

Keagan said, "He made it to retirement. No issues in his records that I'm aware of. If he made it to retirement, then we can assume he was competent at least."

Widow asked, "And then he became a private investigator, right?"

"That's what I told you."

"Did you check to see if he's licensed?"

Keagan said, "Yes."

"Is he licensed in Alaska?"

"No. Utah, California, Nevada, and Colorado. I believe."

Widow said, "So Kloss was a retired FBI agent. He was competent, as you said, but he was probably more than that. He was probably a good agent. Right?"

"At least competent. He was at least average, which would make him good enough."

Widow said, "After he retired, he turned his life into working as a professional private investigator. And he was good enough that he was licensed in four states? Correct?"

"That's right."

"Therefore, we can assume he was good at that job too?"

Keagan said, "Good enough."

"Okay. So it's safe for us to presume that he was good enough at this job too. Wouldn't you agree?"

"He got himself killed."

"That's true. But up till that point, he was at least competent and probably average, right?"

"I'd say that's true."

Widow said, "Look around. What do you see?"

Keagan looked around and said, "I see a cheap hotel room that was nice and neat until you pulled everything out."

"But it was neat before that, right?"

Keagan said, "Yes. Very neat."

Widow said, "It was a little too neat."

"What does that mean?"

Widow said, "This room was searched before we got here."

Keagan looked at him and then looked around again. She let her eyes follow the room, tried to imagine before Widow pulled out all the drawers. She said, "How? It was spotless ten minutes ago."

Widow shook his head and said, "No. It was ransacked."

"How?"

Widow said, "It was ransacked and then put back together. It's called a scrub. This place has been scrubbed. Look how neat everything is."

Widow turned and went to the bathroom. He said, "This hotel is not bottom of the barrel, but it's pretty damn close. Wouldn't you agree?"

Keagan said, "It's the bottom for Kodiak."

Widow pointed at the mirror and said, "A man is staying in this room. He hasn't been here in seven days, and this mirror is spectacularly clean. Look at it."

Keagan moved over to the bathroom and stepped inside. The bathroom was tight enough that she had to brush up against Widow to stand in front of the mirror. He pushed back as far as he could against a towel rack behind him.

She looked at the mirror and at Widow's reflection in it. She said, "That's a clean damn mirror."

They exited the bathroom. Keagan went over to the bed near the door side of the room. Widow went back to the center and stood there. He said, "Here's another thing. We agree Kloss was a decent private investigator. But look around the room."

Keagan looked around.

Widow said, "Where's his laptop? Or his tablet?"

Keagan looked around again and tilted her head. She said, "That is odd."

Widow said, "No way would a guy like this, a private investigator who is licensed in four states, not have a digital device of some type. This guy would have something to record his findings on. He'd need a computer to use the internet, to take notes, to load video files, to store his findings. He'd need email. He'd need Google. But there's no device here."

Keagan said, "Maybe he used his phone for all that. They're basically little computers nowadays, you know? He drowned to death out there in the ocean. His phone is probably in the belly of a fish or something."

Widow shook his head and said, "He probably used his phone, but he wouldn't *only* use a phone. He'd have a laptop, too. Trust me. And the guys who killed him would have his phone, or it's out there in the belly of a shark somewhere. They also would know he had a computer. Hell, he probably told them where it was."

Keagan thought for a moment and said, "Yeah. You're right. Where is it? Maybe the bad guys took it off him before they killed him."

"No. Even if they did, he'd have a backup here. Private investigators keep records and reports and leave things behind—hidden—in case something happens to them. He'd have a backup. He'd have secure records and a secure record-keeping system in place."

She said, "I see nothing like that here. We should check if he has mail at the desk."

Widow said, "Let's go now. We won't find anything else here."

Keagan agreed, and the two of them put everything back the way they found it, locked the room up, and left. They went back to the front desk to find the jittery guy waiting. He took the key. He kept one of his hands behind the counter and out of sight. Widow suspected he went to get a weapon of some sort in case Widow came back. It was probably a baseball bat. Although, it could've been a firearm.

Widow stayed close to Keagan, in case the jittery guy came out with whatever weapon it was. She asked him for Kloss's mail.

The jittery front desk guy said, "No mail."

Widow said, "Did Mr. Hoover ask you to hold anything for him?"

The jittery front desk guy kept his eyes on Keagan and didn't make eye contact with Widow. He said, "Oh, the FBI already picked that up."

Widow and Keagan looked at each other. Their different shades of blue eyes locked for a moment, and then Keagan looked back at the jittery front desk guy.

She asked, "The FBI?"

The jittery front desk guy said, "That's the badge the guy had."

Keagan asked, "Do you remember the guy's name?"

The jittery front desk guy said, "No, ma'am."

Widow asked, "What did this guy look like?"

The jittery front desk guy said, "White guy. Very neat looking. Suit. Tie. Professional. Probably mid-fifties or early sixties. Should I not have given him the package?"

Keagan asked, "Do you remember what this package was?"

The jittery front desk guy scratched his head and said, "It was a small case with a handle."

Keagan asked, "What kind of case? Like a briefcase?"

The jittery front desk guy said, "No. It was like a satchel. It had a shoulder strap on it. And a zipper with a main pocket. It was like something a college professor might carry his papers around in."

Keagan asked, "Like for a laptop?"

The jittery front desk guy said, "Sure. A laptop would fit inside it easy."

Keagan asked, "Do you have security cameras?"

The jittery front desk guy said, "No, ma'am."

Keagan said, "You should get some."

The jittery front desk guy said, "The owners don't want them. The people who come here like their privacy."

The jittery front desk guy paused a beat, and then he said, "I thought it weird that you guys came twice."

Keagan turned to Widow and said, "Come on. There's nothing here for us."

They left the front desk office and the jittery guy and returned to the truck in the lot. They got inside—Keagan behind the wheel and Widow on the passenger side.

She said, "You said the room was 'scrubbed.' Does that mean what it sounds like?"

Widow glanced in the passenger side mirror to see if anyone was watching them from the parking lot. He saw no one. He said, "It's also called a 'clean sweep.' I only saw it when I was in the SEALs doing black ops missions. It's done when the CIA wants to search a room, but they don't want anyone to know they've been there. What they do is they send in a team that takes digital photos of everything so they can remember exactly where everything is. Then they carefully ransack it."

Keagan interrupted and asked, "Carefully ransack?"

"They're very good at it. They move everything around as quickly as possible, breaking nothing, until they find what they're looking for. Then they use the photos to put every-thing back exactly as they found it. Sometimes they clean the room after, erasing all trace evidence that anyone has been there. It works great in hotel rooms. When the occupant returns, they might notice something out of place, but when they see how clean everything is…"

Keagan said, "They chalk it up to maid service."

"Yeah," Widow said.

"And you think that a CIA scrub team came through Kloss's room?"

"Maybe not a team, but I'd bet money it was someone who knew what they were doing. And now we got a guy with an FBI badge going around."

Keagan asked, "So, you don't think it was actually the FBI that took Kloss's laptop?"

"No way. You'd know about it. It'd be in the case files. Plus, whoever the guy was with the badge, he didn't even tell front desk guy Kloss was dead."

Keagan put her hands on the wheel at the ten and two o'clock positions and asked, "What now?"

Widow said, "I'm going to go back in there without you and ask that guy for phone records for the room from the day Kloss checked in till now."

"You think this FBI guy might've used the phone?"

"No, but somebody hired Kloss to be here. That somebody may have called him, or he might've called out using the phone in the room."

Widow thought that Keagan would have better luck getting those phone records, but he couldn't send her back in there when the guy might have a weapon under the counter. He got out of the truck and left her sitting there alone.

Widow was back inside of five minutes with two pages of phone records.

CHAPTER 22

The sky was full of gray and white clouds, but the sun was out. Widow and Keagan drove through the city of Kodiak. Keagan drove, and Widow sifted through the phone records.

Keagan said, "Widow, where are we going?"

Widow kept his eyes on the phone numbers on the paper. He said, "I'm starving. Can we grab some breakfast?"

Keagan looked at a digital clock on the radio, above the center console. It was the middle of the afternoon. She said, "It's late for breakfast. It's more like late lunchtime."

Widow said, "Can we get some lunch, then? Really, I'm starving." He wasn't lying. Just then, his stomach rumbled.

Keagan smiled and glanced over at Widow. She said, "I need to close this case. We don't have time to sit at a restaurant."

Widow's stomach rumbled again, only this time, it was twice as loud. He rubbed it with one hand and said, "See? I'm not kidding. I'm pretty hungry. I work better once I've eaten. I can't think clearly on an empty stomach."

Keagan said, "I have a better idea."

Widow put the papers down in his lap and stared out the window. Keagan took him down a couple more turns and across one major intersection and pulled into the drive-through of a fast-food joint that he had never heard of. It must've been an Alaskan thing. She told him they had the best cheeseburgers. He ordered two of them and fries, no drink. He thought about ordering coffee, but she said there would be coffee at their final destination.

After exiting the drive-through, Keagan handed Widow a big bag of their lunch and took him back to her office. They drove to the US Coast Guard Base Kodiak. They passed through a guard checkpoint and drove along a flight line. There were huge snowcapped mountains in the distance. The flight line had parked aircraft in neat rows and in different sections. Widow saw a pair of HC-130 Hercules planes. One was silent and foreboding. The other one looked like it was being fueled and prepared for a flight. He saw ground crew in coast-guardsmen uniforms tending to their flight checks and examining different parts of the plane.

There were large hangar bays along the back of the flight line. Widow saw several MH-65 Dolphin helicopters parked in a row together. Then he saw numerous MH-60 Jayhawks, like the one that they thought Kloss was dropped from. He didn't point them out to Keagan.

After another two minutes of driving down streets at a slow speed, because speed limits on bases are strictly followed no matter who is driving, they passed several white brick buildings and ended up at another white brick building with a large parking lot. There was one end that was two stories; the rest was one long floor. It kind of looked like a small airport with the tower jutting up in the front.

Keagan parked the truck near an entrance and turned off the engine. She took out the keys, scooped her SIG Sauer from the console, and holstered it.

She said, "Okay. This is it. Take our food and the phone records. We'll look them over inside."

Widow did as asked and got out of the truck. Keagan led him to a door and down a long corridor. Suddenly, lightning cracked outside. They heard a rumble of thunder, and the lights overhead in the hall flickered several times.

Keagan said, "That happens in bad weather. The electrical circuits in this building are terrible."

Widow said nothing to that. He followed her down to the end of the corridor, and they took a right into a large room. There were holding cells to one side. They were empty.

There were two coastguardsmen in uniform. Both sat at desks; both were women. They stood up when they saw Keagan and saluted her.

"At ease, ladies. Get back to work."

She didn't introduce Widow to them or them to him. She shuffled him along and into her office like she wanted to avoid explaining to them who he was. Which made him wonder if they even knew that he was there to help free their bosses. He didn't ask about it.

Keagan's office was small. There was a desk in the room and a window with a view of the parking lot. A MacBook sat on her desk. It was open. There was a single bookcase with many books involving maritime law and Coast Guard topics that were of no interest to Widow.

He took the paperback of *Into the Wild* out of his pocket and set it on the bookcase, bookending one row of books.

Keagan came in behind him and asked, "What are you doing?"

"I finished it. You keep it. It's good."

She shrugged, and Widow took a seat in an empty chair in front of her desk. He saw pictures on the desk of people that looked like Keagan.

He asked, "Are those your family?"

Keagan took her jacket off and draped it over the back of her desk chair. She took her gun and holster off her belt, slid open a drawer, put them inside, closed the drawer afterward, and sat in her chair.

She said, "It's my sisters and their kids."

"You got kids?" Widow asked. He held the fast-food bag on his lap.

She said, "No. You?"

"Nope."

She asked, "You got a wife?"

Widow said, "You already know the answer is no."

"You ever have one?" Keagan asked.

Widow thought about the question. Not that he needed to, but his mind wandered back in time. There were a few faces of women from the past that popped up in his mind's eye, but he pushed them away and said, "About as close as I ever came was live-in girlfriends."

Keagan said, "Oh yeah. How many of those have you had?"

"A few."

"Give me my sandwich," she said, and she held a hand out over the desk for it.

Widow fished out her sandwich, which was easy because it wasn't a double cheeseburger, and so hers was the smallest of the three sandwiches inside. He handed it to her, and she opened it and ate a regular cheeseburger right on her desk over the open wrapper.

Widow made room on his side of the desk and opened one double burger and scarfed it down. A few moments later, he was well into the second one while she was still on her only burger. He emptied the fries out between them and onto the old wrapper from his first burger.

He said, "Have some."

"Thank you," Keagan said, and she scooped up a couple of fries and ate them. After she ate her burger, she reached her hand across the desk and picked up the phone records from Widow. She leaned back in her chair and studied the records.

She said, "I should've gotten a soda."

Widow said, "Didn't you mention something about coffee here?"

"Sure, it's outside the office in the next office over. It's empty. We use it as a break room. Go help yourself."

Widow nodded and scarfed down the last of his second burger. Then he wiped his hands on some cheap napkins and stood up and headed to the door. He stopped in the doorway and asked, "Want some?"

"No, but would you grab me a diet soda out of the fridge? It's in the corner."

"Sure," Widow said, and he left the room.

He found the makeshift break room with no problem and found fresh coffee already in a pot. He took a US Coast Guard coffee mug off a shelf and filled it. He downed the coffee fast, like a man in the desert who just discovered a canteen with water. Then he refilled it and went to the fridge, opened it, and found a diet soda. He took both back to Keagan's office, where she was scanning over the numbers on the phone records thoroughly. He set the can in front of her and popped the tab for her. The soda can fizzed and hissed. The sound filled the silence.

"Thank you," she said, and took a swig from the can. She swallowed and set the can down.

She put the paper down, and said, "Some of the numbers repeated here are local. I googled them, and one is a local diner near the hotel. Kloss was probably ordering out there ... a lot. This other," she said and put her finger on it, "comes back as a local lodge and retreat company called 'Liddy's Lodge.'"

Widow's eyes went wide. He had nearly forgotten about Liddy.

She looked at him and asked, "What?"

"I met him."

"Who?"

"Bill Liddy."

Keagan set the phone records down on the side of her laptop and wiped her fingers on a napkin, and typed away on the keyboard. She googled Liddy and came up with a homepage set up for the business. She looked it over and said, "His business looks legit."

She reversed the screen and showed it to Widow.

She asked, "Is that him?"

Widow saw the website. It looked expensive and well made, like a lot of money was put into the talent that designed it.

There was a picture of two men. They were in hunting gear and holding rifles and posing with a dead animal. It was some kind of elk. Widow didn't know all the different families of horned animals, but it looked like an elk to him. There was snow all around them and mountains. Widow saw one of Liddy's planes in the background. It was parked on the banks of a river.

The two men were smiling. They looked similar ages.

Widow saw the same goggle eye sockets that Liddy had, and the same long white scar down the man's right cheek. He said, "That's him on the left."

Keagan flipped the screen back around.

Widow asked, "Who's the other guy?"

"I don't know. There's no name. Looks like they're personal friends."

Keagan spent some time looking over the website, and Widow sipped his coffee. After a few minutes, she looked up at him. She said, "Liddy charges an arm and a leg for some of these hunting and fishing packages."

Widow nodded, and said, "I've been to one of his lodges. It's pretty nice. His clientele looks international."

"Do you think this guy Liddy is connected to Kloss's murder?"

"How many times did Kloss call Liddy's place?"

Keagan looked at the phone records again and said, "Only once."

"Could be he was thinking about staying there ... maybe."

"Maybe. But also, Liddy could be part of Kloss's case."

Widow said, "Maybe. But it might be nothing."

"It might be related. We should look into Liddy a bit more."

"Totally agree. But what are those other numbers?"

Keagan said, "All the other local ones I've checked out. They're grocers, food delivery places, and a laundromat, where he probably got his clothes dry-cleaned. But this number."

She pointed to a number on the first page and slid the paper around to show Widow. He leaned over the desk and stared at it.

She said, "This number is the only one that's not local. See? The area code is different."

Keagan flipped the page and scanned the next.

She added, "And there's a bunch of calls to and from this number. Kloss was speaking to someone on this line a lot. Hold on and I'll google it."

"It's Northern Utah," Widow said just as Keagan punched the number into google and clicked search.

The number came back. "That's right. Do you recognize it?"

"No," Widow said. "I just remember things. I've seen the area code before. Does Google know the name on the phone?"

Keagan looked at the screen on her MacBook and said, "Buck Garret?"

Widow shook his head and said, "Never heard of him. Call him."

Keagan nodded and took out her cell phone and dialed the number. She put the phone on speaker and set it down. The phone rang and rang and rang, until someone picked it up.

They heard breathing, and a heavy, gruff voice said, "Hello? Who's this?"

Keagan said, "Hello?"

"Yeah. Who is this?" the voice was an older man. That was obvious. He sounded ancient.

"Sir," Keagan said. "My name is Chelsea Keagan."

"Okay, what do you want?"

"Sir, do you know a Gary Kloss?"

"Never heard of him."

Keagan looked at Widow and then said, "Are you sure?"

"What is this? Who are you?"

"I told you. My name is Chelsea Keagan."

The gruff, ancient voice said, "Who?"

"Sir, do you know Gary Kloss?"

"I never heard of him. Who is this?"

Widow shook his head. They were going around in circles.

Keagan asked, "Sir, is there someone else there that I can speak to?"

"Stop calling here. I don't want whatever you're selling," the gruff, ancient voice said and hung the phone up. The line went dead.

Keagan put her phone down and stared at Widow. She said, "That went nowhere."

Widow said, "Sounds like an old guy with old-guy problems."

"You think he might be slipping?"

"He sounded like it. Maybe. You sure about that number?"

"Yes. It's right," Keagan said, and she double-checked her computer screen. She read out the results from her search. "Buck Garret Jr., 231 Old Fort Road, Ruffalo Creek, Utah."

Widow said, "So it's a landline."

Keagan said, "I can reach out to the local police, have them look into this guy."

Widow said, "Will they help us?"

"What does that mean?"

"They don't have any coastline in Ruffalo Creek. Except for maybe the *Creek* part."

Keagan said, "I'm law enforcement."

"I think we should do this ourselves. I think it's best to put eyes on the guy and ask him straight what his connection is to Kloss. Plus, we may have to look around the place. The local cops won't know what they're looking for."

Keagan stared at Widow.

He asked, "What?"

"Protocol would dictate that I need special permission to travel so far away from base to investigate a lead. But ..."

Widow said, "There's no one here to ask permission from?"

"Right. Since my CO is in an Anchorage jail with the other three investigators from this unit, that leaves no one to ask."

Widow said, "That makes you the person to ask."

Keagan said, "I guess we're going to Ruffalo Creek, Utah."

Keagan got up and went out of the office. She spoke to one of her staff and asked them to book a flight for two headed to Ruffalo Creek or as close as they could get. She returned and told Widow they would head out.

CHAPTER 23

The Broadcaster listened in to Widow and Keagan's entire conversation. He used a good old-fashioned bugging device. One of his guys slipped in and put it in her office the moment he got word that she visited Widow at the Kodiak Police Station. The Broadcaster dialed a number and waited for the phone to ring and for another voice to answer.

The other voice said, "This is Babbitt."

"Babbitt, you recognize my voice?"

"Yes. Of course. It's been a long time. How can I help you?"

The Broadcaster said, "I need a loose end tied up. Three of them, actually."

"Really?"

"Yes."

"You know my going rate?"

"Yes."

Babbitt said, "It's not too high for you?"

"Not for this job," the Broadcaster said.

"Okay. Give me the details."

The Broadcaster said, "There's an old man in Utah. I need him taken care of. Also, there's two good-for-nothings snooping around—a man and a woman. They will be headed there tonight. I need you to take care of it."

Babbitt said, "I'm in Denver. I can drive there within eight hours. I have to pack and get ready."

"Okay. Do it. If you can get there before them, take care of the old guy first. I'll text you names, pictures, and the address."

Babbitt said, "Okay. No problem. Any recommendations?"

The Broadcaster said, "The old man shouldn't pose a problem, but the two good-for-nothings, they're here in Alaska. They'll be getting a flight probably tonight. They could be a challenge. One of them is a US Coast Guard investigator. She's got a badge and a sidearm."

"The Coast Guard has investigators?"

"Apparently."

Babbitt asked, "What about the other one?"

"He's the one who might be a challenge. He's a drifter turned Good Samaritan, but he's dangerous."

"What's his interest in this old guy?"

"The two of them are looking into a corpse. It doesn't matter. Just take care of them."

Babbitt asked, "Want me to make it look like an accident?"

"No. Make it bloody. But I need them all to disappear. Maybe burn the remains in a house fire. I don't care. Just get rid of them," the Broadcaster said and clicked off the call.

* * *

BABBITT WAS in an apartment that he rented in Denver under a false name. He was sitting alone at his dinner table in the kitchen. He got up and passed through the kitchen and through his living room, where a TV was playing the news, with the volume all the way down. He went to his bedroom and into the back of his closet, took out a fake panel, and pulled out a duffle bag. He unzipped it and took out a silenced SIG Sauer P365, a compact firearm. Even with the suppressor on it, he could easily tuck it under his coat and keep it hidden from sight until he was ready to pull it out and shoot someone. He knew that for sure because he had done it dozens of times.

He set the weapon on his bed, replaced the wall panel in the closet, took out a small suitcase, and packed a change of clothes in case this turned into an extra day.

Within thirty minutes Babbitt was in his car and on the road, headed to kill three people in Utah.

CHAPTER 24

After eight hours and twenty-nine minutes in airplanes and airports throughout the night, Widow and Keagan stepped off their third plane of the trip and into Salt Lake City International Airport in the early morning hours. They didn't have to wait for baggage because they didn't have any. Widow didn't carry a bag, and Keagan brought a carry-on overnight backpack with a change of clothes, her personal essentials, and her MacBook. She had her SIG Sauer P226 with her, which she'd had to clear and register with TSA. They were on the road in a rented white Chevy Impala within thirty minutes of landing.

The weather was much nicer than in Kodiak. The temperature was in the high seventies. Both Keagan and Widow left their jackets lying across the back seat, along with Keagan's back-pack, and her SIG Sauer in its holster.

Widow rolled the sleeves on his flannel up to his biceps on both arms, revealing his sleeve tattoos. Keagan stared for a long moment before she started the car. Widow noticed, but said nothing.

Keagan drove since Widow didn't have a license, and she wanted to drive fast. If they got pulled over by any cops, she could wave her badge and plead with the officer that she was in a hurry because of the case they were working on, which was all true.

They drove east from Salt Lake City to reach Ruffalo Creek. The whole trip was about four hours. Ruffalo Creek was near the Wyoming and Colorado borders. It was in one of the northeast corners of Utah; the state had two northeast corners because of its shape.

Ruffalo Creek was closer to the Wyoming border than the Colorado one. There was a problem when Keagan first entered Ruffalo Creek into the Chevy's GPS computer. The name of the town did not come up. So she pulled out her phone and double-checked the name. It turned out that Ruffalo Creek had changed its name about thirty years ago to Maiden Creek. She and Widow talked about it for a moment while on the road. It was small talk. What Widow had read online was something about a horrible crime that happened thirty years ago, which involved the Ruffalo family, which the township was named after to begin with. The town changed the name to Maiden Creek, which hadn't been updated on the Chevy's GPS.

They drove with the windows cracked for four hours and came to a small town that was on a large area of land. It was all farms for miles. There were farms to the west, mountains to the north and the east, and a large forest preserve to the west and south. They drove to the town limits, following the GPS's directions to Buck Garret's home address. They drove down long, empty farm roads until they passed an old sign that the township never took down. It read, *Ruffalo Creek*, only the *Ruffalo* part was graffitied over, and a new word was spray-painted above it. Now it read, *Murder Creek*.

Keagan saw it and said, "Charming."

Widow said, "Whatever."

They continued on until they drove through the downtown part of Maiden Creek. It was as small as any small downtown ever was. There were two churches, both the same Christian denominations, both bigger than any other building. They were bigger than city hall, bigger than the town's only convention center. One of the churches doubled as a private school. The only thing they passed that was larger than the churches was one of those mega department stores. It was the kind that sells everything. Where you can go buy your groceries and have the tires on your car rotated all in the same shopping event.

They saw a lone post office made from wood and brick. It also looked old. There was a broken-down Old West wagon parked next to it—the horse-pulled kind. The back end still had its wooden wheels on. The front had nothing. The wooden wheels were gone.

They passed a small police station, and a two-story all-brick bank that had a sign claiming the bank was established in 1891. They passed a huge park for families that was lined with trees and had a large lake. They saw people of all ages walking their dogs and playing in the park. They saw fishermen standing on the shores of the calm lake. They saw a large pavilion on one corner that looked like a small wedding was happening.

The town reminded Widow of where he grew up. He didn't mention it to Keagan.

They drove on past all the town's life and onto another long, winding farm road. Outside the town, they drove past a roadside diner that looked promising, like the kind that Widow preferred. It was a local joint and not a chain. It had a small self-service gas station attached to it.

They passed it and headed down the old two-lane farm road for another ten minutes, when they got closer to the address on the GPS. They had gone farther northeast, making the mountains to the northwest appear smaller and the ones to the northeast appear larger.

At one point, Keagan slowed the Impala so they could stare off to the west at a huge monstrosity in the distance. To the west—down an unmarked road with overgrown grass everywhere and a gate blocking anyone from driving on to it—was an enormous, sprawling industrial plant. There were pipes running everywhere. They were all shapes, all sizes, and headed in multiple directions. From the distance, it was too hard to count them all.

A faint odor lingered in the air and wafted in through the cracked windows.

Keagan smelled it and asked, "Is it a toxic chemical plant or something?"

Widow said, "Oil refinery. See right there?" He pointed at the plant and said, "Those pipes all have different functions. Those are for fluid processing."

"Fluid processing?"

"Yeah. See, those are distillation columns."

"I didn't know oil was a big thing in Utah?"

Widow said, "Apparently, it used to be. At least in this town."

Keagan asked, "If it's shut down, what's that smell?"

"I guess the oil or the chemicals or the waste smell lingers."

Keagan said, "This place looks huge. I bet it was once the crown jewel of the town. I wonder why it closed down."

"Maybe government regulation?"

Keagan shrugged and took her foot off the brake, and they headed back on their way. They drove another four and a half miles and saw not much of anything else but more farmland. And finally, she slowed the Impala at the end of a dirt driveway.

"This has gotta be it," Keagan said. She stared at the dashboard GPS screen and saw it was the end of the line. To their right was a mailbox next to the dirt driveway. It was thin and one lane and all dirt. They turned on to it.

Keagan said, "Maybe we should've picked something with four-wheel drive."

"Just stay in the center of the drive," Widow said.

They drove on the long driveway until they were far into the farm's property.

Widow said, "Not a lot of neighbors. You could fire a gun out here, and no one would hear it."

Keagan said, "That's scary."

They drove a little longer and came up over a hill and past overgrown grass and saw a farmhouse in a large clearing. The clearing was far better maintained than the front of the farm. The grass was cut, and there was a garden with flowers and fruit trees everywhere.

The farmhouse was large, all solid wood. There was a porch with a swing on it and a few chairs. There was a screen door and a front door, which was wide open, probably to let the fresh country air in so whoever was inside could enjoy it.

There was a satellite dish on the side of the house. Widow figured cable TV and internet probably didn't come to this part of Nowhere, Utah.

There was an old truck parked on the side of the house. It looked like it had been handed down from father to son for generations. But it was well-maintained. The tires looked a year old, maybe two. And the coat of paint was only a few years old. The whole vehicle was pretty clean, despite being older than Widow and maybe older than Widow and Keagan combined. The truck was from a generation of farmers from long, long ago.

Widow saw two sets of tire tracks in the dirt, like there was a vehicle missing that normally parked near the truck.

There was a freshwater well with a pump on one corner of the yard. There was a trailer parked off to the other side of the house near the well. It could be used for hauling just about anything.

Once they were more into the clearing, they saw a second drive that veered off to the east. And in the distance they saw the top of the barn that the drive led to.

There was something else. It was something that stuck out a lot, but they hadn't noticed it until they were all the way into the clearing. Keagan put her foot on the brake. The car stopped. Dust kicked up behind them, and she reached her arm out and grabbed Widow by the bicep. But she was reaching for his shirt sleeve to tug on it.

She said, "Look."

Widow looked out the windshield. Off to the west of the house, parked under a huge oak tree, was an old police pickup truck. It was newer than the farm truck by decades, but it was in worse condition. Grass had grown over the tires. Rust had overtaken the frame and much of the external parts of the truck. The windshield was completely gone. A light bar on the roof of the truck was shattered and broken, cracked all over the place. There were words painted on the door of the truck. They were faded and old. The words read, "Ruffalo Creek Sheriff."

Suddenly, they heard a loud, ferocious dog barking. A huge rottweiler appeared from out of nowhere on the side of the house. He had a long chain that was pulled tight as he tried to run at their vehicle. The farm had no fencing, so the dog was chained to a tree in the backyard, but the chain was long enough so he could travel to the front. He barked and foamed at the mouth.

Keagan said, "He looks vicious."

"I'm glad he's restrained. Although, I don't approve of chaining up dogs. I guess when you own this much land, all you can do is fence it in or chain the dog up so he can still run around and get exercise but can't escape."

Keagan said, "Or the chain could prevent him from biting the faces off of strangers."

"There's that too."

They both got out of the Impala. Keagan left her coat and her gun in the back seat. Widow left his coat in the back seat. They shut their doors at the same time and walked around the nose of the Impala and stopped at the front of the hood. They looked at each other once and walked up a stone walkway to the house's porch, but they stopped and froze because someone came out past the screen door.

An old man in his seventies pushed open the door and stepped out onto the porch. Like Widow, he was also in a flannel shirt and blue jeans, but unlike Widow, he wore house slippers. His shirt was tucked into his jeans. He stood about five-ten, with broad shoulders and a slight gut from a retired life filled with long hours of sedentary acts of watching TV and doing not much else. He wore an aged, white cowboy hat on his head.

His face was gruff and worn. He had a trimmed gray beard with black sideburns that threaded into black and gray hair that was thick on his head. His cheeks were wrinkled, like he smiled most of the time. But not then. Right then, he had a look of concern on his face—concern and confusion.

There was one more thing about him that stuck out; perhaps it was the most obvious thing about him. He was holding a gun in one hand.

The gun was a Taurus 444 Raging Bull revolver. It was loaded with forty-four Magnum bullets. The barrel was six-point-five inches long, but that wouldn't have mattered. If the barrel was six inches long or a mile, either way, you didn't want to be on the receiving end of one of the Magnum bullets. One of them could take the head off a horse.

The revolver was gunmetal gray and polished. The old man looked like he sat around all day either watching satellite TV or polishing his weapon, or both at the same time.

The man stopped on the porch and waved the Raging Bull in the air and shouted at them. "Who are you? What are you doing on my farm?"

Keagan said, "Are you Buck Garret?"

The man stared at her. He squinted his eyes. He said, "Is that a woman?"

Keagan said, "Yes, Mr. Garret. Is that your name?"

"Sheriff Garret," he said.

"Are you the town sheriff?" Keagan asked. "I thought this town had a police force." She stayed where she was, in case he started shooting and she needed to duck for cover behind the Impala.

Widow didn't even think to duck behind the Impala because it wouldn't have saved them. Not from one of those bullets.

Garret said, "I used to be the sheriff. But I'm not anymore. Who are you?"

Keagan said, "Mr. Garret, we're with the US Coast Guard Investigative Service. I'm going to reach for my badge and show you. Don't shoot us. Okay?"

Off to the side of the house, the dog barked and pulled on its chain. Widow glanced over at it. He was shocked that the chain held the thing.

Garret said, "I'm not interested in whatever you're selling!"

Keagan said, "No, Mr. Garret, we're with the US Coast Guard Investigative Service. Let me get my badge and show you."

Garret pointed the gun at them, not directly, but in their direction. He said, "Don't make any fast moves! Who are you?"

Keagan said, "I told you, Mr. Garret, we're with the US Coast Guard Investigative Service. We just need to speak to you."

Garret lowered his weapon down to his side. He said, "US Coast Guard? We ain't got no coastline here."

Keagan reached slowly for her wallet and pulled it out of her back pocket. She opened it and showed her badge to Garret.

He squinted and said, "I can't see that far."

Keagan asked, "Can you please lower your weapon. We don't want you to shoot it by accident. You might hit one of us. We're federal agents."

Garret looked at Widow. He could see Widow just fine. Widow knew that. He was a big target.

Keagan said, "Mr. Garret, can we speak to you?"

"What do you want?" he called out.

Keagan said, "We want to talk with you about a man named Gary Kloss."

Garret said, "Kloss? I never heard of him."

Keagan said, "Mr. Garret, can we come inside and talk to you?"

Garret froze and paused a long beat. He started looking around. He looked confused, like he didn't know where he was for a moment. He stared up at the sky like he was getting his bearings.

Widow scanned the farmhouse's windows to see if there was anyone watching. He saw no one. No prying eyes. No fluttering curtains. No movement. He glanced to the right and saw the dog snarling and foaming at the mouth more. It jerked and pulled on the chain.

Suddenly, Garret looked back at Keagan and then over at Widow.

He said, "Who are you? What are you doing on my property?"

He raised the Raging Bull again, same as before, and waved it around, never pointing it directly at either of them, but in their general direction.

He said, "I'm not interested in whatever you're selling."

Keagan looked at Widow. He glanced back at her. Their eyes met. She turned back to Garret and said, "No, Mr. Garret, we're not selling anything. We're with US Coast Guard Investigative Service. We just need to speak to you."

Keagan glanced at Widow one more time. He shrugged.

Garret said, "Who are you? What are you doing on my property?"

Garret stared at both of them, and then he raised the gun and fired a single round into the air. The gunshot was loud and deafening, even in the open. It sounded like a small cannon, which was why the Raging Bull had earned the name "hand cannon."

On instinct, Keagan went for her weapon on her hip and then realized she left it in the back seat of the Impala. Widow didn't move. He didn't flinch. He stayed right where he was. The only thing he did was he raised his hands so Garret could see them. His palms faced out. They were empty.

He said, "Okay, Sheriff. We're leaving."

Garret seemed to recognize him for a moment. Being called Sheriff got his mind wandering back to a time when people called him that. He lowered the Raging Bull.

Widow said, "We're going to leave now. Don't shoot us."

Widow backed up slowly, kept his hands in the air. He glanced over to Keagan and said, "Let's go."

Keagan nodded, and they both got back into the Impala, and Keagan started it up. She reversed it and K-turned, and they drove back down the driveway to the road. She stopped at the end of the drive and in front of the mailbox.

She looked at Widow and asked, "Okay, what now?"

Widow said, "He seems to have lost some of his marbles."

Keagan said. "He really shouldn't even be living alone."

"I'm not sure he does. There were tire tracks near that old truck that didn't belong to the truck."

Keagan asked, "Do you think someone who's normally there is at the store or something?"

"They could be at work. Right now, he doesn't want to talk to us."

"So, what do we do?"

"There was a diner back near town. Let's go back and grab some breakfast and coffee. We can sit and figure it out."

Keagan glanced at the computer screen. It displayed the local time. She said, "Widow, it's nearly lunchtime again."

"Then let's grab lunch."

Keagan couldn't argue. There was nothing else to do. So she turned the wheel. They drove back toward the diner, and she floored it. It was an old country road, after all.

Eleven minutes from when Garret pointed a gun at them, they were seated in a booth at the front window of the diner. Widow had a big mug of coffee. He ordered another cheese-burger and fries, and Keagan ordered a chicken salad dish and diet soda.

The waitress came back with Keagan's diet soda, and Widow asked her a question. He said, "Do you know Sheriff Garret?"

The waitress was in her mid-fifties, so it was a plausible ques-tion. She looked at both of them and said, "Of course. Are y'all friends of his?"

Keagan was about to say something, but Widow spoke first. He said, "Yes, I knew him years ago. But now he doesn't seem to remember me."

The waitress tucked a pencil into her apron and looked Widow over. She didn't recognize him. She looked like she'd known everyone who ever lived there.

She said, "Yeah. His mind has slipped. He forgets things all the time."

Keagan asked, "Does he live out there all alone?"

"No," the waitress said. "He's got someone out there with him."

Keagan asked, "Someone?"

The waitress said, "Yeah."

Widow asked, "Is it his son?"

"Might be. Might be a daughter. We never see whoever it is. But they drive a little car. One of those old Volkswagen bugs," she said.

Widow said, "So, it's probably his daughter?"

"Might be," the waitress said. "Not sure. Whoever it is doesn't come in here."

Keagan said, "Would anybody know?"

The waitress said, "I'm sorry, hon. I don't really know. Garret's lived out there like a hermit for years. Pretty much since everything went down."

Keagan asked, "What went down?"

The waitress paused a beat and put her hand to her head and said, "Oh dear. Nothing. It's just some bad history in this town."

Widow asked, "Is that why the name was changed?"

The waitress looked around the diner. She saw the cook behind the counter staring at her. She said, "Never mind me. You guys enjoy your time here. I'll be back with your food soon as it's ready."

With that, she shuffled away.

Keagan said, "What do you think that's about?"

"Something happened here," Widow said. He took a pull from his coffee and glanced out the window.

He saw a black Mercedes with tinted windows drive by, an expensive car for a town like this one.

As he was putting the coffee mug to his lips to take another pull, he felt something on his shoulder. It was a pair of fingers tapping him. Widow put the mug down and turned around. Sitting in the booth was a kid. Widow guessed he was about ten years old, at the most.

Widow said, "Hello."

The kid was up on his knees in another booth. He faced them. He kept looking back at the counter like he was looking at the waitresses. In front of him were crayons. He had been drawing on the back of one of their takeout menus.

The kid said, "Hello."

Keagan slid all the way up against the window so she could see the kid past Widow's bulk. She said, "Hello. Who are you?"

The kid said, "My name's Jeremy."

Keagan said, "Hi, Jeremy. What are you doing here by yourself?"

"My mom works here. She's the younger waitress. Over there," he said, and he pointed at one of the other waitresses.

His mom was in her twenties. She was seated at the counter-top. She was polishing silverware. Widow had dated a few waitresses in his day. He knew the job. What she was doing was called side work.

Keagan said, "She's very pretty."

The kid said nothing to that. Widow turned all the way around so he could see the kid. He looked at the drawings. He recognized one of them. It was an object he knew well. It was colored green. There was a white star colored on the side.

Widow said, "That's a tank."

The kid said, "Yeah."

"You like tanks?" he asked.

The kid shrugged and looked down at it. There were three crayons in his hand. He said, "They're pretty cool."

Widow said, "I used to work with tanks."

The kid looked up at him. His eyes grew huge in his head. He said, "Did you ever hear one fire? Up close?"

"I have," Widow said. It was true.

The kid said, "That's cool."

Keagan asked, "You know anything about this town?"

"I know some things," the kid said.

Keagan asked, "You know Mr. Garret?"

The kid said, "I seen him once. He's old."

Keagan said, "Yeah. Pretty old."

Widow asked, "You know why this town is called Maiden Creek and not Ruffalo Creek?"

The kid looked around to make sure that no one was listening. Then he looked at Widow and pulled himself close like he was going to whisper it. He said, "It's because of the murders."

Widow asked, "What murders?"

The kid said, "Mr. Ruffalo killed two agents. He drowned them in his pool. Mr. Ruffalo used to own the whole town. He owned the oil plant. Have you seen it? It's haunted."

Keagan ignored the kid's question about the oil refinery and asked, "Two agents?"

The kid said, "Yeah."

Keagan asked, "What kind of agents?"

"They were like police officers or something," the kid said. "It was big news. I think. I don't know. I wasn't alive then."

Widow asked, "How long ago was it?"

The kid said, "Thirty years ago. I think. So long ago."

Thirty years ago, Widow thought.

Just then, the kid's mother, the youngest waitress, was standing up. She was facing them and standing about halfway between them and the countertop. She stared at the kid. He immediately flipped back around and went back to coloring, like he had never spoken to Widow and Keagan.

From across the room, she said, "Jay, keep to yourself."

She turned to Widow and Keagan and said, "I'm sorry about him. He won't bother you. Please, enjoy your lunch."

Their own waitress came out of the kitchen carrying their orders right then. She walked over to their booth and dropped off their food. She left and returned with a pot of coffee to refill Widow's mug. She asked if they needed anything else, and they told her they were all set. She left with a smile.

Keagan stared at Widow. He was somewhere else. In his own head, she guessed.

Widow thought about Maiden Creek. He thought about the post office. He thought back to Kodiak. He thought about the postcard still in his pocket. He thought about the post office there. He had gotten a postcard. He had stopped to look at the FBI's Top Ten Most Wanted list.

He thought about goggle eyes and that white scar on Liddy's face and the familiarity of him. He couldn't put his finger on it, but he had seen Liddy before. And suddenly, like lightning from the sky, it struck him. He returned to the present moment and stared back at Keagan.

Keagan said, "What?"

Widow said, "I might know something."

Keagan said, "What?"

"Can you get your hands on FBI Top Ten lists?"

"Sure. Anybody can. On the internet. It's public information."

Widow said, "Take your phone out and search for the FBI's Top Ten Most Wanted list. Check for all the lists from 1990 through 1995. I need to see their faces."

Keagan didn't protest. She took her phone out and googled the information. It took a couple of minutes because there were dozens and dozens of people on the list from that five-year period.

She handed Widow her phone and said, "Looks like about a hundred people on that list in that time frame."

Widow took the phone and started swiping through the images of faces of the FBI's Most Wanted. He drank his coffee and stared intensely.

After a minute, Keagan asked, "What's up? You're not telling me something."

Widow said, "Let me look through these for a minute. I want to check to see if I'm right before I speculate."

"Okay, I'm going to finish my salad then," Keagan said, and she did just that.

She ate her salad and stared blankly at it until there was nothing left but olives; she never ate the olives. She wasn't a fan.

Keagan looked out the window and saw a black Mercedes with tinted windows and a tinted windshield, which wasn't legal, but she wasn't a cop, not in Maiden Creek. The Mercedes eased into the lot from the street. It drove up to the diner's window, directly in front of them, and right near their rented Impala.

Keagan watched it. The driver seemed to be interested in their car. She was about to tell Widow, but he suddenly stopped looking through the photos.

He said, "So, back in Kodiak, I went to the post office. This was two days ago. I was shopping for a postcard for my friend. I saw that they still put up the FBI's Top Ten Most Wanted poster for the public to see."

Keagan turned her head and attention back to Widow and forgot about the black Mercedes. She asked, "And?"

"In Kodiak, I met this guy, a local. I stayed at his place in a hamlet to the north of the island called Bell Harbor. Do you know it?"

Keagan said, "Sure. It's one of the smaller hubs on the island. There's a bunch of them."

Widow asked, "You know Liddy's Lodge?"

"There's a bunch of those too, not just on Kodiak. They're all over the state."

Widow held his coffee mug in one hand like he was going to take a pull from it at any moment. He held Keagan's phone in the other.

He said, "So I met this guy. We became friendly, and he invited me to stay in one of his rooms. Which I did. He was very nice, but I couldn't help but feel like I'd seen him before. I couldn't remember from where. It was driving me crazy. He insisted we had never met. He said he hadn't left the state for decades. But I knew I knew him. He looked different from when I remember seeing him. Somehow he was different, but I knew his face. He had a long white scar on his cheek. I couldn't shake that I had seen him."

Keagan said, "Okay?"

Widow turned her phone around so that the screen faced her. Keagan looked at it. It was zoomed in on one black-and-white face on the FBI's Most Wanted list. The year was 1993. It was a man with a long white scar on his cheek and deep-set eyes in sockets that could've held a pair of goggles.

Keagan stared at the screen and read the name out loud. She said, "James Thomas Ruffalo."

Widow said, "Read the rest."

Keagan reached across the table and took the phone from Widow. She held it in her hand and read the text aloud. She said, "James Thomas Ruffalo was the owner and CEO of Ruffalo Oil and Gas. He is wanted for the brutal torture and murder of two FBI agents in 1993 in Ruffalo Creek, Utah. He's considered armed and extremely dangerous. Call authorities if you spot him."

Widow said, "Ruffalo. James Ruffalo and Bill Liddy are the same guy. He's the guy I met in Kodiak."

Keagan said, "Kloss was an FBI agent. He was in contact with Sheriff Garret while staying in Kodiak. And now he's dead."

Widow said, "Maybe Garret is his client and doesn't remember. Or maybe he's a witness, and Kloss kept calling him to get him to confirm something or whatever."

Keagan said, "This is the connection. We have to get Garret to talk to us."

"We can go back out there. Maybe he'll be in a friendly mood. He might've forgotten us already."

Keagan saw that Widow still had half his burger. She said, "Finish your lunch first."

Widow nodded and set down his coffee and picked up the other half of his burger and began eating. Keagan set the phone down on the tabletop and glanced back out the window. But the black Mercedes was gone.

CHAPTER 25

Babbitt wasn't his real name, but it was the name he had been known as professionally. Not even the Broadcaster knew his real name.

Babbitt had driven his black Mercedes all morning and all night. He left not long after getting the phone call from the Broadcaster. He was going to Nowhere, Utah, to kill three people. It was important that he get the drop on them. Apparently, one of them was most troublesome. The Broadcaster had said he was a man named Jack Widow.

Babbitt hit a snag on his trip. He had a flat tire back in Colorado, which took him some time to repair. He had a spare, but it was one of those donut tires and not meant for long excursions across state lines. So he had to stop because of the time of night and get a motel room for several hours. He couldn't get a new tire that late at night. He stayed in a cheap motel right off the highway, and as soon as a tire shop nearby was open, which was six o'clock in the morning, he went in and offered double the pay in cash to the mechanic on duty. Within a half hour, he was back on the road with a new tire.

He drove through the town of Maiden Creek, saw the *Murder Creek* sign and the downtown and the two churches and old bank and post office. He saw all the same things as Widow and Keagan. But on his way to the address for the old sheriff that was also on his hit list, he saw a car that was definitely rented, parked at a diner. Being such a small town, he thought it could be possible that the car belonged to two of his targets. Because who really goes to Maiden Creek, anyway?

So he slowed his car and made a U-turn on an old country road and headed back to the roadside diner. He pulled into the lot. The car in question was a rented white Chevy Impala. It was parked right up at the front of the diner. He pulled up behind it and saw the plates and a license plate frame that listed the car rental company. He saw car rental company stickers in the back window. There was another car rental company item that hung from the rearview mirror. It was an air freshener with the car rental company's name on it. And there was a Salt Lake City International Airport permanent parking sticker in the front window. Security issued them to all rental car agencies so their cars could stay parked in the airport's lots.

Babbitt looked up and into the front windows of the diner. He saw his targets. He saw Keagan, and he saw Widow in the same booth, right there in front of him, plain as day. He thought about killing them right there, but he would have to park his car, get out, stand in front of the window in plain view of all the restaurant patrons and staff, and aim his gun and fire through the window. He probably wouldn't get away. Sure, he could do it and be in his car in seconds. He could even be back on the road, but local police and highway patrol would have a description of both him and his car. He would be easy to find.

He could kill them right there, drive off down the road to the sheriff's, kill him, and steal whatever vehicle was on the premises. He could abandon his Mercedes. The plates and the registration would lead the cops to a dead end. But there was no guarantee he'd get away because he didn't know what kind of vehicle the sheriff had. Or even if he had a vehicle. No, it was too risky. He could wait. According to the Broadcaster, Widow and Keagan were there to meet with the sheriff. Since they were at the diner eating, Babbitt felt safe in assuming that they stopped first and would then go on to Garret's place. So they didn't know Garret or anything about him ... yet.

Babbitt smiled and watched them for a moment. He was struck by how attractive the woman was.

Babbitt reversed his Mercedes, K-turned, drove back out of the lot, and turned right onto the old country road, headed off to Garret's address.

CHAPTER 26

After they finished their lunches and paid the waitress, Widow folded a ten under his mug for the waitress and told her to buy the kid a dessert of his choice and for her to keep the change. They left the diner and drove back up the street, past the abandoned oil refinery, and turned back onto Garret's long driveway. They drove back to his farmhouse. They drove up a little farther into the yard this time, with a little more courage than last time. Only this time, it was different. There was a black Mercedes parked in front of the house. It was pulled up off the dirt track and onto the grass. There was something ostentatious about it. It was an expensive car, and it was just thrown up onto the grass off the designated car area, like the owner thought he also owned the house. It was pretentious even, like someone that didn't belong throwing their weight around.

"Whose car is that?" Keagan asked.

"I have no idea."

Keagan put the car into park and turned off the engine. She said, "Maybe it belongs to the younger Garret. The one the waitress told us about."

Widow stayed quiet.

They got out of the car and closed their doors. This time, a breeze came up off the plains, and Keagan shook from it. She went to the Impala's back door, opened it, scooped up her jacket and her weapon, and put on the jacket and fixed the holster and gun to her belt. Before she shut the door, she called out to Widow over the roof of the car.

"You want your coat?" she asked.

Widow stood there a second. He felt the same wind she had felt. The hairs on his arms stood up. He looked back at her and nodded. She grabbed his coat. It was heavier than hers. She tossed it to him over the roof. He took it and slipped it on.

Keagan shut the car door and joined Widow at the nose of the vehicle. They walked past the fruit trees and garden and up to the front porch. This time, the front door was shut.

Widow stayed back a beat and stood there, listening.

Keagan made her way up to the top step and onto the porch landing. She looked back at him. Being elevated, she was finally taller than him, but not much. She said, "Widow? What is it?"

He was looking to the side of the house. He said, "Where's the dog?"

Widow turned his attention to the black Mercedes. It had Colorado plates. He saw the tinted windows. It was the same car he'd seen drive by the diner. He looked at the old farm truck and where it was parked. He looked at the tire tracks from the Mercedes. Then he looked at the ones from a different car, the ones he saw earlier. They were different. They were from a much lighter car. Perhaps they were from the Volkswagen bug the waitress had mentioned.

Just then, the front creaked open, along with the screen door. Standing in the doorway was a man they had never seen before. He stepped out onto the porch, keeping the screen door open.

The man was a white guy of average height, average build, but with a little muscle on him. It was hard to tell because he wore a puffy vest with big puffy pockets. He wore blue jeans, and cowboy boots tucked under the cuff of the jeans so that no one could tell if they were ankle boots, or taller. When he stepped onto the porch, the sound was a distinct boot-on-floorboards sound. The boot heels sounded heavy.

He had fair hair, a little thin in places, but nothing to worry about. He shone them a big white smile. It was all teeth and warmth.

He said, "Howdy. Can I help you all?"

Keagan smiled back, took her wallet out of her pocket, and flipped it open to her badge. She showed it to the man and said, "Hello. We're federal agents. We're here to speak to Buck Garret?"

He looked at her badge from the porch. He didn't ask to see it up close. He continued to smile. He said, "Oh dear. I hope everything is all right? Buck is my father. I'm Bob. Bob Garret."

Keagan said, "Oh, great. We came by earlier, and your father was here alone. He told us to get lost. We thought we might come back and try again."

The guy called Bob Garret said, "He sent you away? Forgive him. He forgets things, including his manners. Why don't y'all come on in, and we can talk. It's getting chilly out here."

Bob Garret stepped back and held the screen door open for them. He signaled them to enter. Keagan went in first, and

Widow took another look back at where he had seen Garret's dog and then went up the steps.

Bob stopped Widow before he crossed into the house and asked, "You looking for that dog? Don't worry, he's tied up behind the barn. He keeps the critters away from the livestock. Come on in."

Widow nodded and passed Bob Garret and entered the farmhouse. Inside, he saw Keagan standing in the middle of a mudroom area. Bob Garret reached for her coat and offered to take it.

Keagan said, "I can take it off."

Bob Garret backed away with his hands up like he didn't mean to offend her and a smile on his face. He turned to Widow and asked, "What about you? Can I take your coat?"

Bob Garret reached for Keagan's jacket and saw her SIG Sauer parked in its hip holster. He stepped back and said, "Oh! That's a serious-looking gun. Do you need me to take that too?"

Keagan smiled and said, "No. I'll keep that on me."

Bob Garret nodded and took her jacket and Widow's coat. He walked over to a bench near the wall. There were boots underneath it. He draped the coats over the top.

Widow saw the shoes and boots underneath. He saw a pair of women's shoes among them. They were pink and small. They were way too small for Bob Garret's feet, which looked to be about a size twelve. The pink shoes underneath looked to be about a size six.

Bob Garret led them through an archway and into a living room, where they saw a large leather sofa and a love seat to match. There was a coffee table, a huge TV that hung above a fireplace, and two more chairs. The floor was Spanish tile. It was immaculately clean, like someone had mopped it recently. Maybe Garret, or maybe he had a maid service that came out, and they had recently been there. The walls were decorated in a Spanish rancher style. Keagan and Widow could see the kitchen to the west. It was opened up enough to see an island and all the appliances.

One of the chairs in the living room was this worn, comfortable-looking rocking chair. It was heavy and cushioned. Sheriff Garret sat in it. This time, he wasn't holding his Raging Bull hand cannon. It was nowhere to be seen.

Keagan introduced herself and Widow without saying that Widow was not technically a member of the CGIS or a federal officer. He smiled at her and greeted them both warmly. He was like a completely different man.

Bob Garret came into the living room behind them and asked them both to sit on the sofa. Keagan sat first, and Widow followed. He dumped himself down beside her. His weight caused Keagan to slide a little toward him. She adjusted herself and re-centered herself on the sofa, far enough away from Widow to not sink in towards him.

Sheriff Garret sat in what Widow guessed was his favorite chair. Even though he didn't have the hand cannon on him and was in his late seventies, he was still an intimidating man. He was tall and thick. Despite the smile on his face, there was a roughness to him like a mountain man. He looked more like he was related to Widow than Bob.

Garret wore the same jeans and flannel shirt as before. He had no shoes on. He was in his socks.

The expression of confusion they saw earlier wasn't there. He looked nervous, like he didn't know why he was being visited by federal agents, maybe.

Bob sat in the chair next to his father's. His back was to the front door. He kept his eyes on Keagan. He asked, "So, what is this all about?"

Keagan glanced at Widow, who was staring at the shoes near the door. She looked back at Bob and smiled. She explained the whole story. She told them they were from Kodiak Island, about the dead guy, about his phone records, and how there were calls to and from Bob's father's house. The whole process took a while to explain.

Widow sat straight up the whole time, his back straight, and his hands flat on his legs, like he was ready to jump up at any moment.

Bob kept his hands in his vest pockets the whole time. Sheriff Garret occasionally would ask who they were. Bob would remind him, and then he would ask who Bob was. Bob reminded him of that, too.

Keagan asked, "So, do you know anything about a guy named Gary Kloss?"

Bob Garret said, "I'm afraid I never heard of him. And my father forgets things, as you can see. I want to get him a live-in nurse, but he keeps refusing."

Sheriff Garret just sat and stared.

Keagan asked, "Maybe he knew Kloss from an old case he worked?"

Bob Garret said, "I doubt it. This is a small town. Not much goes on here."

Bob Garret turned to his father and said, "Pop, do you recognize the name Kloss?"

Sheriff Garret turned and stared at Bob like he didn't recognize his own son. Both Keagan and Widow could see that.

Bob Garret said, "My dad is always calling random numbers. Must be a mistake. Maybe this Kloss guy was just returning the phone call? You know, like a game of phone tag. My dad called him by mistake, and then he'd call back, and then my dad wouldn't answer because he doesn't recognize the number, and then he'd forget and later see the missed call and call him back. And round and round they went. That makes sense, right?"

Keagan said, "Yeah. I guess it could."

Widow looked at Sheriff Garret and said, "Tell us about your daughter."

Sheriff Garret looked up at Widow and stared. His eyes watered up. He started to speak, but Bob Garret interrupted first.

"My pop doesn't have a daughter. It's just me. Right, Pop?" Bob Garret said, and he reached across a short gap between their chairs and patted his father's forearm. Sheriff Garret said nothing for a long moment, and then he cleared his throat and spoke.

He said, "Oh, that's right. Yes. It's just us."

Keagan looked at Widow like she was trying to think of another question. She was about to speak, but Widow interrupted her.

Widow looked at Bob Garret, smiled, and asked, "Got any coffee?"

Bob Garret furrowed his eyebrows. He asked, "Oh, do you think you guys will stay long enough for coffee?"

Widow said, "Yes. We've got a lot more questions. That's if it's not a problem, of course."

Bob Garret glanced at his wristwatch like he had somewhere else to be. He said, "No. Of course, we are happy to help. Let me get some coffee for all of us."

Bob Garret stood up and pointed at Keagan. He asked, "Want coffee too?"

She nodded.

Bob Garret asked, "You guys both want cream and sugar?"

Widow said, "Yes. Cream and sugar for us both, please."

Bob Garret turned to his father and pointed a stern finger at him. He said, "I already know how you want yours. I'll be right back. Now say nothing without me present, Dad. You never know. They might suspect you of murder, and you don't want to incriminate yourself."

Keagan asked, "Oh, are you a lawyer?"

Bob Garret smiled, lowered his stern finger, and said, "Guilty! But not here. I practice in Colorado."

Widow stood up suddenly and asked, "Hey, where's the bathroom?"

"Dad, tell Mr. Widow where the bathroom is. I'm going to make the coffee for us," Bob Garret said, and he headed off to the kitchen.

Sheriff Garret pointed at a hallway in the other direction. Widow nodded, and nodded at Keagan. He whispered to her, "Don't drink whatever he gives you."

She said nothing to that. He left her sitting there and headed to the mudroom. He stopped and took a glance at the shoes again. There was a pair of women's boots along with the pink shoes. He turned and vanished down the hallway. He found the bathroom and stepped in, switched on the light, and ran the water in the sink. He stepped back out into the hall and shut the door behind him. He hugged the wall to stay out of the Garrets' line of sight and headed to one of three closed doors.

He opened one and found a bedroom with a made bed. The room had personal items in it that could've been a woman's. The closet door was open. Widow saw clothes that could've belonged to a woman. He saw no shoes on the floor. He skimmed over the rest of it quickly because he had little time. He found nothing of interest and stepped back out. The second door was a hall closet. He didn't even search it. He closed the door and went straight to the third door.

This one led to the master bedroom, or Sheriff Garret's bedroom. The room was pretty large. The bed was unmade. There were dog toys all over the floor. The bedroom had typical bedroom furniture. There was an open closet. He saw clothes hanging neatly. They all looked like the sheriff's style. There were no shoes on the floor, like the other bedroom. Inside the room there were pictures on the walls, a chest of drawers, a king-sized bed, and carpet on the floor. There were two nightstands, one on each side of the bed. Widow went right for the nightstand that was on the slept-in side of the bed. It had a large white cowboy hat on it. He checked the drawers. He hoped to find a gun, or the Raging Bull, but he found nothing but a box of the bullets. But then he looked at the cowboy hat. He lifted it up, and right there underneath was the Taurus 444 Raging Bull revolver. He tossed the hat onto the bed and lifted the gun. It was heavy. He checked it. It was loaded with forty-four Magnum rounds, six of them. It was in good working order and ready to fire, ready to kill.

Widow left the bedroom and returned to the bathroom and flushed the toilet and turned off the running water in case anyone had been listening. He headed back down the hall and walked into the living room. He saw that Sheriff Garret was still in the same chair. His look of confusion had turned to one of worry. Keagan was on the sofa, same place, and Bob Garret was standing over his chair, his hands in his pockets again. He waited for Widow to sit.

He smiled and said, "Mr. Widow, there's a coffee for you. Cream and sugar, like you said."

On the coffee table was a mug of piping hot coffee in a mug on a saucer. It was not the way he liked it, but he wasn't planning on drinking it, anyway. Keagan held hers in her hands. It was also in a mug on a saucer. Widow imagined that Bob Garret handed it to her that way on purpose to keep her hands full and in plain view since she obviously had a firearm in a holster.

Widow thanked Bob Garret and sat down on the sofa. He didn't touch the coffee.

Widow noticed that Bob's chair was slightly different. It was angled and pointed directly at them both. It hadn't been that way before.

Widow suspected the coffees were drugged. But maybe not. Either way, he saw no reason to keep up the charade. So why wait?

Quickly, Widow heaved his hips forward, lifted his butt up off the sofa, and reached back like he was going to scratch, but he came out with the Raging Bull. The hand cannon looked huge in Sheriff Garret's hands, but it looked like it was the proper fit for Widow's. He shoved the gun out and pointed it directly at Bob Garret.

Bob Garret's face lit up a pale white, like he was shocked. But it died down fast when Widow asked his question.

Widow stared at him and asked, "Who are you really?"

Bob Garret said, "Whoa! What's with the gun?"

Widow thumbed the hammer back, and aimed it at Bob's center mass. He didn't ask again.

Bob Garret kept his hands in his pockets. His smile faded away, and he said, "I'm Bob. This is my father. I told you that."

Keagan said, "Widow, what are you doing?"

Widow said, "You were good, Bob. But not good enough. You shouldn't have denied having a sister so quickly. I looked in both bedrooms and you know what I noticed?"

Bob Garret said nothing.

Widow said, "Look at the Sheriff's feet. He's not wearing shoes. He's wearing his socks. Look at these floors. They're pretty clean. And both bedrooms back there don't have any shoes in the closets. You know why that is?"

Bob Garret said nothing.

Widow said, "Because the Sheriff doesn't want people wearing shoes in his house. Ain't that right, Sheriff?"

Widow kept his eyes on Bob Garret. He kept the Raging Bull aimed at his center mass. He didn't move his eyes away. He didn't flutter. He didn't blink.

Widow asked, "This your son, Garret?"

Sheriff Garret said, "He killed my dog."

That was all Widow needed to hear. He was poised and ready to pull the trigger. But before he could, Babbitt squeezed the trigger to the SIG Sauer P365 that was in his pocket and pointed at Widow.

Before Babbitt squeezed that trigger, Widow watched him. He saw Babbitt's eyes. The look in them switched to a killer's eyes. Widow saw Babbitt's shoulder flinch.

Widow exploded into action. He dodged to his right, slamming into Keagan, pushing her down, and getting between her and any gunfire that came their way.

Babbitt squeezed the trigger, and gunshots punched a hole through his fluffy vest. The sofa cushions behind Widow exploded from the bullet impacts. Once! Twice!

Widow returned fire, but he only shot once.

When the cushions exploded behind Widow, he fired the Raging Bull. It *boomed* in the close quarters of the living room. It took fifty percent of Babbitt's face clean off. The bullet struck his head to the left of his nose. His eye burst, and brain and skull fragments exploded up and out. Some of it was on the ceiling. Most of it was all over the floor, transforming the surface of the Spanish tiles to a deep-red mush.

There was a red mist left in the air. Smoke billowed out of the Raging Bull's muzzle.

Keagan screamed under Widow's weight. He got off her, and she leapt up. She stopped screaming and stared at the mess. She pulled her weapon, not that she needed it out, and she went over to Babbitt's corpse. He was sprawled back on the floor. The chair had gone back with him. Most of him was still sitting in it.

Keagan said, "Oh my God! You killed him!"

Widow said, "Damn. I was aiming at his shoulder."

Garret said, "He's not my son! He would've killed all of us!"

Keagan turned to him. She kept her gun out. She asked, "Are there any others?"

Garret said, "No. He was the only one."

Keagan went over to him and stared at the mess. She holstered her gun and reached into Babbitt's vest pocket where his hand was. She jerked his hand out. And the SIG Sauer P365 that was in it. His fingers were still locked around the gun. She tried to pry it free, but couldn't.

Widow stood up, and said, "Cold dead hands and all."

Keagan said, "This isn't funny. We've killed a man."

Widow said, "It was self-defense. He probably poisoned our coffees."

Keagan searched the rest of the body, touching none of the messier parts. She searched the pockets and came up with nothing other than the keys to the Mercedes. She left them in his pocket. There was nothing else. No cash. No identification. Nothing to help them discover who he was or who sent him.

Keagan said, "He doesn't even have a cell phone on him."

Widow said, "It's probably in the car. It'll be locked, anyway."

Keagan said, "Maybe we can open it with his face. They have facial recognition now."

Widow said, "I doubt this guy had that feature enabled. He probably used a passcode. We won't get in."

Keagan said, "But we need to know who he is. Don't you want to put an end to this?"

Garret said, "You don't need to know who he is. I can tell you who *they* are."

He struggled to stand up. It was a slight ordeal, but he made it. He was old and a little slow. He pushed himself up with his hands. He walked over to Keagan and put his hand on her shoulder.

There was a single tear in his eye. He said, "He killed my dog."

Keagan stopped inspecting the body and turned to him. There was nothing in her training manuals about dealing with dead dogs. But there was a section on dealing with families who've lost a loved one. She recalled what to do. She hugged him. He hugged her back.

She stopped and stepped away, and Garret looked at both of them and said, "He killed my dog. He was a good dog."

Widow said, "I'm sorry. I like dogs."

Garret nodded and said, "You ain't got nothing to be sorry for. He's the one killed my dog."

Widow said, "I'm afraid we may have led him here."

Garret said, "It don't matter. He would've found me, anyway. I'm surprised no one's come for me till now."

Garret stepped over to Widow and reached down and took the gun away. He moved Widow out of the way and told Keagan and him to both move aside. Which they did. He plopped himself down on the sofa, where Widow had sat. He raised the Raging Bull and aimed it toward the front door, over the flipped chair and the heap of dead mess that used to be Babbitt, and he said, "Cover your ears."

Widow and Keagan covered their ears.

Garret fired the gun again. The gun kicked and boomed again. The second bullet exploded a hole in the wall to the front of the house. Now they could see outside.

Keagan asked, "Why did you do that?"

Garret said, "Soon as you all leave, I'm gonna call the police and tell them I shot an intruder. I need to have gun residue on me. They will check. I was an officer of the law, but that was a million years ago. These young guys don't know me. They only think of me as an old good-for-nothing who forgets things. They'll run tests on me to make sure I'm telling the truth."

Keagan asked, "You remember better than you let on?"

Garret nodded.

Widow looked at Garret and said, "You sure about this?"

Garret said, "It's best that no one knows you were here."

Keagan said, "The waitress at the diner knows we came by. But she saw us after you kicked us out earlier."

Garret said, "Don't go back there. Once you leave here, just keep driving."

Garret motioned them to take a seat. Keagan moved as far as she could from the heap and sat on the love seat. Widow took up Garret's favorite chair. He said, "You should pour out those coffees. Don't let them stay out when you call the cops."

Garret said, "I won't."

Widow said, "Where's your dog?"

Garret looked at the back door and said, "I'll deal with him."

"You sure you don't want help to bury him?" Widow asked.

"No. He's my responsibility," Garret said.

Keagan asked, "Do you know Kloss?"

Garret said, "I don't know him. But I know why you're here. Before I go any further, you should know you're dealing with a lowdown horror show of a man."

Keagan said, "We read Ruffalo killed two FBI agents, but we don't know any of the details."

Garret looked at Keagan and then at Widow. He said, "Ruffalo didn't kill nobody."

Garret told them the whole story as best he knew it.

Garret said, "Thirty years ago, James Ruffalo owned an oil and gas company left for him to run by his father. The whole family was a Ruffalo Creek staple. They were one of the original families. They founded the town.

"Ruffalo Oil and Gas was the biggest draw to the area. It supplied thousands of jobs and worldwide opportunity. Locals who wanted to get out of this town could take on a job there and travel with it."

Widow stood and scooped up all the coffees that Babbitt had made and took them to the kitchen. He asked, "You got a dishwasher?"

Garret said, "Yes. You'll see it in there."

Widow asked, "Anybody want any coffee?"

Both Keagan and Garret said, "No."

Widow poured out the coffee and put everything in the dishwasher. He found detergent pods under the sink, and he loaded the dishwasher and started the cycle. He stuck his head back out of the kitchen and called out to Garret.

He said, "Hey, you don't mind if I make some coffee?"

Garret said, "Go right ahead."

They heard the coffeemaker and the drip of the coffee. A minute later, Widow came out with a black coffee in a big white mug, plain. He joined Keagan and Garret back in the living room and sipped on his coffee.

Garret said, "For many years, things were going good for everybody. What happened leading up to the murders we've pieced together ourselves from news articles on the internet and eyewitness accounts. The rest we researched from all over the world to get the whole story."

Keagan interrupted. She asked, "We? You and Kloss?"

"My daughter and I. Well, we'll get to that," Garret said, and he stared at the coffee table, but it looked like he was staring into a deep, deep memory. He said, "Let me ask you both a question."

He glanced up at Widow and then at Keagan. He asked, "What's the most lucrative smuggling operation in the world? Illegal, I mean. What comes to mind when you think of major criminal enterprises?"

Widow and Keagan looked at each other and then back at Garret. Widow said, "Drug trafficking is probably number one."

Garret nodded and said, "It indeed is. But what others are there?"

Keagan said, "Sex trafficking. Trafficking humans. Girls all over the world are kidnapped and sold into slavery."

Garret nodded.

Widow said, "Boys too."

Keagan nodded.

Garret said, "What else, though?"

Widow thought about Rower again. He remembered the criminal enterprise he stumbled into with that whole experience, and he said, "Human organs."

Keagan stared at Widow.

He said, "It's true."

Garret asked, "What else? Any others? Think about what I said: What's the most lucrative smuggling operation in the world?"

Widow sipped his coffee and looked at Keagan. Their eyes met. They both shrugged.

Keagan said, "I don't know. What is it?"

Garret said, "Oil smuggling. Crude black gold."

Keagan stared at Widow, who was pouring more coffee into his mouth. She thought, *Talk about crude black gold*.

Garret said, "Every year, one point seven trillion dollars' worth of oil and gas are traded on the black markets around the world."

Keagan's jaw dropped. She said, "One point seven trillion dollars?"

Garret said, "Yes. That much. It's insane that no one talks about it. And it's one of the oldest criminal enterprises. The oil is mostly smuggled out of a handful of countries in Africa, where the governments are apt to look the other way."

Widow added, "They're called oil pits. They exist in countries where governments are toppled and changed out like underwear."

Garret said, "Precisely. The US government knows all about it. They do nothing about it."

Keagan asked, "Why?"

Garret said, "Lots of senators and other politicians are in the back pockets of oil companies. That's no secret."

Keagan asked, "But why would the oil companies look the other way? Wouldn't they want to stop the competition at least?"

Garret said, "Most of the smuggled oil and the sales on the black market are done by the oil companies. It's not in their official ledgers, but these rogue oil smugglers work for them at some level."

Keagan said, "That can't be true."

Garret started to rebut her, but Widow spoke first. He said, "Finding, digging, refining, and transporting oil costs millions of dollars and thousands of skilled workers. Though much of it is found in Africa with people who know nothing about the process, far more of it is handled by the professionals."

Garret said, "It couldn't happen if the oil companies weren't involved. The process would break down somewhere. There's too much skill and expensive state-of-the-art equipment needed for ragtag rebels to manage all of it on their own."

Widow said, "Plus, someone's got to sell it. I can't imagine a ragtag rebel who probably can't read showing up to a sales meeting in a thirty-year-old suit with no shoes on, trying to sell oil to people who have the money to buy."

Garret nodded and said, "This is true."

Keagan asked, "So, who buys black-market oil?"

Garret said, "Rogue nations, warlords, countries that have major sanctions against them, like North Korea."

Widow said, "Al-Qaeda. ISIS."

Keagan nodded and said, "Okay, and Ruffalo was in this business too?"

Garret said, "Not at first. After his father died, people doubted he could run the company properly. Which turned out to be sort of true. The company's profits dwindled for a while. Until a stranger approached Ruffalo with a deal. Ruffalo trusted this man. He had impeccable credentials. He had worked in Africa in these unstable countries for years."

Keagan asked, "The countries with the oil pits?"

Garret said, "Yes. This stranger was an expert in the region. It would turn out he was an expert in many, many things. He asked Ruffalo to make him the controlling partner of his family's oil company on the down-low. In exchange, he would save the company and the town."

Keagan asked, "And Ruffalo took the deal?"

Garret said, "In all honesty, he had no choice. He was terrified of this stranger. Everyone who ever met him was terrified of him. Including me."

Keagan asked, "Who is this stranger?"

Garret said, "I'm getting there."

Widow took another gulp of the coffee.

Garret said, "Ruffalo took the deal, and everything was going okay. Like the stranger said, the profits doubled and even tripled, and things went well for a long time. But the more time passed, the more Ruffalo was hearing about murders, and regimes being changed in military coups and so on from Africa, in the countries where he was sending resources and money on behalf of his new partner. Eventually, the FBI caught on."

Garret paused a beat and looked at Widow, who took another pull from his coffee.

Keagan asked, "What happened?"

Garret said, "The short of it, and that's all I know, is that a special task force was onto the stranger. Turned out he's special."

Keagan interrupted and asked, "How special?"

Garret said, "Hold on. I'll tell you. So two FBI agents ambushed Ruffalo in secret. They picked him up. They took him to an undisclosed location, and they showed him they knew everything. They threatened him with a life sentence. Ruffalo was no gangster. He was scared shitless. I wouldn't be surprised if he pissed his pants."

A smile came over Garret's face like he had seen such a thing before from his days as the town's sheriff.

He said, "Anyway, they worked Ruffalo over so badly that he couldn't think straight. So they offered him a deal to save himself. They wanted his partner, the stranger. He agreed to do it. I should also mention that Ruffalo was the wealthiest man in all of Ruffalo Creek. He had a huge house across town. In the back of the house, he had this enormous swimming pool. I mean it was really something. There were statues of Greek gods all around it. It was really something to see.

"Also, Ruffalo had a wife. She was pregnant with their firstborn. And she was far along."

Widow said, "What happened?"

Garret swallowed and said, "The FBI thought they were so clever. They had Ruffalo on the hook, and he was the perfect witness, the perfect whistle-blower. But they were thinking they were dealing with an ordinary international criminal. They weren't. The stranger got wind of the whole plot. One day, Ruffalo thought he was heading home to meet with the FBI agents. Instead, he came home to a scene out of a horror movie.

"The stranger, with some of his men, was there. They were armed. They had his pregnant wife at gunpoint. And the stranger invited everyone out to the pool. At the pool, Ruffalo walked out and saw the two FBI agents who made a deal with him. They were the heads of the task force. They were duct-taped to metal chairs. They were gagged. The stranger tortured them in front of Ruffalo."

Garret took a break and rubbed his beard like he was haunted by what he saw that day. Another tear came down his cheek. This one was different. It wasn't a tear for his dog. It was a tear of guilt.

Widow saw it. He recognized the difference. He stayed quiet.

Garret said, "The stranger put the scare into Ruffalo, who cried and sobbed and begged for their lives. But the stranger wasn't having it. So he had his guys put these heavy chains across the two FBI agents, and one by one, the stranger kicked them into the pool. They sank like rocks. Ruffalo pleaded for the stranger to let them live. He swore he would never tell. He swore everything just to save their lives. But the stranger didn't help them.

"In fact, he pulled a gun and put it to Ruffalo's pregnant wife. His men held her tight, and the stranger put a gun to her head and then to her belly. The stranger told Ruffalo to watch the FBI agents drown. He told him if he looked away, he'd murder both his wife and baby right there in front of him."

Garret looked away for a moment and cleared his throat like he was trying to stop himself from crying. Keagan looked at Widow and then back at Garret.

She asked, "What happened next?"

Garret said, "The two FBI agents died. The stranger made Garret and his wife swear never to tell anyone. They left them. The Ruffalos had to get rid of the bodies and everything. Of course, they didn't know how or what to do. They buried the bodies, and deep too. But we got a real problem out here with coyotes. And they love to dig. The two dead agents turned up a month later. It didn't take long for the Feds to see that there was a deal in place to protect Ruffalo, and the two agents had a meeting with him just before they died.

"The stranger took Ruffalo from his home, his life, and gave him a new one somewhere else. Of course, I thought he was dead all these years, but he's not. The stranger kept him alive and under guard."

Widow said, "For thirty years, Bill Liddy has been hiding in plain sight, but as someone else. Who would suspect?"

Keagan said, "Why though?"

Garret said, "I guess the stranger needed him. Probably used his knowledge and connections or whatever. Ruffalo Oil and Gas is still a large international oil company. The offices and refinery here were only the beginning. The company itself has a CEO and a board, but really, it's run by Ruffalo and the stranger."

Widow asked, "What happened to his wife?"

Garret said, "After what had happened, she wanted to flee and take their kid as far away from Ruffalo and the stranger as possible. A month after the FBI agents went missing, before their bodies were found, she gave birth, but there was a complication, and she died during labor."

Keagan asked, "What about the baby?'

Garret said, "She gave birth to a daughter."

Widow said, "Earlier, you said, 'eyewitness accounts.' Whose did you mean?"

Garret said, "Mine. I was there. I saw him murder those agents. I wanted nothing to happen to Silvia or the baby."

Keagan asked, "Silvia?"

Garret said, "Ruffalo's wife. Her and I were having an affair. I got mixed up in it. I didn't know the stranger was going to kill those agents, though! I swear! I thought he was going to scare us. It was later that I learned who he really was."

Widow asked, "Is the girl really Ruffalo's, or is she yours?"

Garret turned and leaned over the sofa to a side table. He scooped up a picture in a frame. He handed it to Widow, who got up off the chair and took it. He looked at it and passed it to Keagan. It was a photograph of a young woman as a teenager. She was in a soccer uniform.

Garret said, "That's Tessa. She's Ruffalo's biological daughter, but I raised her. Here. As my own."

Keagan asked, "Where is she now?"

Garret didn't answer that.

Widow said, "She's the one who hired Kloss. She wanted to find her dad."

Garret said, "I had to tell her the truth someday. She's a grown woman now. I couldn't lie to her forever."

Keagan said, "That's why Kloss called here. He was calling her, not you."

Garret nodded and said, "Kloss wanted to help. He wanted to find the stranger as badly as Tessa wanted to find her real dad. She has a right to know him. He's not the monster that the FBI said he was. I'm as guilty as he was."

Widow said nothing to that. Instead, he repeated Keagan's question and asked, "Where is she now?"

Garret said, "She's in Kodiak. When she didn't hear from Kloss for several days, she insisted she go after him. I couldn't stop her."

Keagan said, "We have to call her. What's her cell number?"

Garret said, "It's no use. She turns her phone off unless she's using it. She does it so he can't track her."

Keagan asked, "Who?"

Garret said, "The stranger. His real name is Efrem Voight. He was a bureau chief in Africa for decades."

Keagan asked, "A bureau chief?"

Widow asked, "He's CIA?"

Garret nodded and said, "He was. That's how he made the connections he needed to run a black market oil empire. He's been doing it for thirty years now. And no one has a clue he even exists anymore. He's ruthless and dangerous."

Keagan asked, "Has she called you? Is she safe?"

Garret said, "Yes. She calls me every night. She's staying in something called an Airbnb?"

Keagan stood up, looked at Widow, and said, "We got to get back to Kodiak. I can call my guys to keep an eye out for her."

Widow said, "I thought all your guys are locked up?"

Keagan said, "We still got uniformed police. We got the CGPD."

Widow said, "Better call the local cops too."

Keagan pulled out her phone and said, "We should send someone out to Liddy's."

Widow said, "No! Don't tell them about Liddy. We can't take the chance of spooking this Voight guy. If he's former CIA or whatever, he's too dangerous. We can't tip him off. We don't know how connected he is. He could already have her. If he sees cops, he'll kill her."

Keagan said, "Okay. Then we need to be in the air right now."

Widow said, "Agreed."

Keagan told Garret that they would call him as soon as they knew something. She thanked him for his help, and Widow told him to call Keagan's phone the second that Tessa made contact. Before they left, Garret gave them a thick folder with article cutouts, testimonies, and background files all pieced together over the last thirty years. It told the story of Voight, the CIA, the oil scheme, and Ruffalo.

Keagan took it and thanked him. They wished him luck and went back on the road and headed back to the Salt Lake City Airport.

CHAPTER 27

Widow and Keagan sat at a Starbucks, waiting on their flight back to Anchorage. Predictably, Widow had coffee and Keagan had a bottled water.

She looked through all the material that Garret had collected over the years. She finally closed it and said, "It looks like Garret was building a case to exonerate Liddy."

Widow stayed quiet and sipped his coffee.

Keagan said, "We should've moved Garret to a safe house or gotten local cops involved."

Widow said, "He wouldn't go for that. We can't make him do it. My guess is he doesn't trust the local cops any more than the FBI. Plus, he wouldn't have left his house. He was going to wait by that phone with his firearm for her to call no matter what. Besides, I killed that guy who pretended to be his son. That guy was an assassin. Probably a pretty good one. The cops won't believe our story."

"I guess you're right," she said. "He loves that girl."

"Yeah, I wouldn't worry about him. He can take care of himself."

"Still, I feel like we should tell someone. My authority is limited here."

Widow said, "Who we going to tell?"

"The Feds. They'll be interested in the fact you found Ruffalo."

"We can't involve them. Not yet. If Voight is who Garret says he is, we don't know who we can trust. We don't know if he's got Tessa or not. If he gets her, he'll use her to get us."

Keagan asked, "Then what?"

"Voight will kill all of us. Let's not sound the alarm just yet. Not until we get our hands on her. Then we can call the Feds."

On the next plane, Widow closed his eyes and leaned his head against the window. He fell asleep, and slept until they touched down back in Anchorage.

CHAPTER 28

The wheels to the plane from Seattle came down, and Widow woke up from the mechanical sound of the landing gear. But Keagan was fast asleep on his shoulder.

The flight attendant told him to buckle up, which he did. She also woke up Keagan with a tap on the shoulder. She woke up. Her hair was disheveled, and there was a confused look on her face, like she forgot where she was for a moment. She sat up straight and buckled her seat belt.

Twenty minutes later, they were on the ground, and she checked her phone. There was a voicemail from Garret. They got off the plane and started making their way over to the last plane that would take them to Kodiak. Keagan called Garret back. He told her that Tessa called him, and he got the address to her Airbnb, but she turned her phone off after in case Voight was trying to track her.

Keagan got off the phone with Garret. She walked alongside Widow to their next plane. She said, "Tessa is safe. She's staying at a private bungalow down by the water in Kodiak. She's gonna stay put until we get there."

Widow said, "Is Garret sure she is going to wait?"

"Garret said he thinks so because she was seeing cars cruise around her street. She said it was a private dead-end street, so there should be no one driving around it. She might just be a little paranoid."

Widow said, "We should get there as fast as we can though."

"I agree."

They boarded their last plane and took off.

* * *

THEY LANDED in Kodiak by nightfall. They got off the plane and headed to Keagan's Coast Guard truck, which they had left parked in short-term parking at Kodiak Airport. They got in. Keagan did her usual driving rituals—gun and holster in the cupholder, backpack in the footwell, behind Widow. But she kept her jacket on because it was cold again. She put her key in the ignition and fired up the engine.

She said, "We should pick up Tessa before we do anything else."

Widow said, "Agreed."

Keagan put the address to the Airbnb that Garret gave her into the GPS on a screen embedded in the truck's dash. Once the coordinates were up, she drove, and they exited the airport. They drove down the highway and the main roads through town, following the instructions on the screen for about thirty minutes until they were led out of the main township of Kodiak City. They kept on going, taking winding streets and two-lane roads, staying close to the shoreline. They drove west from town until there weren't many cars on the streets. Eventually, there wasn't much of anything. No businesses. No gas stations.

They ended up turning on a road that led into a secluded cove. The street ended at a dead end. They took a turn onto a private drive and found the Airbnb bungalow. The lights were on. It was a small building with a front door and lots of windows. The shades were drawn on all of them. There was no car in the driveway.

They stayed at the end of the drive for a moment and stared out the windshield at the property. The landscaping looked impressive and expensive. There was plenty of green—trees and properly cut grass and flowers and shrubbery. All of it was neat and well kept. It made Widow think about Hawaii.

Keagan said, "What do you think?"

Widow said, "I don't see a car."

"Would she have a car?"

"She probably rented one. She's gotta get around somehow."

Keagan said, "We have this thing called Uber. Maybe you've heard of it?"

Widow said, "I thought you Alaskans all rode around on bears?"

"Ha. Ha."

Widow asked, "Would Uber come all the way out here?"

"Sure, they would. They gotta make a buck too."

Widow said, "Maybe she's not here."

"I don't know. Garret said she would stay put till we got here. He said she sounded scared enough. I don't think she'd leave on her own."

"Maybe she went out to grab some pizza?"

"Well, come on. Let's have a look," Keagan said, and she pulled the truck up into the driveway all the way and drove to the end of it and parked in front of the bungalow. She grabbed her SIG Sauer and un-holstered it. She checked to make sure a round was in the chamber. They both got out. Keagan took the lead since she was the cop and had the gun.

"Stay behind me," she told Widow. He was unarmed.

Widow found that if a woman with a gun gives an order, the best thing he could do was follow it. He stayed close to her. He could smell her perfume. It smelled good. He hadn't noticed it before. They left the truck running and walked off the paved driveway and stepped onto a stone walkway. They followed it to the front door.

They heard ocean sounds in the distance. Widow glanced back and saw waves crashing in the distance, beyond the trees.

At the front door, Keagan lowered her weapon to keep it out of sight from anyone who might be inside. She didn't want to scare Tessa. She rang the doorbell. They heard it chime and echo through the whole bungalow. They waited and listened. They heard nothing from inside.

Widow said, "Ring it again."

Keagan rang it again. She leaned into the front door and listened. Widow stepped back and over to the nearest window. He stepped off the stone walkway and onto the grass. The house, the yard, all of it was dimly lit. He looked up and saw plenty of stars in the sky, but the moon under cloud cover, and the bungalow was surrounded by trees. The leafy canopy above the bungalow blocked out a lot of the starlight. Widow looked east and saw the lights from Kodiak City.

He made his way over to a large window and cupped his hands and leaned in and looked.

Keagan rang the doorbell again, but got no answer. She heard no one inside. She called out to Widow.

She said, "You see anything?"

He stepped back and away from the window. He said, "Yeah, an empty house. She's definitely staying here. I can see a suitcase on the kitchen table. There's some girly stuff hanging out of it."

"Girly? Like what? Underwear?"

Widow said, "No. There's a pink scarf, and I saw a stuffed animal."

"Hmm. She's thirty years old and has a stuffed animal?"

"A lot of people keep that stuff."

Keagan asked, "Did you ever have a stuffed animal?"

Widow said, "My mother's idea of a childhood toy was a Glock."

Keagan stepped back and headed several feet out into the yard. She looked over the house. She saw a few other windows. There was another light on in one, but no signs of movement. She walked around the house to the back. Widow followed. She kept her weapon drawn. They found a backyard with a patio and outside furniture and a grill. But no signs of Tessa.

Keagan holstered her gun and stared into a set of sliding glass doors. Widow joined her.

She said, "She's not here."

Widow went over to the sliding doors and tried to open them. They slid open. He looked back at Keagan.

"Not locked," he said. They went into the bungalow.

"Tessa?" Widow called out. He stopped and glanced at Keagan. He said, "No signs of a struggle."

Keagan nodded and followed him through the rest of the bungalow. They walked around, looking in every room and every corner and every closet. The bungalow was pretty simple. There was a living room, kitchen, bathroom, and two bedrooms. Both beds were made. The place was empty. Only her stuff was there.

Keagan asked, "What now?"

Widow said, "We should stay here and wait for her to return."

Keagan said, "I need to get the evidence from Garret's files logged and locked up. It's my ticket to get my guys off the hook. Plus, at some point, the FBI and local cops should be notified about all of this."

Widow said, "Okay, you take the evidence. Take it back to the base. Log it. I'll stay here, wait for her. I'll call you when she shows up. There's a house phone right there."

Widow pointed at a portable phone in a cradle.

Keagan asked, "Why do I get the feeling you're ditching me?"

"It's not like that. You got to get that evidence logged and protected. For your guys and also in case."

"In case what? Something bad happens to you?"

Widow said, "Don't worry about me. I'll be here. You can call me when you're done."

Widow stepped over to the phone. There was a note by it from the owner to whoever stayed in the bungalow. It had the phone number for the house on it. He read it off to Keagan, and she programmed it into her phone.

"Okay, but you call me as soon as she shows," Keagan said, and she recited her number to Widow. He didn't write it down.

She asked, "You gonna remember my number?"

"I'll remember it till the day I die," he said.

"What is it?"

Widow recited the number just as she relayed it to him.

Keagan smiled and took her SIG Sauer out again. She handed it over to him and said, "Take my gun."

Widow waved it away and said, "No. You keep it."

She said, "Widow, I'm not kidding. I want you to take it. I won't need it. I'm going to be on base surrounded by eighty-seven officers and five hundred and seventeen trained and armed enlisted coastguardsmen. I'll be completely safe. You could be in danger here by yourself."

Widow frowned and stayed quiet. Keagan walked over to him and placed her gun on top of the bar in the kitchen near the cradled phone. She brushed her hand across his chest after.

She said, "Please. Take it for me. You've got to protect this girl at all costs. She's our proof and our witness. I'll be in my truck and at my desk in thirty minutes. I won't need a gun. Besides, I have a spare in a desk drawer."

Widow nodded, stayed quiet.

Keagan pushed up onto her tippy-toes and kissed him on the cheek. Widow reacted and put a single hand on her waist. He held her up and kissed her on the mouth. She kissed him back. It wasn't an earth-shattering kiss like in the movies. That sort of thing is rare, like a unicorn. But there was a spark. They both felt it.

Keagan backed off, and he removed his hand. She had her eyes closed, but stepped back and opened them.

She said, "That was nice. When this is all over, maybe I'll let you take me out."

Widow stayed quiet.

Keagan said, "What's a matter, Commander? Cat got your tongue?"

He smiled at her and said, "When this is over, I might have to stick around."

Keagan smiled and turned to the sliding glass door. She shut it and locked it. She headed to the front door, opened it, and walked out. Widow followed her back out to the truck. She got in, closed the door, and buzzed the window down. She leaned out and looked at him.

Widow stood inches from the door. The wind blew a cold chill. He was glad he had his coat on.

She said, "Kiss me once more before I go."

When a woman with a loaded gun gives him an order, Widow follows it. So he kissed her again. Another kiss that wasn't earth shattering, but it was definitely on the Richter scale.

Afterward, he pulled back and stepped away. Keagan smiled at him, buzzed the window back up, and K-turned and drove back out the driveway and back down the dead-end road.

Widow stood there watching her taillights until they were gone from sight. He went back into the house and shut the door behind him. He started searching through Tessa's stuff, but didn't want to be too nosy. He just wanted to make sure she had left on her own volition, and not at gunpoint. He already established that there was no sign of a struggle. He just wanted to be sure.

He looked through all the rooms again. He checked all the windows to make sure they were locked. Everything seemed normal. Everything but the sliding glass door at the back. It had been unlocked. But that meant nothing necessarily.

Widow went to the kitchen and picked up the SIG Sauer. He checked it and tucked it into the waistband of his pants.

He went back to one of the bedrooms, the one he assumed Tessa slept in because she had stuff in it, and he looked it over. He found a laptop under the pillow. Maybe she had been watching something on it and stuffed it under the pillow.

He took it to the kitchen and sat at the table and opened it. He tried to access it, but it was password protected. He decided he didn't want to be sitting in her house and searching through her stuff when she got back. Seeing a giant strange man who looked the way he looked might terrifying for a young woman.

He grabbed the portable phone out of the cradle, took it with him, and went out the front door. He left it unlocked so he could get back in and sat in an outside chair set up near the door. He listened to the ocean surf crashing in the distance and waited.

CHAPTER 29

Keagan raised the driver's side window back up before she left Widow back at the Airbnb where Tessa Garret was supposedly staying. She was glad she did, because by the time she passed through the guard checkpoint and drove past their hutch at one of the gates to get onto Base Kodiak, the rain started. It was drizzle at first, but by the time she parked her Coast Guard pickup in the lot behind her station, the rain started pounding like the sky was engaging in a liquid bombing raid on her base.

She didn't make it to the door dry. She stopped under a covering and shook her head, ran her hands over it, but it was no good. Her hair was completely soaked. Her jacket was wet. She was grateful that her socks were dry, but more grateful that Garret's file on Ruffalo and this Voight guy were also dry.

She went to the door. It was locked, which made sense because it was nighttime. Her support staff would've gone home hours ago, and the other members of her unit were in jail still. So she fumbled around with her keys until she found the right one, and she unlocked the door. She jerked it open and stepped inside the long hallway. She left the light off because there were twenty-four ambient lights all along the baseboards. She walked the long hall until it opened up to her unit's bullpen.

She stepped in and went right for her office. She flipped the light on, dropped her keys on the desktop, and tossed the file on her desk. She took off her coat and draped it over the back of her chair. She went into the makeshift break room next door and switched on the light in there, too. She went to the fridge and opened it and pulled a diet soda out. She popped the tab open. The can fizzed, and she put her lips to it and slurped up the fizz before it spilled over the lip of the can. She got it all up and took a pull from the soda. She let out an audible sound, like one of those supermodels from the commercials after drinking a cold soda from a machine in the middle of the desert.

Keagan glimpsed herself in the reflection of a dark window to the outside world. She looked pretty good.

Eat your heart out, Cindy Crawford, she thought, and she smiled to herself. She left the light on in the makeshift break room and returned to her desk in her own office.

She sat down at her desk, placed the diet soda on the desktop, and she flipped open the files. She wanted to get more of a look at the details. She had her phone on her, so if Widow found Tessa, he could call her.

She looked through the documents and photographs that Garret gave her. There was a flash drive in the folder as well. It contained everything that was printed out, as well as more things that he and Tessa had collected on her dad and this Efrem Voight character, who she was really hoping she would never meet.

Keagan stayed in her seat for ten minutes, looking through the files, before she heard the sound of a door opening and closing at the other end of the long hallway. She heard it and stopped and listened. She realized she had left the door unlocked. She listened and waited. She heard nothing but the rustle of hard wind on the exterior walls and the rain pounding on the roof. Dim white lights danced on the floor in the bullpen from the windows. She heard the rain pound on the glass. She waited and listened. She heard no footsteps, no sounds of someone in the hall.

She called out from her desk.

"Hello?"

There was no answer. Keagan went back to looking at the papers. Seconds later, she heard footsteps. They were coming down the hallway. It was boots on tile. She called out again.

"Hello?"

No answer. The footsteps stopped. She paused a beat and called out again.

"Hello?"

No answer. She listened. Lightning struck outside, and a loud thunderclap *boomed* in the stillness. It startled her, and she nearly jumped out of her seat. She might've yelped out loud. She wasn't sure. She put a hand over her heart, a reactionary measure. She tried to breathe, and she smiled at how silly she felt being startled like that.

She listened again and heard the footsteps. They were moving closer to the bullpen. She went for her weapon on her hip holster, but it wasn't there. She remembered she left it with Widow. She went for her keys and fumbled with them and found the right one and put it into the lock on her desk drawer, where she kept her backup firearm. She got the key in the lock, but right as she was about to turn the key, she heard a voice. She looked up. And there was someone standing at the far end of the bullpen. It was a male. He wore the US Coast Guard operational dress uniform, the uniform for everyday work. It was navy blue.

The guardsman was of lower rank than her—she knew that—but he was too far away and too shadowed in darkness for her to make out his insignia and rank.

The guardsman stood at the mouth of the bullpen, at the edge of the hallway. He had his hat in his hand. He called out to her. He said, "Ma'am?"

Keagan stopped what she was doing and stood up from her chair. She called back.

She said, "Yes? Can I help you?"

The guardsman stayed where he was. The top half of his face was covered in shadow and darkness. She could see that he was tall. He was built kind of like Widow. He was taller than most. He had a thin midsection but massive broad shoulders. She saw his hands. They were big. If he had fanned them out, he could've blocked the muzzle of a tank's main cannon.

The guardsman said, "Are you Keagan?"

In a stern voice, Keagan said, "Ensign Keagan to you, Seaman."

The guardsman fidgeted with his hat like he was nervous. He said, "Sorry, ma'am. That's what I meant."

Keagan asked, "What can I help you with?"

Keagan glanced down and saw her keys were hanging out of the lock on the drawer where her gun was.

The guardsman asked, "Are you the one working on the case of that drowned private investigator?"

Keagan said, "Step into the light, Seaman, so I can get a better look at you."

The guardsman stayed where he was. In a nervous voice, he said, "The guys they arrested for it. Our guys, they're innocent."

Keagan repeated, "Come on in and tell me about it, Seaman."

The guardsman said, "I've got proof, ma'am."

Sensing that he was nervous, Keagan moved. She stepped out from behind the desk and stepped closer to the doorway to her office. She still couldn't make out his face.

She said, "Why don't you come on in? Sit with me. We can talk about it. Tell me what you got?"

The guardsman stayed where he was a long second, like he was contemplating doing as she asked.

Keagan didn't want him to leave, but she also didn't want him disobeying her direct orders. In this situation, in this room, she outranked him. She knew that much without seeing his rank. So she said, "That's an order, Seaman. Come on in. I won't hurt you. If you know something, come on in and speak up."

The guardsman stayed where he was and fidgeted with his hat. Finally, he put it back on his head and said, "Never mind. I can't. This is a mistake. I'm no rat."

He turned around and walked away, fast and hard. She heard his wet boots moving back down the corridor like he was fast-walking.

She called out from behind him. But lightning struck some-place outside again, and the windows lit up with a white flash and a loud thunderclap *boomed* again. The sound muted anything she was calling out to him. He couldn't hear her.

Keagan didn't want to lose a potential witness, so she ran after him. She hoped she could catch him before he vanished into the rain. She chased after him and ran through the bullpen and into the hall. She turned the corner just in time to see the door to the building flap shut. She ran down the hall, slipping and sliding a bit because he had left massive wet boot prints everywhere.

She ran harder. She reached the door at the end of the hall, but didn't slow her speed. It had a push bar on the inside. She slammed right into it, barreling out into the rain and wind. She stepped out onto the concrete and under the covering. Rain pounded on the covering's metal roof.

She turned to the direction of the parking lot and walked down the concrete ramp to the end of the covering. The rain was really something. It poured so hard that she could barely see her own truck in the lot. The lights from the base were dim, with concentric circles of light coming off the light poles over the parking lot.

Keagan strained her eyes to see the guardsman, but she couldn't. She saw a second vehicle parked to her left. It was a four-door sedan. It was in the first spot, pulled up close to the side of the building. The headlights were on, and the rear lights were on, but not the brake lights, indicating that the car was in park. The engine was idling. She saw the car was empty and the trunk lid was ajar.

Confused, she turned back around, and the guardsman stood there. He was right in front of her. Up close, he was even bigger than she had thought. Before she could react, before she could say a word, the guardsman clobbered her across the face with a vicious right hook. She twirled and stumbled off the walkway out into the rain and hit the gravel. The guardsman stepped behind her. She heard his footsteps on the gravel. The rain pounded on his uniform. He knelt fast and put a knee in her back. He pinned her. She struggled, but his weight was too much. Before she could scream, he jabbed a needle in her butt and plunged the contents into her bloodstream.

Within seconds, Keagan was out like a light. The guardsman tossed the needle out into the gravel lot and took his knee off her. He knelt again and scooped her up and carried her in the rain toward the tail of his car. He lifted her and dumped her down into the trunk and stepped back and closed the lid.

The guardsman returned to her office and took Garret's files. He left her keys dangling in the lock to the drawer with her backup gun. The guardsman went back out into the rain and got into his sedan and drove away. He headed back out the gate he came in, past the guards.

CHAPTER 30

Widow heard the same thunderclaps and heavy rain Keagan heard. He waited at Tessa's bungalow for two more hours. He stayed outside until the rain became too hard and the air got too cold. He moved indoors and sat on the sofa in the living room. Widow got pretty bored waiting around. He thought about turning on the TV, but he hadn't watched a TV on purpose in over a decade. Plus, he didn't know what the etiquette was for him in this situation. Was it okay for him to watch a strange TV in someone else's house?

He wished he had kept his paperback copy of *Into the Wild*. He could reread it. Not that he thought it was the bee's knees or anything. He just was that bored. Widow ended up playing Solitaire with a deck of playing cards he found in a drawer in the kitchen. He was at the kitchen table playing a second round of Solitaire when the phone in the cradle rang. He jumped up and stumbled around, trying to thread his way through a tight space of dining table chairs and barstools until he got to the phone. He scooped it up and clicked the button and put the phone to his ear.

He said, "Hello?"

"Hello?" a gruff old man's voice said.

"Yeah?"

"Who is this?" a gruff old man's voice asked.

Widow recognized the voice. He asked, "Garret? Is that you?"

"Widow?"

"Yeah, it's me."

Garret asked, "Where's Tessa? You found her okay?"

"No. Actually, we've not found her yet."

"Why are you answering her phone?"

Widow said, "I'm at her Airbnb. I'm waiting around for her to return. She wasn't here when I got here."

"How did you get into her place, then?"

Widow said, "Slider in the back. It wasn't locked."

"Huh? That's not like her. She's usually pretty careful. So, where the hell is she?"

"I don't know. I figured she went out for pizza or something. But don't worry. There's no sign of break-in or a struggle here. And I don't see her wallet, cell phone, or her keys. So she probably stepped out. She'll be back."

Garret was silent for a long beat, like he was imagining all the worst-case scenarios about his adopted daughter's whereabouts.

Widow sensed Garret's worry and said, "Buck, don't worry. She's okay. I'm going to find her and protect her. You have my word."

Garret said, "Okay. But she missed our phone time."

Widow said, "How did you get this number? I thought you said you only had her cell phone number?"

"No. I said she turns her cell phone off. You never asked for this number. But that's not why I didn't give it to you. I forgot I had it. I actually forget things, you know? It's just not as bad as I let on."

Widow said, "Well, don't worry. She'll turn up."

Garret asked, "Okay. Well, you guys can answer your phone every once in a while."

"What phone?"

"Keagan's phone. The number she gave me to call. I've called it like four times. I left two voicemails. She still hasn't called me back. I was getting worried."

Widow listened and thought that wasn't good news. He realized that Garret probably thought Keagan was with him.

He said, "Okay. I'll tell her to check for your voicemails."

"Okay. Call me as soon as Tessa is safe and sound. Okay?"

"I will," Widow said, and he clicked off the call. He then dialed Keagan's number from memory and listened to the phone ring. It rang and rang and finally went to voicemail. He heard Keagan's voice.

"This is Keagan. I'm not available. Leave a message."

Widow stayed quiet a brief second, debating on if he should leave a message or not. Then he said, "Chelsea. It's me, Widow. I'm worried about you. Call me back at this number."

He clicked off the phone and set the portable phone back in the cradle and turned his back on it. He went back to the kitchen table.

Suddenly, the phone buzzed and rang in its cradle. It was an annoying sound. He turned back to it and walked over, and scooped it up. There was the number of the caller showing in a little digital box on the back of the phone. It was Keagan's cell number. He clicked on the call and put the phone to his ear.

He said, "Keagan? Where are you?"

A voice that sounded like a broadcaster, like Dan Rather, spoke. The male voice on Keagan's phone made Widow think he must've read the caller ID wrong. It wasn't Keagan.

The Broadcaster said, "Hello. Who is this?"

Widow thought, *You first, pal.* But he didn't say that because he didn't know if it was just a guy calling for Tessa. She was a thirty-year-old grown woman and not a kid. She could have gentleman callers. It wasn't illegal, and he wasn't her father.

Widow asked, "Are you calling for Tessa?"

"No," the Broadcaster said. He lingered on the word like he was teasing Widow.

Widow said, "Oh, then maybe you got the wrong number?"

"I don't think so. I know who Tessa is. I know where she is. I'm asking who you are."

Widow stayed quiet.

The Broadcaster said, "So, who are you?"

Widow thought for a moment. Held his breath and then let it out. He asked, "Is this Efrem? Efrem Voight?"

"Hey. You got my name. Very good," Voight said.

"Where's Tessa?"

"Don't worry. Everyone's safe and sound for now."

"Everyone?"

"Yeah. I got all of our pals: Ruffalo, his daughter, and your friend."

"My friend?" Widow asked. He felt his fist clench Keagan's gun tight. His index finger danced around the trigger guard like he might slip it in and start shooting.

Voight took a moment and spoke like he was reading off an ID, his broadcaster voice making it sound like Widow was getting a lecture from a Harvard-educated newsman.

Voight said, "Junior Officer Ensign Chelsea Keagan of the United States Coast Guard. Look here, she's an investigator with CGIS."

Widow clenched his fist around the gun even harder. He squeezed his eyes shut. He felt rage coming on. But he breathed in and breathed out. He composed himself, kept his cool.

He asked, "Is she okay?"

Voight said, "Don't worry. They're safe and sound. Whether or not they stay that way depends entirely on you."

"What do you want? The file on you? That's with the Feds by now."

"No. It's not. I have Garret's so-called *evidence*. The only thing I need now is the last loose string to be tied off. Can you guess what string that is?"

Widow said, "Me?"

"Yes. That's right. You're the last loose string. Well, you and that pesky old sheriff, but no one's going to believe him."

Widow said, "Come get me."

"If I knew exactly where you were, I would've already."

Voight didn't know he was at Tessa's bungalow. Maybe they didn't even know where it was or that she had one, which told him they hadn't tortured her yet. Widow realized she must have gone out to Liddy's lodge on the other side of the main island in Bell Harbor. But was she still there?

Voight asked, "Widow, are you listening to me?"

"I'm listening."

"Good. Here are the rules. If you deviate from them, Tessa, Liddy, the lovely Ensign Keagan, they all die. And Widow, when I say they die, I don't mean a quick and fast bullet to the head. Do you understand me?"

Widow said, "Yes."

"Good. First rule: no cops! Got it?"

Widow said, "First rule: no cops."

"Good. Second rule: go to the same dock where Peter left you. He'll pick you up there. Got it?"

"Yes."

Voight said, "Repeat it back to me, please?"

"Second rule: I go to the same dock where Peter left me."

"Excellent. Now, the third rule is leave any gun you have behind. Got it?"

Widow stared at Keagan's SIG Sauer and said, "I got it."

"Widow, if Peter finds a gun on you, I will kill them all. Do you understand?"

"I said I got it all," Widow said. "I don't have a car. So I gotta walk. It'll take me some time. I'm outside of town."

"You've got forty-five minutes. Get moving," Voight said, and he clicked off the phone.

Widow immediately dialed Garret's phone number. He told Garret about the call and that he would take care of it. He told him to get into his truck and go stay at a motel. He left off the part about Tessa being captured. He told him she was hiding out and not to worry. No reason to spook the old guy to death. Widow wanted him focusing on his own safety.

After that, Widow hung the phone up, took the SIG Sauer, and left it in the bungalow's mailbox at the end of the drive. He turned left on the dead-end road and started walking in the rain back to Kodiak and the docks where Peter had left him two days earlier.

CHAPTER 31

T he rain battered the surrounding pavement. Widow walked the dead-end road until he got back to the main two-lane road, which he followed for a long time. He feared he might not make it in the forty-five minute time frame that Voight had given him. He started jogging, which was hard in the weather, the harsh conditions, and also because he hadn't kept up with his SEAL PTO. However, he got lucky and got a ride from two old guys in a truck that was as old as they were. The back had a camper on it, and the bed was empty. Since Widow was soaked from head to toe from the rain, the old guys told him to climb in the back, and they'd drop him off downtown, which was close enough. They dropped him off near Kodiak Espresso, where his love for coffee felt like it was thrown into a cage match with his relentless thirst for justice, because he was sorely tempted to go inside and get a coffee. He knew the right thing to do was to keep on, but his addiction to coffee seriously made him stop and pause a beat.

Of course, he went on foot to meet Peter at the docks. He came walking down the wharf to the place where Peter had landed Liddy's plane two days before. He saw Peter standing in the rain in front of the same red seaplane from before.

Widow walked out of the wet darkness and stopped ten feet from Peter. He shivered in the rain.

Peter stood there in a rain poncho, the hood pulled over his head. He called out loud because the hammering raindrops on the wharf muted normal speech. He said, "You barely made it."

Widow said, "I'm here."

Peter said, "Put your arms out."

Widow raised his arms and held them out. He shivered in the wet, cold air, despite wearing a warm coat.

Peter went over to him and patted him down. He found no weapons, no gun, no knife—nothing but Widow's passport, the postcard for Gray, and some cash. He left all of it on Widow and gestured for Widow to get in the plane. Widow did and Peter followed.

The waves rocked the plane pretty hard. Peter shut his door and lowered the hood of his poncho.

Widow asked, "Is it safe to take off in this weather?"

Peter said, "No."

He started the engine, and the propeller fired to life. It spun hard and fast. The engine spurted and then hummed normally. Peter reversed the plane, and within seconds, they were speeding out to sea. Widow gripped the seat beneath him hard. The seaplane started bouncing on the waves until it took off and was airborne.

Peter piloted the plane up and up. It climbed up to the low clouds and a little above. The plane climbed until the weather was safer. Peter leveled the plane off and flew northwest. Widow didn't stop gripping the seat.

Between Widow and Peter, on the ceiling of the cockpit, there was a CB radio. It suddenly clicked and sputtered to life. Widow listened to the radio chatter. It sounded like the US Coast Guard. Two coastguardsmen talked to each other. There was nothing about Widow's situation or Keagan missing from base.

Peter reached up and switched the radio off. They flew in silence until about halfway there, when Widow spoke first.

He asked, "How long have you babysat Liddy?"

Peter stayed quiet.

Widow said, "Might as well talk to me. Especially if you think Voight is going to kill me."

Peter spoke but didn't look at Widow. He kept his eyes forward on the rainy sky. He said, "He *is* going to kill you. I can't even understand why you volunteered to come back."

"You wouldn't?"

"No way! Not if I knew I was walking to my own death."

Widow paused a beat and asked, "Not for anyone?"

Peter said nothing.

Widow asked, "Not even for Liddy?"

Peter glanced over at him. It was a quick look, like a glance just to make sure Widow was still seated there. Peter said, "Maybe."

Widow asked, "How long have you been with him?"

"Ten years now."

"What did you do before?"

Peter said, "I was in the clink."

"Really?"

"Yes. Also ten years. When I got out, Mr. Voight found me. Gave me a job, a life, and a fresh start."

Widow asked, "You military?"

"Once."

"Is that where you learned to fly?"

Peter said, "Yes."

"Did you do time in military prison or civilian?"

Peter said, "I was in civilian prison. Armed robbery gone wrong."

Widow asked no more about it. He said, "You know, Voight will kill Liddy too. Probably tonight."

Peter shot Widow a sideways look. He said, "No, he won't."

"I bet he does. Honestly, I don't know why he kept him alive this long."

Peter said, "You don't know what you're talking about. He won't kill him."

"I hear the doubt in your voice. You already suspect it, don't you? Liddy's long since outlived his usefulness for Voight. Now he's caused all this ruckus. Easier just to kill him. I mean, why keep him alive? So he can run the Liddy's Lodge business in Alaska? From what I understand, Voight doesn't need the money from that. The oil thing is where all his fortune comes from. How much do you think Voight is worth, anyway? Gotta be a lot of money selling oil to dictators all around the world, right?"

Peter said, "I wouldn't know about any of that."

Widow said, "What do you think he'll use you for next? After he kills Liddy."

Peter said, "Enough talk."

Widow turned his head and stared out the window.

Thirty-seven minutes later, they landed in Bell Harbor, back through the hard rain. Widow saw lightning strikes in the distance, in the river's direction where he first met Liddy. He thought about it, and for a second he wished he had let the bear just eat him.

Peter landed the plane on the bay, and they rode it back in to Liddy's wharf, and different dock workers from the ones he saw previously were there to help them park the plane at the dock.

Widow got out first and was helped onto the pier, and Peter followed. He got in front of Widow and said, "This way."

Liddy's Lodge looked different at night. It was slower than the night he was there. There were far fewer people around. Widow glanced up to one end of a flight of stairs, and he saw the same girl that was in his room three nights back. She was still pale, still covered in tattoos, and still rail thin. She stared at him. He recalled her name. It was Miley. He lifted a hand and waved at her. She grimaced in his direction and turned and vanished between two buildings.

Peter led Widow back up the stairs and behind the lodge to the four-wheelers. The rain pounded on them both. He stopped in front of them and took out a set of keys. He sat on one and started it. He revved up the motor and got off the saddle.

Peter said, "Take this back down that path. Keep heading straight until you get to the trees and can't go any farther.

Park it, leave the keys on the seat. Walk back to the river where you met Liddy. They'll pick you up there."

Widow shivered in the rain. He asked, "Who will?"

Peter stared at him. He paused a beat, and then he took off his rain poncho and handed it to Widow.

He said, "Take this. I've got more."

Widow took it and slipped it on, put the hood up. He didn't thank Peter. And it made only the smallest difference because he was already soaked.

Peter turned and walked away. He stopped halfway and turned back to Widow.

He said, "I'm sorry."

Widow stayed quiet. He sat on the four-wheeler and looked forward and took off down the path into the darkness.

* * *

WIDOW DROVE on for what seemed like forever. The four-wheeler had a set of headlamps on the front, and they were on, but they might as well have just been off because of the rain and the darkness. Everything was still hard to see.

Widow followed the winding path and drove as fast as he could, while trying to stay upright. One wrong move, or if he hit the wrong bump, and he could flip the four-wheeler and crash. Potentially, he could break a leg or something, and then what would he do?

Finally, he came to the end of the path. He parked the four-wheeler and killed the engine, and left the keys on the seat. He looked around, and nothing looked familiar. He tried to remember the direction of the river, and he headed that way. He walked on until he felt mud under his shoes.

He stopped and listened. It was hard to hear with the rain pounding on his poncho. But he could hear the river running wild. He walked toward the sound and found it. It was the same bank that Liddy had fished on.

Peter had told him to wait where he and Liddy had met, but there was no way for him to find that exact spot. Not in the dark. So he waited there even though he didn't know what he was waiting for.

Widow didn't have to wait too long. About ten minutes after he stopped at the river's bank, he heard it. It was distant but audible. It was the mechanical sound of a vehicle. He looked around and saw nothing. He knew that the path he came on was the only road for miles. He knew that because he spent a lot of time traversing this area before he met Liddy and that bear.

He watched the path, thinking it was a truck or something, but there was nothing there.

As the mechanical sound got closer, he heard *whop, whop*. And he knew what it was. He ran over to a hill next to a clearing and stood there. He looked up to the sky toward the southwest, and he saw the navigational lights of a helicopter. It came closer and closer. He started waving his arms in the air, hoping it would see him. He wished he had road flares, but he had nothing. He thought about running back to the four-wheeler and switching on the headlamps, but he didn't have to.

The helicopter pilot must've seen him because the lights pointed in his direction, and the helicopter lowered. The blades rotated above. As it drew near, he recognized the helicopter. It was a Sikorsky MH-60 Jayhawk rescue chopper. It had twin engines. It looked like the ones he saw on the runway at the Coast Guard base, only this one was different. The paint on it was different. There were words on the side.

As it lowered, Widow read the inscription on the helicopter. It read, "Ruffalo Oil and Gas."

The helicopter lowered and landed in the clearing. The cabin door swung open, and two large men got out. They both wore rain ponchos. They both switched on flashlights. One of them drew a gun. He pointed it at Widow. Both flashlight beams shone on his face. He saw nothing beyond the lights and the muzzle of the gun.

A voice shouted, "Put your hands in the air!"

Widow put his hands up. The guy without a drawn firearm lowered the flashlight and approached him. He said, "I'm going to search you. Do you have any weapons?"

"No," Widow said.

The guy searched him and found no weapons. He nodded at his partner, and the two of them stepped back. The one who searched him took a set of handcuffs out of his pocket. He tossed them to Widow, who didn't catch them. They fell at his feet into the mud.

The guy said, "Put those on."

Widow knelt slowly and scooped them up out of the mud. He stood back up, slow. The rain washed away most of the mud from the cuffs, and the steel glimmered from the flashlight beams.

Widow clicked one around his wrist, and then he put the other on the other wrist. He kept them in front of him because they didn't order him otherwise.

The one who searched him said, "Tighten them. All the way."

Widow tightened them. The second guy lowered his gun and holstered it on his belt, on his hip under the rain poncho. The two of them approached Widow, turned around, and put hands around his biceps, which reminded him of the cops from Kodiak Police Station.

They escorted Widow to the Jayhawk, loaded him onboard, and slammed the door shut. Before they slammed the door, Widow noticed a winch on the side of the Jayhawk. He saw the cable, the hook, but no rescue litter. It was gone. He knew instantly that this was the helicopter that Kloss was thrown from.

The Jayhawk took off from the clearing. It yawed and banked and came back around until the nose faced southwest. The rain pounded on the steel skeleton, and the Jayhawk took Widow over the island and out to sea.

CHAPTER 32

The Jayhawk rotors *whopped* above Widow. He heard them even over the rain and thunder. The flight crew numbered two in the cockpit and two in the cabin with Widow—if you counted the two big pit-bull guys that Widow was sandwiched between on a bench as flight crew.

The two pit bulls wore rain ponchos, which made them even more menacing in a certain way to a certain person. But Widow wasn't a certain person. He continued looking straight ahead, unfazed, watching the skies through the windshield. The rain hammered on the glass, but the pilots seemed to not care. Normal helicopters wouldn't traverse this kind of weather on purpose, but the Jayhawk was designed for harsh elements, making it the preferred rescue helicopter for the Coast Guard.

They flew over Kodiak Island, past it, and out to sea. They flew fast. The Jayhawk could clock in at speeds of two hundred and seven miles per hour, but in this weather, pilots normally didn't go that fast. It was dangerous. But the two pilots sitting in the cockpit didn't seem to mind the risk. They didn't seem to mind so much that Widow was convinced they even had a death wish. The thought made him crack a smile because if they were a part of Voight's operation and helped him kill Kloss, then Widow would oblige their death wish— no problem. They had made their beds.

Widow kept on staring out the windshield. He tried to remember landmarks in case he had to fly back. That only lasted fifteen minutes, while they were still over Kodiak Island. When they flew over the Gulf of Alaska, he stopped worrying about landmarks. He tried to keep up with the distance in his head. After about thirty minutes over the ocean, Widow figured they were about fifty miles out to sea. That's when he saw their destination through the clouds and rain and darkness.

Just ahead in the ocean, Widow saw lights, lots of them. Including a light that blinked at the top of something that couldn't have been the crow's nest of a ship. It was too high off the surface of the water. As they drew closer, he knew what he was staring at.

In the middle of the ocean, far from shore, there was an enormous offshore oil platform. It looked practically out of use, or maybe it was out of use because there were large sections of the hull that were completely gone. They looked ripped off by something even bigger than the platform, like an alien creature from the deep. Or maybe that prehistoric shark had taken giant bites out of it.

Even with all the damage to the hull, the rig still had power. That was for damn sure, because every light in the thing was on. However, most of them didn't work right. Widow saw bulbs flashing and sparking all over the place. Then there were large patches of complete darkness. That's where he suspected there were more giant shark bites out of the hull.

The layers underneath the platform, beneath the hull, looked like large construction beams. They crisscrossed all over the place. Some of them were damaged and even missing and broken. The legs for the platform were enormous. They stretched down into the sea. Elevating racks doubled as a set of legs. At the bottom, over the ocean surface, were giant spud tanks.

There were tanks and gear units and gear boxes and seawater pumps all neatly placed along the platform. There was an old building to the north. It must've been living quarters for the workers. Only, there were no workers—Widow figured because there was too much damage to the external parts of the entire rig.

Widow saw that scrawled across the top of the platform, written for passing aircraft, was the name of the oil company: "Ruffalo Oil and Gas."

An enormous crane jutted out from one side, but it wasn't as large as the derrick, which shot straight up into the air. It had the flashing light on top. The crane's neck hung out over the water. The body was a thick, double-layered structure, and the derrick was enormous, bigger than the crane. The derrick's neck stretched up so high, Widow imagined that without the blinking light on top it would look like the derrick vanished into the clouds.

Widow imagined enormous drills that went down from the center of the legs, below the spud tanks. He pictured the drills at the leg centers going all the way below the ocean surface and down to the floor. He imagined several, if not dozens, of oil wells below. He had no idea how deep the water was right there, but the oil rig looked to be four hundred feet from the top of the derrick to the ocean surface.

Lightning struck the ocean off in the distance. It was directly behind the oil platform but miles away. The light illuminated the rig. Widow saw a helipad on the platform deck. That's what the pilots aimed for. The helicopter yawed and shook as the pilots turned it and hovered for a moment and then began lowering the Jayhawk, aiming at the helipad.

Widow saw waves crashing below the rig. The landing was rough. They came in low; the wind swayed the helicopter a bit, but the pilots were pretty good. They maneuvered and kept the Jayhawk on target, like they had done it a thousand times before. The landing wheels touched down on the helipad, safe and sound.

A moment later, Widow was on deck with the pit bulls and the pilots. They were greeted by a third pit bull in a rain poncho. They took Widow down a flight of stairs into the hull. The two pilots came along behind the rest of them. Widow counted five guys so far.

They passed a large torn-out section of the hull and then back to covered walls.

At the bottom of the stairs, Widow passed into the belly of the beast. He heard the waves crashing far below. They took him into a lit hallway and passed a couple of closed doors until they came to a bridge of sorts. It was a control room with computer terminals all over the place. Some terminals blipped and whirred. Some of them were completely off. They either had no power or had been destroyed long ago. There was water damage on the tiled floors and on the ceilings.

The inside of the hull looked more like the inside of an office building than it did an offshore oil rig in the middle of the ocean. Except for all the large swaths of missing walls, and the water damage. The giant holes and missing walls made it feel chilly in the hull. Widow felt the heating system was on full blast to accommodate. His body temperature switched between cold and hot almost every step he took.

Widow saw a working CB radio station on one of the terminals. He knew it worked because he could hear radio chatter. Plus, it was lit up like someone had been listening to it or using it.

They passed through the control room and stepped into an office suite that looked like it belonged to a fancy executive. No wall missing from in there. It was toasty inside, too. The two pit bulls holding his biceps pushed him through the doorway, and the third shut the door behind them. Inside the office, there was an old executive desk and cushioned armchairs sprawled in front of it. There was a high-backed chair behind the desk with a leather jacket draped over it.

Widow saw a cobweb in the ceiling's corner.

There was a room to the right with a door open and a light on.

The two pit bulls shoved Widow down in one of the armchairs. He sat there for a long minute in silence. He felt the rig rattle and grind under his feet. He imagined the giant metal beams below him were strained from both the hard wind outside and the rig's enormous weight. Then he heard water running from a sink in the open doorway. He looked up and saw that it was a private bathroom. Probably from years ago when the rig boss worked from this office.

Just then, a man in his fifties, of average height and well-built, stepped out of the bathroom. He wore a crinkled dress shirt and a loose tie and black chinos. Widow had never seen him before, but he felt he had because the guy looked a lot like James Ruffalo, only it wasn't. He was younger, and he didn't have the white scar on his face, but he had those goggle eye sockets. His eyes were a different color, though. They were blue and his hair was neater. It was gray, but combed and slicked back. He was clean-shaven, whereas the Ruffalo he knew probably hardly ever shaved. This guy was in much better shape physically than Ruffalo.

The guy came out and glanced at Widow and smiled a big smile. He walked out into the room and around the desk. He stopped right in front of Widow and reached a hand out for Widow to shake.

He said, "Mr. Jack Widow. Or is it Commander Jack Widow? How do you prefer to be addressed?"

Widow stayed quiet and stayed still. He didn't take the guy's hand.

The guy looked up at one of the pit bulls and nodded. The pit bull drew a gun and shoved it into Widow temple. He pressed it hard. Widow stayed quiet.

The pit bull said, "Shake his hand!"

Widow reached a hand up and took the Ruffalo clone's hand and shook it, then released. The pit bull lowered the gun and holstered it somewhere behind his rain poncho.

Ruffalo's clone walked back behind the desk and over to a table. The table had rocks glasses and a bottle of expensive whiskey. The guy poured himself a drink—neat—and stepped to the desk. He didn't take a seat behind it, like Widow expected. Instead, he ambled around to the front and sat on the edge. He put the glass to his lips and took a swig.

He stared at Widow. There was something in his eyes, something Widow had seen before and something Widow recognized. It was malevolence—evil, pure, and simple.

Widow didn't flinch away. He stared back.

Ruffalo's clone said, "I'll just call you Widow. I got ahold of some information about you. I gotta say, I'm impressed. An undercover agent pretending to be a Navy SEAL, all while you're really investigating them. Was that how it went?"

Widow stayed quiet.

Ruffalo's clone said, "My name is Efrem Voight, in case you hadn't figured that out yet."

Widow stayed quiet.

Voight said, "You don't have to talk with me. Soon, we won't be able to shut you up. Trust me. I've seen it a million times. I wanted to have a drink with you and talk. It's not every day I meet someone who's lived a life like I have."

Widow stayed quiet.

Voight said, "See, Widow, like you, I also lived a double life. I was a spy for the CIA for two decades. I worked all over the world, but it was when I was in Africa that I discovered the oil business. The CIA sent me to meet with a warlord in the mountains. They sent me on a peace mission. They sent me to deliver a briefcase as a gift, a sign of good faith. You know what was in the case?"

Widow knew, but didn't answer.

Voight said, "Money. It was a million dollars in unmarked bills—currency, Widow. Have you ever seen a million dollars in cash?"

Widow said nothing.

Voight said, "Well, that changed the course of my life. I'm sure that explains the complicated life I have lived. You might wonder, 'Why Ruffalo? And why not just kill him? Why keep him alive all these years?' I often asked myself that."

Widow stayed quiet.

Voight took a hefty swig from the whiskey. He asked, "Widow, have you read the Bible?"

Widow stared at him blankly.

Voight said, "No. I'm guessing not. You strike me as a man without a country, without a God. All the information I could get on you suggests you're a man with a high sense of morality. You literally think you're a one-man army, taking out people who you think are bad.

"Since you don't read the Bible, I assume you never heard the story of Isaac and Ishmael?"

Widow stared at him, into his eyes, but stayed quiet.

Voight said, "Abraham and his wife couldn't get pregnant no matter how hard they tried. Desperately wanting a child, Abraham and their slave girl had a baby—a son. His name was Ishmael. Shortly after that, however, Sarah, Abraham's wife, got pregnant with a boy—Isaac. Not wanting anything to do with Ishmael, Sarah convinced Abraham to force them out. Ishmael and his mother were banished into the desert. Isaac was given all the love and riches of his father, while Ishmael was left in the desert to suffer and die, but he did not die. Do you know what happened to him?"

Widow finally spoke. He said, "Ishmael grew up to build his own kingdom, rivalling that of his half brother. Ishmael represents the Arabs; Isaac the Jews. Two brothers warring over old grudges."

Voight smiled and said, "One was the rightful heir! The other came second, but he got all of his father's love! His fortune! The other went to the desert, living a life of double-crosses and betrayal."

Widow said, "But in the end, the two brothers joined to bury their father." Right then, it clicked in Widow's head. He was slow getting there, but he got there. He said, "You and Ruffalo are half-brothers."

"Same father. Different mothers, just like in the Bible," Voight said, and he sucked down the rest of his whiskey. He said,

"So I took over the family business. I killed our father. James's whore mother was already dead. My mother died long ago. I confronted him with a gun and a proposition. Instead of accepting it, right off the bat, he got the FBI involved. I took care of that and let him live. I set him up in a good life. His wife died giving birth and that sheriff took his daughter. Everything was great for thirty years until my niece started asking questions, hired Kloss, and you know the rest."

Widow stayed quiet.

Voight said, "I'm sorry. But I can't afford to leave you alive. I'm going to give you the same treatment that Kloss got. And you will tell us everything you know. Who have you told? All of it. Do this, and maybe we'll let your friend die fast. And maybe I'll let my brother and his daughter live. Resist and we'll give your woman far worse than you'll get. And I'll be forced to kill Jimmy and his kid. Family or no family."

Widow said nothing.

Voight said, "Take him down, show him the others, and then set him up. I'll be down in a minute."

The two pit bulls in rain ponchos scooped Widow up by his arms and hauled him up to his feet out of the chair. They must've been pretty strong because Widow was no sack of hair. Right then, he weighed two hundred and thirty pounds of solid mass. He got to his feet, and they pushed him back through the door, through the control room, where they passed the two pilots. They were sitting in front of one of the control consoles, feet up on the desk. One of them was drinking a coffee, and the other shoveled a donut into his mouth.

The third pit bull stayed behind with Voight.

They hauled Widow out into a hallway and took him over to an elevator. They hit the button, and the elevator came up, and they got on. They hit a button for a floor that was down. Widow had no idea how far down. The buttons were all smeared and cracked. One of them was missing completely.

The doors closed, and they rode down. The elevator cables echoed above them.

Widow asked, "What the hell happened to this rig?"

At first, the pit bulls said nothing, but one of them apparently decided, *What could it hurt?* and he answered. He said, "The rig's old. It's been through earthquakes and blizzards and storms, but a major earthquake mixed with the tsunami that followed destroyed a lot of structural integrity."

They stayed quiet the rest of the way down. Finally, the doors opened, and hard wind blew at them. Widow's hair danced around the top of his head. Rainwater whipped into his face.

The two pit bulls took a second and pulled their hoods back up. They half carried, half led Widow out onto catwalks beneath the hull. They walked, and turned corners where they had to. A lot of the railing was missing. There were even parts of the metal floor grating missing. The two pit bulls had to point out different areas to Widow so he wouldn't slip and fall through. One of them quipped they didn't want him to die before they could kill him. It was lame but rehearsed, like he had made the same joke before.

Widow looked down. He saw the ocean below. The waves crashed into the stud tanks and the legs.

He asked, "What happens if someone falls over the railing?"

"*If* you don't die, then you could swim and climb up on the bottom of that leg," the pit bull said and pointed at one of the legs. "The elevator will go down there. There's also a ladder over there. But it's missing rungs, and I wouldn't want to climb it."

Duly noted, Widow thought.

Finally, they turned another corner and went down a few metal steps and came to an alcove. Everything was metal. A large section of the railing was missing there. The wind was stronger than earlier.

Widow saw it—the place where Kloss was tortured.

At the center of the alcove there was a metal chair. It was welded to the flooring. It was covered in dried blood. There was a bucket beneath the chair that also had blood on the lip. Next to it, there was a large, open toolbox. Inside, Widow saw all kinds of bloodstained tools—hammers, knives, pipes, wrenches, a length of chain. There was even a battery-powered heavy-duty drill. There was blood on the bit.

Widow's eyes didn't linger on the chair or the toolbox because behind them, at the far end of the alcove, he saw Keagan, Tessa, and Liddy. They were all handcuffed to the railing. They sat on their butts on the floor. And they were each gagged with duct tape over their mouths.

Widow made eye contact with Keagan. She had a black eye on one side of her face. Her hair was completely disheveled, and she looked terrified, but otherwise, she was in one piece. Tessa looked fine, just scared, as did Liddy.

One of the pit bulls stepped out in front of Widow. He was going to grab Widow by the handcuffs and force him to sit in the chair, which was the way it went last time with Kloss. But Widow had other plans. He knew that if he got strapped to that chair, he wasn't coming out in one piece.

Widow bent his knees—fast—and heaved his shoulders back and catapulted forward like he was fired out of a cannon and head-butted the first pit bull right in the face, full force. He used all of his leg muscles and core strength and delivered a colossal headbutt. The pit bull's nose broke instantly. His front teeth shattered like glass. He was blinded by the splatter of blood from the top of his nose, and he swallowed more blood from the bottom of his nose. It gushed blood everywhere. Blood splashed onto Widow's face.

Lightning cracked in the distance.

Widow whipped around and saw the second pit bull already had his gun out. It was a Glock. He raised it to fire. He was fast, but Widow was faster.

The guy pulled the trigger blindly. But Widow was on top of him. The gunshots blasted out, but the wind and rain and thunder meant that no one above them would hear them.

Widow danced right and came in at the guy and grabbed his gun hand two-handed because of the cuffs. The Glock fired multiple times. The bullets all went out into the night.

Widow rushed forward while holding the pit bull's gun hand and slammed the guy into the railing. He danced back, released the Glock, and kicked the pit bull right in the groin. He used all his force. The kick was as hard as his headbutt to the first guy had been. Widow was no doctor, but if the first pit bull's nose had busted wide open, he could only imagine what happened to the second pit bull's lower regions. The pain on the guy's face said it all.

The second pit bull wasn't out of the fight, though. He raised the Glock toward Widow. Widow slapped it out of the guy's hand, and it bounced once on the floor grate and under the railing and plummeted off the platform completely. Widow grabbed the second pit bull by the rain poncho and pulled him and twirled on his feet, spinning both of them. And then he released the guy, catapulting him over to the railing that was broken. The second pit bull went flying off the platform. He slammed into the water and never came back up.

Keagan was shouting at Widow, only he couldn't hear her because of the duct tape. But he knew she was warning him. So Widow turned to the first pit bull, who was scrambling to find his Glock under his poncho. He brandished it. Only he couldn't see a thing, because blood kept spurting into his eyes from his nose. He blind-fired in the direction he thought Widow was in.

The Glock fired once. Twice. Three times.

Widow ducked and dodged as best he could. One bullet nearly hit him in the arm. He got low and charged the guy— full speed, full force. Widow slammed into him like a line-backer. He charged and lifted the guy off his feet and took the two of them past the railing, past the hole in it, and off the platform.

They both plummeted more than two hundred feet to the ocean below.

* * *

THE WATER WAS COLD. Widow felt himself getting shivers before they hit it. He used the pit bull's body to break his fall into the water, which prevented him from breaking any bones on impact, but it didn't prevent the freezing water.

He didn't know how many bones were broken in the first pit bull's body when he hit the water, but he knew the guy wasn't dead because he kept trying to point the Glock at Widow underwater.

They sank deeper and deeper and struggled over the Glock. Widow wasn't sure if it would fire or not. There was no reason it shouldn't. At least, it would fire once. The bullet would be slowed down, but at close range, it could still kill him. He used both hands to keep it from aiming at him. The first pit bull was determined to shoot Widow in the gut.

They sank and sank. Widow slapped the guy's hand away, setting his gun hand free, but Widow twisted and pushed off the guy and rotated around him. He put the handcuff chain over the guy's head and around his neck before the pit bull knew what he was doing.

It was already too late. Widow got his knees into the guy's back and wrenched the handcuff chain as hard as he could. The pit bull released the Glock and reached up and tried to pull the chain. The Glock sank into the darkness beneath them. They thrashed around and around.

Widow pulled and jerked as hard as he could. He did it until the guy went limp, and then he did it some more. Finally, he released and moved the handcuff chain off the guy's neck and spun him around and looked into his eyes. He was dead. His eyes bulged out of his head and blood pooled around his face from the busted nose.

Widow searched the guy's pockets, hoping he was the one who had the keys to the handcuffs. And he did. He pulled them out and let go of the corpse. It sank away slow like heavy driftwood.

Widow unlocked himself and let go of the cuffs, watched them sink. He pocketed the key and swam as hard and as fast as he could. He broke the surface, and a wave crashed down on him, stealing his breath for a moment. He broke the surface again and took a deep breath before he was covered by more ocean water. Widow got his bearings and swam toward the nearest leg.

He reached it after a minute of fighting the swells. Widow pulled himself up onto the concrete block at the base. He was lucky that the first leg he tried was the one with the elevator and ladder. He sat there, feet dangling off the side of the block, then collapsed back. He closed his eyes and just breathed.

He didn't get one of their guns, but he was alive.

After a long minute, Widow caught his breath and tore off his coat. It was soaked through and through. He actually felt warmer without it. He took out his passport, which was wet, but it could be salvaged. His postcard for Gray was a different story. It was soaked and ruined. He tossed it and pocketed his passport. He went to the elevator and pressed the call button. The elevator cables whined and echoed throughout the lower structure of the rig. He watched it come down and prepared himself to leap at anyone who might be on it. But it was empty. He got on board and pressed the button he remembered the pit bull had pressed.

The elevator whined and lifted back up. The elevator stopped, the doors opened, and Widow spilled out. He breathed deeply. He could feel a lot of his energy was gone from fighting and swimming, and he shivered from the cold. He followed the path from memory back to the torture alcove and found Keagan, Tessa, and Liddy all still there, still hand-cuffed and gagged.

Widow scrambled over to them and fished the key out of his pocket, and started with Keagan. He undid her cuffs. She ripped the duct tape off her mouth. Widow tried to do Tessa next, but Keagan leapt on him and hugged him too tight.

She said, "I was so scared. They were going to kill us."

"They didn't."

"Thank you! Thank you!" she whispered in his ear. She pulled back and kissed him again, only this time it was more like the movies. It was powerful and passionate. He figured it was probably the adrenaline and emotion, but he didn't fight it.

Finally, he pulled back, and Keagan stepped aside. He unlocked and un-gagged Liddy and Tessa, who both rushed to hug each other for the first time. Then Liddy hugged Widow.

He pulled Liddy off and said, "Okay. Let's get the hell out of here first. Then we can celebrate."

Keagan said, "We don't have any guns."

"I know," Widow said.

Liddy said, "What about my brother?"

"He's still up there," Widow said. "There's three more guys with him too."

Keagan said, "What do we do?"

Widow looked over at the toolbox. He said, "The elevator only goes up to the hull. So I'll go up and take care of them. Stay here."

He went to the toolbox and looked inside. It was like a dungeon master's dream of weapons. In the end, he went with a clawhammer.

Widow went to the elevator and got in and hit the button for the hull. The doors shut, the cables echoed again, and the elevator rode up. He stood there at the center of the elevator. He squeezed the clawhammer's handle and waited. The elevator came to a stop, and the doors opened. No one was there. He stepped into the hall quietly and looked left, looked right. He went right for the control room. He stopped in the doorway and peeked in. He heard the pilots laughing and talking. He saw they were still at the same control panel. They still had their feet up, only this time, they had music playing on an iPhone. It was an old rock and roll song by Black Sabbath called "Iron Man." The song was just getting going.

One of the pilots said, "Turn that up. I love this song."

The other turned the volume up.

Widow walked straight into the control room. One of the pilots had his back turned to Widow. The other sat across from him about ten feet away. He could see Widow in his line of sight, but instead of shouting out a warning, he was frozen in terror.

Widow marched into the room, walked straight over to the pilots. His coat was gone. He was soaked from head to toe. He looked like something that crawled out of the swamp, something that they had tried to bury.

The pilot that could see Widow lifted a hand and pointed his finger at him. He tried to say something but couldn't speak.

The pilot with his back turned said, "What is it, man?"

He put his feet down and turned his head just in time to see Widow raise the clawhammer and slam it down hard into his face. Widow used all his strength, and the blunt end of the hammer broke through the guy's skull and submerged into his brainpan.

Widow looked at the second pilot, who still couldn't speak but was trying to scream. Widow jerked the clawhammer out of the first pilot's skull and released him. His body slunk down in the chair. Blood and bone and brain fragments dripped off the hammer. The first pilot was dead.

Widow lifted the clawhammer, reversed it, and threw it at the second pilot. The sharp end of the claw stabbed the second pilot right in the eye socket. He fell back and slid off a control panel. He was also dead.

Widow heard Voight from the inner office. He called out, "Hey! Turn that music down!"

Widow checked the first pilot's pockets and found another Glock. He checked it and chambered a round. He stood up and walked past the computer consoles, past the CB radio station, and straight into Voight's office.

The last pit bull leaned against the far wall. He was staring at his phone. Voight was sitting behind the desk, drinking a fresh whiskey. The leather jacket was on him this time and not hanging off his chair.

Voight saw Widow and saw the Glock in his hand. He said, "No! Wait!"

Widow raised the Glock and shot the last pit bull twice in the chest. The guy was dead before his body slid down the wall to the floor.

Widow spun and pointed the Glock at Voight, who he knew right then was unarmed because he never went for anything —no gun, no weapon of any kind.

Widow pointed the Glock at Voight's center mass and stepped around the desk.

Voight said, "I'm unarmed."

Widow knocked the glass out of his hand and bunched up Voight's tie and wrenched him up on his feet by it. He quickly checked his pockets and waistband for a gun and found nothing.

Widow turned and dragged Voight out of the office and back into the control room.

Voight choked from the pressure of how tight Widow pulled his tie. He clawed and grabbed at Widow's forearm, but kept slipping off because Widow was wet.

Widow stopped dead center in the control room and looked around. He listened for the sound he was looking for, and he found it. He dragged Voight out of the control room and into the hallway. He followed the sound of wind and rain. He pulled Voight room to room until he found the right one. He dragged Voight over to a room that was missing half the floor and the wall. All there was left was exposed rebar at one side of the room.

Voight struggled to speak and finally got some words out. He said, "Wait. I can make you rich! I can cut you in!"

Widow hauled Voight up and held him out in front. He held him there and stared into his eyes. That evil look was gone and replaced with fear.

Voight talked some more, but Widow didn't listen. He said nothing and dragged Voight to the edge and let go of his tie.

Widow stepped back and shot Voight twice in the gut. Voight stared at him in horror. He didn't fall back, so Widow kicked him. Voight went flying back, into the wind and the rain. Lightning flashed once far off in the distance, but just enough for Widow to see Voight's eyes one last time. And then he was gone. He fell three hundred feet to the ocean water.

CHAPTER 33

None of them knew how to fly the Jayhawk, but that was okay because Keagan knew exactly how to use the CB radio. She called the US Coast Guard, and within forty minutes, they were surrounded by Jayhawk rescue helicopters. These had "United States Coast Guard" plastered on the sides. It looked like they sent their entire fleet of helicopters out to the oil rig, and just for four survivors.

The Ruffalo Oil and Gas company closed its doors forever the following month.

The FBI released Keagan's unit with their apologies. They also dropped the old charges against James Ruffalo, but that made no difference to Ruffalo because he elected to keep the name Liddy.

Liddy and Tessa Garret started a new father-daughter relationship from scratch. She stayed in Alaska and got hired on to his business, where she would learn to help him run it.

Peter got arrested, but Liddy hired the best lawyers to help fight his case. He ended up with a five-year prison sentence. But Liddy promised to hold a job for him when he got out.

Keagan received commendations for her bravery and police work. She found Widow's paperback copy of *Into the Wild* that he left on her bookshelf in her office. From time to time, when she felt lonely, she would glance over at it and know he was out there somewhere.

Widow left town to avoid questions and to move on, as he always did. But before he left, he made one last stop in Kodiak. He stopped at the post office and bought the same postcard he had ruined on the oil rig. This time, he sent it to Sonya Gray's home address in Virginia.

He signed it, *From Widow. I'm back here again. Thinking of you.*

NOTHING LEFT: A PREVIEW

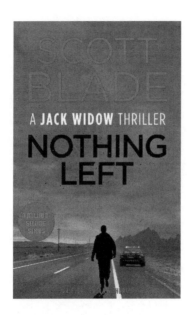

Coming Soon!

NOTHING LEFT: A BLURB

Two murdered cops.

A lone policewoman.

One suspect—Jack Widow.

A cold night in the middle-of-nowhere, in a vast county in New Mexico, a lone patrolwoman comes across a pair of dead cops sitting in their cruiser. And who does she find standing over their corpses? A giant, lone drifter with one stark trait; he is menacing like a nightmare. His name? Jack Widow.

To find the real killer, she'll have to partner with Widow. What seems like an ambush and execution might turn out to be something conspiratorial and far more sinister.

*Coming Fall 2021.

Readers are saying about Scott Blade and the Jack Widow series...

★ ★ ★ ★ ★ Scott Blade and Lee Child are cut from the same cloth! Do yourself a favor and check this series out!

CHAPTER 1

Two cops. Both dead. Murdered by twenty-six bullets, between them. Twenty-six shots fired. Twenty-six shell casings ejected. Twenty-six bullet holes suggest they were killed with extreme prejudice. Without remorse. Without hesitation. Without fear of consequence. But also, without experience. Without planning. Without expertise. Because the whole scene was overdone. Overreach. Overstated. Overkill.

The shooter wanted to kill them, resurrect them, and kill them again.

The corpses were slumped over the front seats of an unmarked white Ford police cruiser, like deflated tires. Blood dripped off the driver's side door panel. It dripped slowly off the steering wheel, like a loose bathroom faucet. The blood soaked everything. Broken glass littered the interior and the ground around the vehicle. Fluids leaked from the car's undercarriage and pooled in the dirt. Dust clouds lingered in the air like a car just sped off, and I missed it.

Someone shot both cops in their heads, shoulders, necks, and chests—straight through the driver's side windshield. Large sections of the windshield remained intact. But other sections were broken and gapped and scattered about where glass used to be. Jagged edges of broken glass on the ground reflected the moonlight, the clouds, and the stars.

Bullet holes riddled the remaining glass, the hood, the metal, the dash, the seats, and the rear bench. There were probably spent bullets in the trunk. The headlamps were shattered. Small plastic pieces were scattered across the ground under the grille. Countless veiny cracks splintered across the windshield, fracturing off in thousands of directions, like an infestation of spiderwebs. The windshield slowly cracked in places. I heard it under the wind. It sounded like someone tiptoeing over broken glass.

I stood in the middle of nowhere, in the middle of the night, about sixty yards off an old road in the distance behind me. It was a forgotten two-lane highway, just a line on a map with no real interest to anybody but the people who passed through, like an abandoned tunnel or an ancient bridge. It wasn't used all that often anymore because newer interstates and roads emerged and took away the need for it.

Besides the locals—which there weren't many of—this road was mostly used as the *scenic route*. Some travelers are into that sort of thing. No one stopped to see what was in the middle of it. They just passed through it as fast as they could and went onward to their final destinations.

I was in the middle of New Mexico, on the Great Plains. Low hills rolled in all directions. Huge mountains loomed in the distance. Billowing Indiangrass stretched out for miles. To the west, a herd of huge, shadowy objects moved like slow-rolling boulders. It was a herd of grazing buffalo. The highway and the police cruiser were the only signs of human existence for a few miles, with one exception.

Hovering over me, and all around me, were huge wind turbines. They spread out for a hundred thousand acres. They towered over everything at around five hundred feet high. The long blades *whooshed* and spun, like enormous helicopter rotors. They looked pretty new. My guess was less than five years old. Some were only months old, maybe. They were all well-maintained. I must've been surrounded by a giant wind farm. Some kind of multimillion dollar project to cheapen power for the state, as well as help the environment.

I *was* headed to Roswell, hunting for aliens—the little green men, not the migrants. It was a simple curiosity, one of those things where the stars aligned.

This morning, I stopped at the Four Corners Monument, a quadripoint where four states merge at a crossing with four perfect right angles. You can stand in two states at once, one foot in each. You can step from one state to the next and twice more, a total of four states. Crossing the borders of Arizona, Colorado, Utah, and New Mexico in a single second. I saw younger people trying to time each other to see who could traverse the four states the fastest. It was like a kids' game. It was one I'd seen before. Only, that game is drawn on a street with chalk. There are squares and each player hops on one foot to the next square. The young people seem to enjoy it. I think it's called Hopscotch.

I'd never been to the Four Corners before. That's where I met a young couple who were on their way back to wherever they came from. They drove an old Bronco covered in alien and UFO bumper stickers. One sticker was of a UFO beaming a man up. It read: *Get in Loser*.

There was a mural painted all over the Bronco. It was like a collage of alien stuff. There were little green men, UFOs, and drawings of space. The couple smelled of marijuana. I was looking for a ride, which they offered me, but they were headed north, and I was headed southeast. Although, I could've changed my direction. I was headed down toward Texas for no particular reason. Like the wind hitting sails on a boat, I could change course. No problem.

We got to talking, and they told me all about how much fun they had doing an alien tourist thing down in Roswell, New Mexico. I asked if they had tried Area 51, in Nevada. There's a small town there, not even sure if it's a town, more like a settlement. The whole thing is built around the allure of Area 51. There's an alien diner, alien museum, and a mysterious black mailbox where visitors can leave mail for the aliens. It's not marked on any map. It's a big black mailbox stuck on the side of the road. It's easy to miss. They told me they had been to Las Vegas many times and visited all that stuff before. But this was their first time in Roswell.

I'm not a believer in aliens or past visits. But I also can't rule it out either. This couple got me curious, but the thing that pushed me to decide to stop here was what happened this past summer. The U.S. Navy released a report that admitted to more than a dozen cases of pilots coming across UAPs over the ocean. UAP stands for Unidentified Aerial Phenomena. The powers that be renamed the technical term from UFO to UAP. There are plenty of conspiracy theories about that too. It's the official position of the Navy that these flying crafts, or whatever they are, can't be determined. But several retired pilots—men I never met, but respected—have come forward and described things that sound an awful lot like aliens. This public admission has caused quite the fervor in the alien community, in an *I told you so* kind of way. But it's also affected regular people, as well. The whole planet talked about it. So I decided, why not follow in the footsteps of my new acquaintances and pass through Roswell?

It was at a gas station close to the state border that I got a ride from the woman who abandoned me several miles back down the highway. I passed through an abandoned town, with empty rundown buildings and one major intersection with a half of a stoplight dangling from a cable.

And that's how I ended up here.

Roswell, New Mexico was more than twenty miles southwest, but less than fifty, from where I ended up. The driver who abandoned me had overshot Roswell. So I had to backtrack, which was what I was doing now. I hitched a ride with the mission of discovering aliens. Instead, I found two dead cops.

Two hours ago, the driver who picked me up had dropped me off without explanation. Right at that moment, she was blasting Sheryl Crow on the stereo. Ironic.

The driver's decision had been a last-minute sort of thing, like she just changed her mind about me, suddenly. It was bad luck for me, because we were outside the realm of civilization, and it was after nightfall. In hindsight, she ditched me. Maybe she suddenly didn't like the look of me. Or maybe it was something I said, or didn't say. Either way, it's fine. That's part of road, part of the rules of nomadic life. You take your chances, like Sheryl Crow said: *Every day is a winding road.*

You got that right, Sheryl.

So I walked a while and ended up here—lost. I saw the unmarked police cruiser's faded red brake lights in the distance. I stepped off the main road to check it out. I thought maybe there was someone here who could help me out. Maybe someone who could give me a ride to a service station. I expected to discover some campers, or a couple of teenagers out here drinking and thinking they wouldn't be bothered. Instead, I stumbled upon two dead cops. But they wouldn't help me. They wouldn't help anyone. Ever again.

The wind blew around me, turning the massive turbine blades. They droned with each rotation. The grass *whooshed* and rustled. Darkness surrounded me. Nighttime prairie sounds thrummed across the landscape. It was quiet, but not silent. Crickets chirped all around me. Coyotes, or wolves, howled far off in the distance. A rattlesnake rattled somewhere between the howls and where I stood, somewhere off in the tall grass. Nightbirds fluttered their wings overhead. Their flight path was below the massive blades. I couldn't see them. Judging by the sounds, they were probably birds. But they could've been bats. I prayed they were owls.

Above, the moon was full. Heavy clouds streamed across the sky quickly, like time was fast-forwarding. There was still plenty of moonlight to see, clouds or no clouds. I could see the scene pretty well, even without a flashlight. The nearest city lights were faint on the horizon, but the darkness was soft enough and the moonlight bright enough to make the visibility pretty good.

I concentrated on the dead cops and examined the murder scene. Bullet holes honeycombed the cruiser's hood. Thin plumes of smoke wafted out of the bullet holes, like parts of the engine were smoking. *Hopefully, the thing wouldn't catch fire.* I double checked the engine was off. And it was.

The front tires were flat from bullet punctures. Water from the radiator leaked out under the car and soaked into the soil.

Gunsmoke lingered in the air. I smelled blood on the wind. The whole thing smelled like it went down not that long ago. Tire tracks were smeared back down the track. The killer peeled out before speeding away. He left behind all kinds of tire tracks, and probably, rubber from the tires for the forensic guys. There were clear skid marks all across the highway, which would be easier seen in daylight.

The cruiser's headlamps were off, but the brake lights were lit up, tinging the hills behind the cruiser in a low red hue, like faded blood. The cruiser was in park, but the driver died with his foot on the brake pedal, and it stayed there after he was dead. Thus, the lingering brake lights.

I was the only living person around in the nighttime gloom. I looked around in all directions, and saw no one else. No signs of other humans. No traces of anyone else, except for the aggressive tire tracks the killer left behind, the looming city lights of the nearby town, and, of course, the giant rotating wind turbines.

I leaned over the open driver's side window, careful not to touch the corpse. A coffee napkin from my pocket made a great tool to cover my fingerprints. With the napkin covering my hand, I reached into the window, grabbed a knob, and twisted it for the headlamps. They flickered on. Dust hazed through the beams. I leaned back out of the car and walked around to the cruiser's nose, out several yards to the killer's vehicle's tire tracks.

I knelt and studied the tire tracks in the dirt. I was no expert on tires, but I knew the FBI could identify everything about the vehicle easily from these. I stood up and turned back to the police cruiser. I saw the dead cops as dark figures, staring back at me. They looked more like heaps of bones than humans.

I stayed where I was and scanned the ground between the killer's vehicle and the police cruiser. Instantly, I realized I had missed the shell casings on the ground. But I saw them now. Luckily, I hadn't stepped on them. Out in front of the cruiser's headlamps, there were numerous shell casings. They littered the ground. I counted them up, as I had the bullet holes. I accounted for twenty-six, matching the number of bullet holes.

I crept closer to them, squatted, and looked, staying careful not to step on them. The killer's footprints were right there with them, several feet away from me. His gun had spat out the bullet casings in the same direction, indicating one firearm used.

I inched closer again and looked at them. The bullet casings were all the same—all nine-millimeter. I recounted them and stared at each to be sure of the number and caliber. I got twenty-six again. Near the shooter's footprints, I found one empty magazine. It was too dark to count the notches, which marked how many bullets each magazine held. The killer was sloppy to leave the magazine behind. Criminals forget to pick up their casings all the time, but a magazine? That was dumb.

The same gun fired them. There was one shooter. I dared not get any closer. I didn't want my footprints mixing in with the shooter's. So I stood up and retreated to the cruiser.

I got close to the dead cops, but touched nothing. Like my fingerprints, I didn't want my DNA on any part of the crime scene. I didn't want anyone to mistake me for having any part of it. I studied the dead cops from an observer's distance. Their wounds appeared to be scattered kill shots. They weren't random, but they weren't professional either. It was just sloppy work. Plain and simple. The shooter knew how to fire a gun. Probably because they watched it on a bad prime time cop show. But they weren't a trained professional. My guess was they had fired a weapon before, but had zero training. This was no assassination for pay. No professional hit. It was just a run-of-the-mill criminal homicide, except the victims were cops.

There are a few things that really piss me off. One is injustices, like when bad guys get away with bad things. The second is cop killers. The same goes for anyone who kills our military service members. Cop killers, and enemy combatants who kill service members, struck a vengeful nerve with me.

The cruiser was unmarked, but I knew it was a police car because there was an array of antennas sticking up along the trunk lid. The kind police needed to stay in contact with dispatch, especially when driving out in the middle of nowhere.

Both dead bodies had that cop look about them. They wore street clothes, but were definitely off-duty cops, or federal agents in plain clothes. They could've been on a stakeout, or having a clandestine meeting with an informant, or doing any of those things that cops do.

I've spent the last several years hitchhiking from one state to the next, never stopping for long, and never getting too used to staying in one place. I started drifting after I left my under-cover job in the NCIS. And I'm addicted. Not unlike a drug or alcohol addict, but my addiction isn't going kill me—probably.

I'm addicted to two things: coffee and nomading. My addic-tions have no cure. Not that I'd want to cure them. I love them both. Why live paycheck to paycheck? Why stay in one place your whole life? Why work for someone else, paying taxes, paying rent, paying bills? Why settle for any of that? Why settle at all? I didn't get it.

I love not knowing what's around the corner. You never know what the tide will bring. Sometimes that's a good thing and sometimes it's a bad thing. On the road ahead of me, there could be anything. I could meet a beautiful woman. I could meet a stranger with a gun. I could run into danger. I could run into adventure. That's the magic. The spontaneity. The improvisation of life. The unknown. That's what I love.

But, right then, all of those things happened to me all at once, like some kind of twisted ambush.

Right then, a pair of headlights appeared in the darkness. A car approached from down the two-lane highway. I froze where I was and watched it. It grew larger in a long moment as it headed in my direction. *Was it the killer? Was he returning to the scene of the crime?*

At first it passed by, but then the brake lights came on. And the driver slammed to a stop. The tires skidded, and the brakes howled. Dust rose behind the tires.

Once the headlights had passed, I got a better look at the vehicle. And it was bad news for me.

Shit, I thought.

The oncoming car was another police cruiser, but a regular one, not an unmarked one. I could tell because the light bar on top lit up and blue lights washed through the darkness, over the terrain. The blue light bounced off the nearest wind turbine's white base, illuminating a wide stretch of ground beneath it.

The driver left the siren off. The car reversed, and the engine whined until the cruiser made it back to the track I stood on. The car stopped, and the engine whine died away as the driver switched the car into drive and turned onto the dirt track. The new police cruiser sped up as fast as it was safe to. The headlights bounced up over dips in the track.

The cop must've seen the brake lights from the dead cops' car. Not knowing what to do, I froze. Technically, I didn't kill them. There was nothing for me to fear. But in my experience, I had been arrested more often than your average drifter for crimes I didn't commit. It was mostly because of how I looked and partially out of convenience.

I was six foot four, two hundred and twenty pounds of concrete muscle mass. And I stood over two dead cops in the middle of nowhere. *What would this new cop think when he saw me?* He'd arrest me. No doubt about it. I'd do the same thing if I were in his shoes.

I could run. So far, he hadn't seen me. Not from the highway. *But where would I go?* There was nothingness in every direction. Plus, running would get me more than arrested. It'd probably get me beaten with nightsticks in a room with no cameras and no witnesses. It'd get me charged and probably stuffed into a jail cell. In some rural areas, in some states, it'd get me killed. Cops don't like cop killers. Even though I had killed nobody. At least not in New Mexico. Not yet.

I stayed where I was.

The newly-arrived police cruiser continued up the track. As it got closer, I got a better look at it. The cruiser was old, but had once been a state-of-the-art machine. The driver must've spotted me, and spotted the bullet holes in the police car in front of me. Maybe he saw the two dead bodies inside because he buzzed the siren, not turned it on, just blipped it, like a warning to me to stay put.

The cruiser swayed and bounced as it sped toward me from out of the darkness. A coyote howled somewhere behind me. The giant wind turbine *whooshed* overhead. The police cruiser slammed to a stop again. The tires screeched, and the brakes squealed as the thing came skidding to a stop ten feet from where I stood. The rear of the car skidded clear across the dirt. Dust sprayed up into the air behind it. The wind gusted a huge dust cloud out past the cruiser. It engulfed both of us for a moment, before dissipating into the gloom.

The siren blipped again, and the blue lights lit up the low, hilly grassland around me, like little blue lighthouses on the sea. The night sky brightened and the beams from the light faded into hazy clouds. More dust rose up from the tire skid, but this time slow and somber.

The headlamps washed over me, and stayed there. But the light stopped at my neck, just below my chin. My head and face remained in darkness above the beams.

I stayed where I was.

The cop inside threw the car's transmission into park. The police cruiser's driver's door burst open, and the cop jumped out and pulled a department-issued Glock on me. The cop had excellent moves. It all went down as I had predicted. Except I was wrong about one important detail. The cop wasn't a he. He was a she.

She steadied her arms over the top of her car door, the Glock held out and pointed directly at me. She locked her arms straight out and stood strong—textbook stance. She aimed her weapon at the dead center of my chest. There was no laser sight, but I felt it. This cop was well-trained.

I didn't know if it was bad luck on my part that she appeared out of nowhere or if she'd pulled up to answer a distress call from the two dead cops. I hadn't thought to check the police radio, or look to see if their hands were empty. The latter was plausible. Maybe one of them stayed alive long enough to radio for help. Maybe the radio was still in the palm of his hand.

What I knew for sure was, to this cop, I was a total stranger. She was a cop staring at a police cruiser with two dead cops in it, and me, a stranger, standing over them. Not a dream scenario. To her, I was just a giant hitchhiker with black, gas-station-bought clothes on.

Factor in the black clothes, my large stature, and the middle-of-nowhere scene, and she probably looked at me and saw the thing from outer space from many eighties alien invasion/horror movies. One of those movies where a giant alien, who never dies, hunts man for sport. The kind of alien giant who keeps returning from the dead after being shot with shotgun rounds, nine-millimeter parabellums, or whatever else the local cops could throw at it.

The policewoman aimed down the barrel of her Glock at me, and shouted, "Hands up!"

Without objection, I raised my hands high above my head and kept my fingers limp and still. As my arms went up, she followed them with her eyes slowly. Like uniformed sailors watching a flag rising up a flagpole in front of them. It was a long route. Her eyes flicked back down to my face. I doubted she could see much detail because of the darkness.

She shouted, "Keep them up!"

Her voice was calm, yet firm. It was a seasoned cop-voice. She had used it hundreds of times, maybe thousands.

She shouted, "Turn around! Face the other direction! Do it slow!"

I turned around, slow and calm. My head pivoted back to look over my shoulder as I turned so I could maintain eye contact with her. Not that she could tell.

She shouted, "Face forward!"

I turned my head back toward the front and faced the direction of the silent cop car with the two dead cops inside. My eyes washed over their bodies again, closely. I got a better view of the damage. There were bullet holes all over the place —the front hood, the backseat, the rear windshield, and even through the headrests.

The policewoman walked up behind me, slow and steady, with her boots scuffling in the dirt. She stopped directly behind me, but outside of my reach, which was a smart move on her part. She had sized me up like a veteran law enforcement officer would. She determined it best to stay clear of my long reach in case I spun around and snatched the Glock from her hands, which I could've done.

She said, "Place your hands behind your back! Do it slow!"

I did as she asked. Knowing what she was going to do, I jetted my thumbs out. A half-second later, she grabbed my wrist and locked it in a handcuff. She followed with the other wrist and cuff. I heard the *clicks* from the handcuffs. The cold metal chilled my skin as it coiled over my wrists. I glanced back at her from over my shoulder. Not fast and not slow, just a steady glance. I kept my expression friendly. I had been arrested many times before, and by female officers before. I knew the drill.

In my experience, officers in arresting situations are hopped up on adrenaline and training, which told them to be aggressive, to make their voices sound full of authority and strength. They were trained to sound like they meant business. When an officer tells you to freeze, what they are really saying is *freeze or I'll shoot you*. And ninety-nine point nine percent of the time, they *will* shoot you.

I didn't know this woman from Eve. So far, she seemed professional, level-headed, and competent, but I wasn't a hundred percent sure she wasn't a bad apple. Lots of police departments have them. Bad apples would be just as quick to shoot you and sort it out later, instead of following procedure. Especially out in the middle of nowhere. No witnesses. And two dead cops as probable cause. So I gave her no provocation to shoot me.

I kept my voice friendly, but more toward the side of neutrality than familiarity. I said, "You're making a mistake. I didn't do this. I just found them."

She said, "Right. Now, turn around. Slow. Let me see your face."

I turned around, dawdling, and gazed down at her. She squinted her eyes, but not in the way that said she couldn't see me. It was more like she couldn't believe her eyes, like something amazed her, like she recognized me. She took one hand off the Glock and covered her mouth with it. She stayed like that for a long second and held the gun one-handed, pointing at my center mass. Then, she reached down and grabbed a small flashlight from her police belt, quickly, like she had rehearsed it many, many times.

She lifted it up and clicked the light on in one fluid motion. The beam was bright, white like a surgeon's light. The beam spotlighted straight at my chest and then moved up to my face. She stopped it, held it on my face. The flashlight beamed a powerful light on me. It blinded me.

I couldn't make out her features behind the beam.

The police officer suddenly broke protocol and stepped forward, closer to me than she should have. She stared at me for another long second. Suddenly, she did something completely unexpected. She lowered the Glock, a fraction of the way down. But she kept it pointed at me and kept her finger inside the trigger guard, in case she had to draw it up fast and put a bullet in me.

I could make out her face, but not enough to pick her out of a lineup. I saw just enough to know she was probably about forty, not much older than I was.

She looked at me strangely—strange for this situation. Strange for any situation where a stranger is pointing a Glock at you one second, and the next, she's greeting you with the eyes of someone from the past.

The officer lowered the flashlight enough for me to see better. I saw her face. She had pale blue eyes and fair skin. I believe the tone was called porcelain. I imagined it wasn't a natural look in New Mexico, where there is plenty of sunlight. Maybe she only worked the night shift. And she had been doing so for a long time, judging by how pale her skin was.

She was about five-four, not short for an average woman, but an entire foot shorter than I was. She wore a bulletproof vest over her uniform. It looked bulky around her chest, like her breasts stretched the vest more than the design was meant for. Bulletproof vests are traditionally designed with men in mind. Men make up most of the vocational forces that utilize bulletproof vests. There are some companies out there with more female form-fitting designs in their catalogue. Apparently, whatever department she belonged to in New Mexico didn't offer those.

Her uniform shirt had long sleeves. I could see a hint of a tattoo cropping out of her sleeve, over her wrist. It rode up the back of her gun hand. There was another tail of it poking out of the collar of her shirt. It came up her neck about a third of the way. I imagined it was all one enormous piece. I had a lot of tattoos myself. So I knew two things about it. First, the procedure was long and painful, which told me she had patience, and probably a high threshold for pain. And two, it was expensive. Big tattoos like that could cost thousands of dollars and take weeks or months to complete.

All of this told me she was tough and patient. She probably had thick skin, with a radar for bullshit. Most female cops like her do. There's an extra layer of bullshit for women to go through in male-dominated industries. Law enforcement was no different. It's far from a perfect world.

I glanced at her name patch. It was just a flick of the eyes. Her name patch was sewn above her right breast on the bullet-proof vest. It read: *Voss*.

I took a second glance, with another flick of the eyes to see her badge. It glimmered faintly from the moonlight. It was a small, gold star-shaped badge, engraved with symbols, representing New Mexico Law Enforcement. And there was a badge number. The symbol was probably the crest for the local city she worked out of, and not the county, because the side of her car read: *Angel Rock: Police* and not *Angel Rock: Sheriff*. She was a part of a police force and not a sheriff's office, which meant that she was on the force for a township or city, and not for a county, because sheriffs policed the counties of America, and police worked the municipalities.

Her flashlight flicked back up to my face. The light was bright in my eyes. I recoiled from looking at her badge. She lowered the beam, so it was no longer blinding me.

I returned my eyes up to her face. Her expression had completely changed from one of strangeness, to one of perplexity. *But, why?*

She looked at me like she had seen a ghost, someone from years ago that she had thought was dead by now. And then, I knew why, because she spoke.

She said, "Widow? Jack Widow?"

A WORD FROM SCOTT

Thank you for reading THE DOUBLE MAN. You got this far —I'm guessing that you liked Widow.

The story continues…

The next book in the series is *NOTHING LEFT*, coming Fall 2021.

To find out more, sign up for the Scott Blade Book Club and get notified of upcoming new releases. See next page.

SCOTT BLADE BOOK CLUB

Building a relationship with my readers is the very best thing about writing. I occasionally send newsletters with details on new releases, special offers, and other bits of news relating to the Jack Widow Series.

If you are new to the series, you can join the Scott Blade Book Club and get the starter kit.

Sign up for exclusive free stories, special offers, access to bonus content, and info on the latest releases, and coming-soon Jack Widow novels. Sign up at ScottBlade.com.

THE NOMADVELIST

NOMAD + NOVELIST = NOMADVELIST

Scott Blade is a Nomadvelist, a drifter and author of the breakout Jack Widow series. Scott travels the world, hitchhiking, drinking coffee, and writing.

Jack Widow has sold over a million copies.

Visit @: ScottBlade.com

Contact @: scott@scottblade.com

Follow @:

Facebook.com/ScottBladeAuthor

Bookbub.com/profile/scott-blade

Amazon.com/Scott-Blade/e/B00AU7ZRS8

ALSO BY SCOTT BLADE

The Jack Widow Series

Gone Forever

Winter Territory

A Reason to Kill

Without Measure

Once Quiet

Name Not Given

The Midnight Caller

Fire Watch

The Last Rainmaker

The Devil's Stop

Black Daylight

The Standoff

Foreign & Domestic

Patriot Lies

The Double Man

Nothing Left

The Protector

Kill Promise

The Shadow Club

Printed in Great Britain
by Amazon